ICONS

ICONS

MARGARET STOHL

LITTLE, BROWN AND COMPANY
NEW YORK BOSTON

Copyright © 2013 by Margaret Stohl, Inc.
Excerpt from *Idols* copyright © 2014 by Margaret Stohl, Inc.
Excerpt of *Dangerous Creatures* © 2014 by Kami Garcia, LLC, and Margaret Stohl, Inc.

Little, Brown and Company

Hachette Book Group
237 Park Avenue, New York, NY 10017
Visit our website at lb-teens.com

Little, Brown and Company is a division of Hachette Book Group, Inc.
The Little, Brown name and logo are trademarks of Hachette Book Group, Inc.

The publisher is not responsible for websites (or their content)
that are not owned by the publisher.

First Paperback Edition: April 2014
First published in hardcover in May 2013 by Little, Brown and Company

Library of Congress Cataloging-in-Publication Data
Stohl, Margaret.
Icons / by Margaret Stohl. — First edition. pages cm
Summary: After an alien force known as the Icon colonizes Earth, decimating humanity, four surviving teenagers must piece together the mysteries of their pasts—in order to save the future.
ISBN 978-0-316-20518-4 (hc)—ISBN 978-0-316-24721-4 (international)—
ISBN 978-0-316-20519-1 (pb)
[1. Science fiction. 2. Survival—Fiction. 3. Insurgency—Fiction.
4. Extraterrestrial beings—Fiction.] I. Title.
PZ7.S86985Ic 2013   [Fic]—dc23   2012040163

10 9 8 7 6 5 4 3 2 1
RRD-C
Printed in the United States of America
Design by Andrea Vandergrift

For Lewis,
writing partner and writer's partner
on and off the page

GIVE
SORROW
WORDS.

—William Shakespeare, *Macbeth*

NOTE: THIS BOOK, LIKE MOST BOOKS, IS
NOT AUTHORIZED FOR CIRCULATION.

If a Sympa finds you with this book,
he will destroy it and you.

Consider yourself warned.

ICONS / BOOK 1
THE HUMANITY PROJECT

Pressed by Hand
Circa Spring 2080 ATD

PROLOGUE
THE DAY

One tiny gray dot, no bigger than a freckle, marks the inside of the baby's chubby arm. It slips in and out of view as she cries, waving her yellow rubber duck back and forth.

Her mother holds her over the old ceramic bathtub. The little feet kick harder, twisting above the water. "You can complain all you want, Doloria, but you're still taking a bath. It will make you feel better."

She slides her daughter into the warm tub. The baby kicks again, splashing the blue patterned wallpaper above the tiles. The water surprises her, and she quiets.

"That's it. You can't feel sad in the water. There is no sadness there." She kisses Doloria's cheek. "I love you, *mi corazón*. I love you and your brothers today and tomorrow and every day until the day after heaven."

The baby stops crying. She does not cry as she is

scrubbed and sung to, pink and clean. She does not cry as she is kissed and swaddled in blankets. She does not cry as she is tickled and tucked into her crib.

The mother smiles, wiping a damp strand of hair from her child's warm forehead. "Dream well, Doloria. *Que sueñes con los angelitos.*" She reaches for the light, but the room floods with darkness before she can touch the switch. Across the hall, the radio is silenced midsentence, as if on cue. Over in the kitchen, the television fades to sudden black, to a dot the size of a pinprick, then to nothing.

The mother calls up the stairs. "The power's gone off again, *querido*! Check the fuse box." She turns back, tucking the blanket corner snugly beneath Doloria. "Don't worry. It's nothing your *papi* can't fix."

The baby sucks on her fist, five small fingers the size of tiny wriggling earthworms, as the walls start to shake and bits of plaster swirl in the air like fireworks, like confetti.

She blinks as the windows shatter and the ceiling fan hits the carpet and the shouting begins.

She yawns as her father rolls down the staircase like a funny rag doll that never stands up.

She closes her eyes as the falling birds patter against the roof like rain.

She starts to dream as her mother's heart stops beating.

I start to dream as my mother's heart stops beating.

HAPPY BIRTHDAY TO ME

"Dol? Are you okay?"

The memory fades at the sound of his voice.

Ro.

I feel him somewhere in my mind, the nameless place where I see everything, feel everyone. The spark that is Ro. I hold on to it, warm and close, like a mug of steamed milk or a lit candle.

And then I open my eyes and come back to him.

Always.

Ro's here with me. He's fine, and I'm fine.

I'm fine.

I think it, over and over, until I believe it. Until I remember what is real and what is not.

Slowly the physical world comes into focus. I'm standing on a dirt trail halfway up the side of a mountain—staring down at the Mission, where the goats and pigs in the field below are small as ants.

"All right?" Ro reaches toward me and touches my arm.

I nod. But I'm lying.

I've let the feelings—and the memories—overtake me again. I can't do that. Everyone at the Mission knows I have a gift for feeling things—strangers, friends, even Ramona Jamona the pig, when she's hungry—but it doesn't mean I have to let the feelings control me.

At least that's what the Padre keeps telling me.

I try to control myself, and usually I can. But I wish I didn't feel anything, sometimes. Especially not when everything is so overwhelming, so unbearably sad.

"Don't disappear on me, Dol. Not now." Ro locks his eyes on me and motions with his big tan hands. His brown-gold eyes flicker with fire and light under his dark tangle of hair. His face is all broad planes and rough angles—as solid as a brambled oak, softening only for me. He could climb halfway up the mountain again by now, or halfway down. Holding Ro back is like trying to stop an earthquake or a mud slide. Maybe a train.

But not now. Now he waits. Because he knows me, and he knows where I've gone.

Where I go.

I stare up at the sky, spattered with bursts of gray rain and orange light. It's hard to see past the wide-brimmed hat I stole off the hook behind the Padre's office door.

Still, the setting sun is in my eyes, pulsing from behind the clouds, bright and broken.

I remember what we are doing and why we are here.

My birthday. It's my seventeenth birthday tomorrow.

Ro has a present for me, but first we have to climb the hill. He wants to surprise me.

"Give me a clue, Ro." I pull myself up the hill after him, leaving a twisting trail of dried brush and dirt behind me.

"Nope."

I turn to look down the mountain again. I can't stop myself. I like how everything looks from up here.

Peaceful. Smaller. Like a painting, or one of the Padre's impossible puzzles, except there aren't any missing pieces. In the distance below, I can see the yellowing patch of field that belongs to our Mission, then the fringe of green trees, then the deep blue wash of the ocean.

Home.

The view is so serene, you almost wouldn't know about The Day. That's why I like it here. If you don't leave the Mission, you don't have to think about it. The Day and the Icons and the Lords. The way they control us.

How powerless we are.

This far up the Tracks, away from the cities, nothing ever changes. This land has always been wild.

A person can feel safe here.

Safer.

I raise my voice. "It'll be getting dark soon."

He's up the trail, once again. Then I hear a ripple through the brush, and the sound of rolling rock, and he lands behind me, nimble as a mountain goat.

Ro smiles. "I know, Dol."

I take his calloused hand and relax my fingers into his. Instantly, I am flooded with the feeling of Ro—physical contact always makes our connection that much stronger.

He is as warm as the sun behind me. As hot as I am cold. As rough as I am smooth. That's our balance, just one of the invisible threads that tie us together.

It's who we are.

My best-and-only friend and me.

He rummages in his pocket, then pushes something into my hands, suddenly shy. "All right, I'll hurry it up. Your first present."

I look down. A lone blue glass bead rolls between my fingers. A slender leather cord loops in a circle around it.

A necklace.

It's the blue of the sky, of my eyes, of the ocean.

"Ro," I breathe. "It's perfect."

"It reminded me of you. It's the water, see? So you can always keep it with you." His face reddens as he tries to explain, the words sticking in his mouth. "I know—how it makes you feel."

Peaceful. Permanent. Unbroken.

"Bigger helped me with the cord. It used to be part of a saddle." Ro has an eye for things like that, things other people overlook. Bigger, the Mission cook, is the same way, and the two of them are inseparable. Biggest, Bigger's wife, tries her best to keep both of them out of trouble.

"I love it." I thread my arm around his neck in a rough hug. Not so much an embrace as a cuff of arms, the clench of friends and family.

Ro looks embarrassed, all the same. "It's not your whole present. For that you have to climb a little farther."

"But it's not even my birthday yet."

"It's your birthday eve. I thought it was only fair to start tonight. Besides, this kind of present is best after sundown." Ro holds out his hand, a wicked look in his eyes.

"Come on. Just one little hint." I squint up at him and he grins.

"But it's a surprise."

"You're making me hike all this way through the brush."

He laughs. "Okay. It's the last thing you'd ever expect. The very last thing." He bounces up and down a bit where he stands, and I can tell he's practically ready to bolt up the mountain.

"What are you talking about?"

He shakes his head, holding out his hand again. "You'll see."

I take it. There's no getting Ro to talk when he doesn't want to. Besides, his hand in mine is a good thing.

I feel the beating of his heart, the pulse of his adrenaline.

Even now, when he's relaxed and hiking, and it's just the two of us. He is a coiled spring. He has no resting state, not really.

Not Ro.

A shadow crosses the hillside, and instinctively we dive for cover under the brush. The ship in the sky is sleek and silver, glinting ominously with the last reflective rays of the setting sun. I shiver, even though I'm not at all cold, and my face is half buried in Ro's warm shoulder.

I can't help it.

Ro murmurs into my ear as if he is talking to one of the Padre's puppies. It's more his tone than the words—that's how you speak to scared animals. "Don't be afraid, Dol. It's headed up the coast, probably to Goldengate. They never come this far inland, not here. They're not coming for us."

"You don't know that." The words sound grim in my mouth, but they're true.

"I do."

He slips his arm around me and we wait like that until the sky is clear.

Because he doesn't know. Not really.

People have hidden in these bushes for centuries, long before us. Long before there were ships in the skies.

First the Chumash lived here, then the Rancheros, then the Spanish missionaries, then the Californians, then the Americans, then the Grass. Which is me, at least since the Padre brought me back as a baby to La Purísima, our old Grass Mission, in the hills beyond the ocean.

These hills.

The Padre tells it like a story; he was on a crew searching for survivors in the silent city after The Day, only there were none. Whole city blocks were quiet as rain. Finally, he heard a tiny sound—so small, he thought he was imagining it—and there I was, crying purple-faced in my crib. He wrapped me in his coat and brought me home, just as he now brings us stray dogs.

It was also the Padre who taught me the history of these hills as we sat by the fire at night, along with the constellations of the stars and the phases of the moon. The names of the people who knew our land before we did.

Maybe it was supposed to be like this. Maybe this, the Occupation, the Embassies, all of it, maybe this is just another part of nature. Like the seasons of a year, or how a caterpillar turns into a cocoon. The water cycle. The tides.

Chumash Rancheros Spaniards Californians Americans Grass.

Sometimes I repeat the names of my people, all the people who have ever lived in my Mission. I say the names and I think, *I am them and they are me.*

I am the Misíon La Purísima de Concepción de la Santísima Virgen María, founded in Las Californias on the Day of the Feast of the Immaculate Conception of the

Blessed Virgin, on the Eighth Day of the Twelfth Month of the Year of Our Lord One Thousand Seven Hundred Eighty-Seven. Three hundred years ago.

Chumash Rancheros Spaniards Californians Americans Grass.

When I say the names they're not gone, not to me. Nobody died. Nothing ended. We're still here.

I'm still here.

That's all I want. To stay. And for Ro to stay, and the Padre. For us to stay safe, everyone here on the Mission.

But as I look back down the mountain I know that nothing stays, and the gold flush and fade of everything tells me that the sun is setting now.

No one can stop it from going. Not even me.

RESEARCH MEMORANDUM:
THE HUMANITY PROJECT

CLASSIFIED TOP SECRET /
AMBASSADOR EYES ONLY

To: Ambassador Amare
From: Dr. Huxley-Clarke
Subject: Icon Research

We still can't be sure how the Icons work. We know, when the Lords came, thirteen Icons fell from the sky, one landing in each of the Earth's mega-cities. To this day, we still can't get close enough to examine them. Our best guess is that the Icons generate an immensely powerful electromagnetic field that can halt electrical activity within a certain radius. We believe it is this field that enables the Icons to disrupt or disable all modern technology. It appears the Icons can also shut down any and all chemical processes or reactions within the field.

Note: We call this the "shutdown effect."

The Day itself proved the ultimate demonstration of this capability, when, as we all know, the Lords activated the Icons and ended all hope of resistance by making an example of Goldengate, São Paulo, Köln-Bonn, Cairo, Mumbai, and Greater Beijing...the so-called Silent Cities.

By the end of The Day, the newly arrived colonists gained complete control of all major population centers on the Seven Continents. An estimated one billion lives ended in an instant, the greatest tragedy in history.

May silence bring them peace.

2 PRESENTS

By the time we reach the top of the hillside, the sky has turned dark as the eggplants in the Mission garden.

Ro pulls me up the last slide of rocks. "Now. Close your eyes."

"Ro. What have you done?"

"Nothing bad. Nothing *that* bad." He looks at me and sighs. "Not this time, anyway. Come on, trust me."

I don't close my eyes. Instead, I look into the shadows beneath the scraggly trees in front of me, where someone has built a shack out of scraps of old signboard and rusting tin. The hood of an ancient tractor is lashed to the legs on a faded poster advertising what looks like running shoes.

DO IT.

That's what the bodiless legs say, in bright white words spilling over the photograph.

"Don't you trust me?" Ro repeats, keeping his eyes on the shack as if he was showing me his most precious possession.

There is no one I trust more. Ro knows that. He also knows I hate surprises.

I close my eyes.

"Careful. Now, duck."

Even with my eyes shut, I know when I am inside the shack. I feel the palmetto roof brush against my hair, and I nearly tumble over the roots of the trees surrounding us.

"Wait a second." He lets go of me. "One. Two. Three. Happy birthday, Dol!"

I open my eyes. I am now holding one end of a string of tiny colored lights that shine in front of me as if they were stars pulled down from the sky itself. The lights weave from my fingers all across the room, in a kind of sparkling circle that begins with me and ends with Ro.

I clap my hands together, lights and all. "Ro! How—? Is that—electric?"

He nods. "Do you like it?" His eyes are twinkling, same as the lights. "Are you surprised?"

"Never in a thousand years would I have guessed it."

"There's more."

He moves to one side. Next to him is a strange-looking contraption with two rusty metal circles connected by a metal bar and a peeling leather seat.

"A bicycle?"

"Sort of. It's a pedal generator. I saw it in a book that the Padre had, at least the plans for it. Took me about three months to find all the parts. Twenty digits, just for the old bike. And look there—"

He points to two objects sitting on a plank. He takes the string of lights from my hand, and I move to touch a smooth metal artifact.

"Pan-a-sonic?" I sound out the faded type on the side of the first object. It's some sort of box, and I pick it up, turning it over in my hands.

He answers proudly. "That's a radio."

I realize what it is as soon as he says the words, and it's all I can do not to drop it. Ro doesn't notice. "People used them to listen to music. I'm not sure it works, though. I haven't tried it yet."

I put it down. I know what a radio is. My mother had one. I remember because it dies every time in the dream. When The Day comes. I touch my tangled brown curls self-consciously.

It's not his fault. He doesn't know. I've never told anyone about the dream, not even the Padre. That's how badly I don't want to remember it.

I change the subject. "And this?" I pick up a tiny silver rectangle, not much bigger than my palm. There is a picture of a lone piece of fruit scratched on one side.

Ro smiles. "It's some kind of memory cell. It plays old songs, right into your ears." He pulls the rectangle out of my hand. "It's unbelievable, like listening to the past. But it only works when it has power."

I shake my head. "I don't understand."

"That's your present. Power. See? I push the pedals like this, and the friction creates energy."

He stands on the bike pedals, then drops onto the seat, pushing furiously. The string of colored lights glows in the room, all around me. I can't help but laugh, it's so magical—and Ro looks so funny and sweaty.

Ro climbs off the bicycle and kneels in front of a small black box. I see that the string of lights attaches neatly to one side. "That's the battery. It stores the power."

"Right here?" The enormous ramifications of what Ro has done begin to hit me. "Ro, we're not supposed to be messing with this stuff. You know using electricity outside the cities is forbidden. What if someone finds out?"

"Who's going to find us? In the middle of a Grass Mission? Up a goat hill, in view of a pig farm? You always say you wish you knew more about what it was like, before The Day. Now you can."

Ro looks earnest, standing there in front of the pile of junk and wires and time.

"Ro," I say, trying to find the words. "I—"

"What?" He sounds defensive.

"It's the best present ever." It's all I can say, but the words don't seem like enough. He did this, for me. He'd rebuild every radio and every bicycle and every memory

18

cell in the world for me, if he could. And if he couldn't, he'd still try if he thought I wanted him to.

That's who Ro is.

"Really? You like it?" He softens, relieved.

I love it like I love you.

That's what I want to tell him. But he's Ro, and he's my best friend. And he'd rather have the mud scrubbed out of his ears than mushy words whispered in them, so I don't say anything at all. Instead, I sink down onto the floor and examine the rest of my presents. Ro's made a frame, out of twisted wire, for my favorite photograph of my mother—the one with dark eyes and a tiny gold cross at her neck.

"Ro. It's beautiful." I finger each curving copper tendril.

"She's beautiful." He shrugs, embarrassed. So I only nod and move on to the next gift, an old book of stories, nicked from the Padre's bookcase. Not the first time we've done that—and I smile at him conspiratorially. Finally, I pick up the music player, examining the white wires. They have soft pieces on the ends, and I fit one into my ear. I look at Ro and laugh, fitting one in his.

Ro clicks a round button on the side of the rectangle. Screaming music streams into the air—I jump and my earpiece goes flying. When I stick it back in, I can almost feel the music. The nest of cardboard and plywood and tin around us is practically vibrating.

We let the music drown out our thoughts and occupy

ourselves with singing and shouting—until the door flies open and the night comes tumbling inside. The night, and the Padre.

"DOLORIA MARIA DE LA CRUZ!"

It's my real name—though no one is supposed to know or say it—and he wields it like a weapon. He must be really angry. The Padre, as red-faced and short as Ro is brown and long, looks like he could flatten us both with one more word.

"FURO COSTAS!"

But I've given Ro his own turn with the earphones, and the music is so loud he can't hear the Padre. Ro's singing along badly, and dancing worse. I stand frozen in place while the Padre yanks the white cord from Ro's ear. The Padre holds out his other hand and Ro drops the silver music player into it.

"I see you've raided the storage room once more, Furo."

Ro looks at his feet.

The Padre rips the lights out of the black box, and a spark shoots across the room. The Padre raises an eyebrow.

"You're lucky you didn't burn down half the mountain with this contraband," he says, looking meaningfully at Ro. "Again."

"So lucky." Ro snorts. "I think that every day, right before dawn when I get up to feed the pigs."

The Padre drops the string of lights like a snake. "You realize, of course, that a Sympa patrol could have seen the lights on this mountain all the way down to the Tracks?"

"Don't you ever get tired of hiding?" Ro glowers.

"That depends. Do you ever get tired of living?" The Padre glares back. Ro says nothing.

The Padre has the look he gets when he's doing the Mission accounting, hunched over the ledgers he fills with rows of tiny numbers. This time, he is calculating punishments, and multiplying them times two. I tug on his sleeve, looking repentant—a skill I mastered when I was little. "Ro didn't mean it, Padre. Don't be angry. He did it for me."

He cups my chin with one hand, and I feel his fingers on my face. In a flash, I sense him. What comes to me first is worry and fear—not for himself, but for us. He wants to be a wall around us, and he can't, and it makes him crazy. Mostly, he is patience and caution; he is a globe spinning and a finger tracing roads on a worn map. His heart beats more clearly than most. The Padre remembers everything—he was a grown man when the first Carriers came—and most of what he remembers are the children he has helped. Ro, and me, and all the others who lived at the Mission until they were placed with families.

Then, in my mind's eye, I see something new.

The image of a book takes shape.

The Padre is wrapping it, with his careful hands. My present.

He smiles at me, and I pretend not to know where his mind is.

21

"Tomorrow we will speak of bigger things. Not today. It's not your fault, Dolly. It's your birthday eve."

And with that, he winks at Ro and draws his robed arm around me, and we both know all is forgiven.

"Now, come to dinner. Bigger and Biggest are waiting, and if we make them wait much longer, Ramona Jamona will no longer be a guest at our table but the main dish."

As we slide our way back down the hillside, the Padre curses the bushes that tug at his robes, and Ro and I laugh like the children we were when he first found us. We race, stumbling in the darkness toward the warm yellow glow of the Mission kitchen. I can see the homemade beeswax candles flickering, the hand-cut paper streamers hanging from the rafters.

My birthday eve dinner is a success. Everyone on the Mission is there—almost a dozen people, counting the farmhands and the church workers—all crammed around our long wooden table. Bigger and Biggest have used every cracked plate in the shed. I get to sit in the Padre's seat, a birthday tradition, and we eat my favorite potato-cheese stew and Bigger's famous sugar cake and sing old songs by the fire until the moon is high and our eyes are heavy and I fall asleep in my usual warm spot in front of the oven.

When the old nightmare comes—my mother and me and the radio going silent—Ro is there next to me on the floor, asleep with crumbs still on his face and twigs still in his hair.

My thief of junk. Climber of mountains. Builder of worlds.

I rest my head on his back and listen to him breathe. I wonder what tomorrow will bring. What the Padre wants to tell me.

Bigger things, that's what he said.

I think about bigger things until I am too small and too tired to care.

EMBASSY CITY TRIBUNAL AUTOPSY

CLASSIFIED TOP SECRET

Performed by Dr. O. Brad Huxley-Clarke, VPHD

Note: Conducted at the private request of
Amb. Amare

Santa Catalina Examination Facility #9B

Also see adjoining DPPT in addendum file.

Deceased Personal Possessions Transcript

Deceased classified as victim of Grass Rebellion uprising. Known to be Person of Interest to Ambassador Amare.

Gender: Female.

Ethnicity: Indeterminate.

Age: Estimate mid-to-late teens. Postadolescent.

Physical Characteristics:
Slightly underweight. Brown hair. Blue eyes. Skin characterized by some discoloration indicative of elemental exposure. Exhibits human protein markers and low body weight indicative of predominantly agrarian diet. Staining

patterns on teeth consistent with consumption habits of local Grass cultures.

Distinguishing Physical Markings:
A recognizable ███ marking ██ appears inside the specimen's right wrist. At the Ambassador's request, a ████ ████ specimen of the ███████████████ has been removed, in observance of ███████ security protocols. ████████████████.

Cause of Death: ████████████████████████████████.

Survivors: No identified family.

Note: Body will be cremated following lab processing.

Embassy City Waste Facility Assignment: Landfill ████.

THE PIETÀ OF LA PURÍSIMA

Feelings are memories.

That's what I'm thinking as I stand there in the Mission chapel, the morning of my birthday. It's what the Padre says. He also says that chapels turn regular people into philosophers.

I'm not a regular person, but I'm still no philosopher. And either way, what I remember and how I feel are the only two things I can't escape, no matter how much I want to.

No matter how hard I try.

For the moment, I tell myself not to think. I focus on trying to see. The chapel is dark but the doorway to outside is blindingly bright. That's what morning always looks like in the chapel. The little light there prickles and stings my eyes.

Like in the Mission itself, in the chapel you can pretend

26

that nothing has changed for hundreds of years, that nothing has happened. Not like in the Hole, where they say the buildings have fallen into ruins, and Sympa soldiers control the streets with fear, and you think about nothing but The Day, every day.

Los Angeles, that's what the Hole used to be called. First Los Angeles, then the City of Angels, then the Holy City, then the Hole. When I was little, that's how I used to think of the House of Lords, as angels. Nobody calls them *alien* anymore, because they aren't. They're familiar. We never see them, but we've never known a world without them, not Ro and me. I grew up thinking they were angels because back on The Day they sent my parents to heaven. At least, that's what the Grass missionaries told me, when I was old enough to ask.

Heaven, not their graves.

Angels, not aliens.

But just because something comes from the sky doesn't make it an angel. The Lords didn't come here from the heavens to save us. They came from some faraway solar system to colonize our planet, on The Day. We don't know what they look like inside their ships, but they're not angels. They destroyed my family the year I was born. What kind of angel would do that?

Now we call them the House of Lords—and Ambassador Amare, she tells us not to fear them—but we do.

Just as we fear her.

On The Day, the dead dropped silently in their homes, never seeing what hit them. Never knowing anything about our new Lords, about the way they could use their Icons to control the energy that flowed through our own bodies, our machines, our cities.

About how they could stop it.

Either way, my family is gone. There was no reason for me to have survived. Nobody understood why I did.

The Padre suspected, of course. That's why he took me.

First me, and then Ro.

I hear a sound from the far end of the chapel.

I squint, turning my back to the door.

The Padre has sent for me, but he's late. I catch the eye of the Lady from the painting on the wall. Her face is so sad, I think she knows what has happened. I think she knows everything. She's part of what General Ambassador to the Planet Hiro Miyazawa, the head of the United Embassies, calls the old ways of humanity. How we believed in ourselves—how we survived ourselves. What we looked up to, back when we thought there was someone up above.

Not something.

I look back to the Lady a moment longer, until the sadness surges and the pain radiates through me. It pulses from my temples and I feel my mind stumble, folding at the edge of unconsciousness. Something is wrong. It must be, for the familiar ache to come on so suddenly. I press my hand to my temple, willing it to stop. I breathe deep, until I can see clearly.

"Padre?"

My voice echoes against the wood and stone. It sounds as small as I am. An animal has lurched into my leg, one of many more entering the chapel, and my nostrils fill with smells—hair and hides and hooves, paint and mold and manure. My birthday falls on the Blessing of the Animals, which will begin just hours from now. Local Grass farmers and ranchers will come to have the Padre bless their livestock, as they have for three hundred years. It is Grass tradition, and we are a Grass Mission.

Appearing in the door, the Padre smiles at me, moving to light the ceremonial candles. Then his smile fades. "Where's Furo? Bigger and Biggest haven't seen him at all this morning."

I shrug. I can't account for every second of Ro's day. Ro could be lifting all the dried cereal cakes out of Bigger's emergency supplies. Chasing Biggest's donkeys. Sneaking down the Tracks toward the Hole, to buy more parts for the Padre's busted-up old *pistola*, shot only on New Year's Eve. Meeting people he doesn't want me to meet, learning things he doesn't want me to know. Preparing for a war he'll never fight with an enemy that can't be defeated.

He's on his own.

The Padre, preoccupied as always, is no longer paying attention to himself or to me. "Careful..." I catch his elbow, pulling him out of the way of a pile of pig waste. A near miss.

He clicks his tongue and leans down to chuck Ramona Jamona on the chin. "Ramona. Not in the chapel." It's an act—really, he doesn't mind. The big pink pig sleeps in his chamber on cold nights, we all know she does. He loves Ro and me just as he does Ramona—in spite of everything we do and beyond anything he says. He's the only father we have ever known, and though I call him the Padre, I think of him as my Padre.

"She's a pig, Padre. She's going to go wherever she wants. She can't understand you."

"Ah, well. It's only once a year, the Blessing of the Animals. We can clean the floors tomorrow. All Earth's creatures need our prayers."

"I know. I don't mind." I look to the animals, wondering. The Padre sinks onto a low pew, patting the wood next to him. "We can take a few minutes to ourselves, however. Come. Sit."

I oblige.

He smiles, touching my chin. "Happy birthday, Dolly." He holds out a parcel wrapped in brown paper and tied with string. It materializes from his robes, a priestly sleight of hand.

Birthday secrets. My book, finally.

I recognize it from his thoughts, from yesterday. He holds it out to me, but his face is not full of joy.

Only sadness.

"Be careful with it. Don't let it out of your sight. It's very rare. And it's about you."

I drop my hand.

"Doloria." He says my real name and I stiffen, bracing myself for the words I fear are coming. "I know you don't like to talk about it, but it's time we speak of such things. There are people who would harm you, Doloria. I haven't really told you how I found you, not all of it. Why you survived the attack and your family didn't. I think you're ready to hear it now." He leans closer. "Why I've hidden you. Why you're special. Who you are."

I've been dreading this talk since my tenth birthday. The day he first told me what little I know about who I am and how I am different. That day, over sugar cakes and thick, homemade butter and sun tea, he talked to me slowly about the creeping sadness that came over me, so heavy that my chest fluttered like a startled animal's and I couldn't breathe. About the pain that pulsed in my head or came between my shoulder blades. About the nightmares that were so real I was afraid Ro would walk in and find me cold and still in my bed one morning.

As if you really could die from a broken heart.

But the Padre never told me where the feelings came from. That's one thing even he didn't know.

31

I wish someone did.

"Doloria."

He says my name again to remind me that he knows my secret. He's the only one, Ro and him. When we're alone, I let Ro call me Doloria—but even he mostly calls me Dol, or even Dodo. I'm just plain Dolly to everyone else.

Not Doloria Maria de la Cruz. Not a Weeper. Not marked by the lone gray dot on my wrist.

One small circle the color of the sea in the rain.

The one thing that is really me.

My destiny.

Dolor means "sorrow," in Latin or Greek or some other language from way, way before The Day. BTD. Before everything changed.

"Open it."

I look at him, uncertain. The candles flicker, and a breeze shudders slowly through the room. Ramona noses closer to the altar, her snout looking for traces of honey on my hand.

I slip my finger through the paper, pulling it loose from the string. Beneath the wrapping is hardly a book, almost more of a journal: the cover is thick, rough burlap, home-made. This is a Grass book, unauthorized, illegal. Most likely preserved by the Rebellion, in spite of and because of the Embassy regulations. Such books are usually on subjects the Ambassadors won't acknowledge within the world of the Occupation. They are very hard to come by, and extremely valuable.

My eyes well with tears as I read the cover. *The Humanity Project: The Icon Children.* It looks like it was written by hand.

"No," I whisper.

"Read it." He nods. "I was supposed to keep it safe for you and make sure you read it when you were old enough."

"Who said that? Why?"

"I'm not sure. I discovered the book with a note on the altar, not long after I brought you here. Just read it. It's time. And nobody knows as much about the subject as this particular author. It's written by a doctor, it seems, in his own hand."

"I know enough not to read more." I look around for Ro. I wish, desperately, he would walk through the chapel door. But the Padre is the Padre, so I open the book to a page he's marked, and begin to read about myself.

Icon doloris.

Dolorus. Doloria. Me.

My purpose is pain and my name is sorrow.

One gray dot says so.

No.

"Not yet." I look up at the Padre and shake my head, shoving the book into my belt. The conversation is over.

The story of me can wait until I'm ready. My heart hurts again, stronger this time.

I hear strange noises, feel a change in the air. I look to Ramona Jamona, hoping for some moral support, but she is lying at my feet, fast asleep.

No, not asleep.

Dark liquid pools beneath her.

The cold animal in my chest startles awake, fluttering once again.

An old feeling returns. Something really is wrong. Soft pops fill the air.

"Padre," I say.

Only I look at him and he is not my Padre at all. Not anymore.

"Padre!" I scream. He's not moving. He's nothing. Still sitting next to me, still smiling, but not breathing.

He's gone.

My mind moves slowly. I can't make sense of it. His eyes are empty and his mouth has fallen open. Gone.

It's all gone. His jokes. His secret recipes—the butter he made from shaking cream together with smooth, round rocks—the rows of sun tea in jars—gone. Other secrets, too. My secrets.

But I can't think about it now, because behind the Padre—what was the Padre—stands a line of masked soldiers. Sympas.

Occupation Sympathizers, traitors to humanity.

34

Embassy soldiers, taking orders from the Lords, hiding behind plexi-masks and black armor, standing in pig mess and casting long shadows over the deathly peace of the chapel. One wears golden wings on his jacket. It's the only detail I see, aside from the weapons. The guns make no noise, but the animals panic all the same. They are screaming—which is something I did not know, that animals could scream.

I open my mouth, but I do not scream. I vomit.

I spit green juices and gray dust and memories of Ramona and the Padre.

All I can see are the guns. All I can feel is hate and fear. The black-gloved hands close around my wrist, overwhelming me, and I know that soon I will no longer have to worry about my nightmares.

I will be dead.

As my knees buckle, all I can think about is Ro and how angry he will be at me for leaving him.

EMBASSY CITY TRIBUNAL
VIRTUAL AUTOPSY: DECEASED PERSONAL
POSSESSIONS TRANSCRIPT (DPPT)

CLASSIFIED TOP SECRET

Performed by Dr. O. Brad Huxley-Clarke, VPHD

Note: Conducted at the private request of
   Amb. Amare

Santa Catalina Examination Facility #9B

See adjoining Tribunal Autopsy, attached.

Contents of personal satchel, torn, army-issue, found with deceased.

See attached photographs.

1. Electronic device, silver and rectangular. Appears to be some form of contraband pre-Occupation music player.

2. Photograph of woman, similar in feature and stature to deceased. Possible predeceased family member?

3. ██████████████████████████████████████ .

4. ███████████████████████████████████
███████████████████████████████████.

5. Dried plant leathers. Substantiates finding of probable vegetarianism in deceased.

6. One blue glass bead. Significance unknown.

7. One length of muslin cloth, stained with biological and natural material consistent with body wrapping, presumably of the wrist, as is customary for ████████████.

4 TRACKS

I am alive.

When I open my eyes I'm on a train—alone in a prison transport car, gunmetal gray, pushed by an old coal-fueled steam engine. Nothing but four walls lined with metal benches, bolted to the floor. A door to my left, a window to my right. A pile of old rags in the corner. That's it. I must be on the Tracks, hurtling toward the Hole. The dim blue waters of Porthole Bay flip in and out of sight, rhythmically punctuated by shuffling old comlink poles. They stick up from the land like so many useless skeleton fingers.

I watch my reflection in the window. My brown hair is dark and loose and matted with dirt and bile. My skin is pale and barely covers the handful of small bones that are me. Then I see my reflection twist, and in the plexi-window I look as sad as the Lady in her painting. *Because the Padre is dead.*

I try to hold on to his face in my mind, the grooves by his eyes, the mole on his cheek. The cocky spike of his thinning hair. I'm afraid I'll lose it, him—even the memory. Tomorrow, if not today.

Like everything else, there's no holding on to the Padre. Not anymore.

I look back out at the bay, and I can feel the bile churn inside me, strong as the tides. Usually the water calms me. Not today. Today, as I clutch the blue glass bead at my throat, the ocean is almost unrecognizable. I wonder where the Tracks are taking me. *To my death? Or worse?*

I see a glimpse of the rusting, abandoned cars on the highway along the rails, junked as if all life stopped and the planet froze in place, which is pretty much what happened on The Day. After the House of Lords came, with their Carrier ships, and the thirteen Icons fell from the sky, one landing in each of the largest cities in the world.

The Padre says—said—that people used to live all over Earth, spread out. There were small towns, small cities, big cities. Not anymore. Almost the entire population of the planet lives within a hundred miles of a mega-city. The Padre said this happened because so much of the world has been ruined by people, by the rising waters, rising temperatures, drought, flooding. Some parts of Earth are toxic with radiation from massive wars. People stay in the cities because we are running out of places to live.

Now everything people need to live is produced in or near the cities. Energy, food, technology—it's all centralized in the cities. Which makes the Lords' work that much easier.

The Icons regulate everything with an electronic pulse. The Padre said the Icons can control electricity, the power that flows between generators and machines, even the electrical impulses that connect brains and bodies. They can halt all electrical and chemical activity at any time. Which is what happened to Goldengate, on The Day. And São Paulo, Köln-Bonn, Greater Beijing, Cairo, Mumbai. The Silent Cities. Which is why we gave in to the Lords and let them take our planet.

But out in the Grasslands, like at the Mission, we have more freedom. The Icons lose their strength the farther away you go. But the Lords and the Ambassadors are in control, even then, because they have the resources. They have weapons that work. And there's no power in the Grass, no source of energy. Even so, I have hope. The Padre always tried to reassure me—everything has a limit. Everything has an end. Beyond the borders of the cities and the frequencies of the Icons, life goes on. They can't turn everything off. They don't control our whole planet. Not yet.

Nothing in the Grass works that isn't pulled by a horse or cranked by a person. But at least we know our hearts will be beating in the morning, our lungs pumping air, our bodies shivering from the cold. Which is more than I know about myself tomorrow.

The pile of rags groans from the floor. I was wrong. I'm not alone. A man, lying facedown, is splayed across from me. He smells like a Remnant, which is what the Embassy calls us, another piece of worthless garbage like me. He even smells like he lives with the pigs—drunk pigs.

My heart begins to pound. I sense adrenaline. Heat. Anger. Not just the soldiers. Something more.

Ro's here.

I close my eyes and feel him. I can't see him, but I know he's near. *Don't*, I think, though he can't hear me. *Let me go, Ro. Get yourself somewhere safe.*

Ro hates Sympas. I know if he comes after me the rage will come after him, and he will probably be killed. Like the Padre. Like my parents, and Ro's. Like everyone else.

I also know he will come for me.

The man sits up, groaning. He looks like he is going to be sick, leaning against the swaying side of the car. I steady myself, waiting by the window.

The comlink poles go slapping by. The Tracks turn, and the watery curve of the Porthole shoreline comes into view, the Hole beyond it. A few crude skiffs float on the water nearest the shore. Beyond them, rising above the water, is the Hole, the biggest city on the west coast. The only one, since Goldengate was silenced. I don't look at

41

the Icon, though I know it's there. It's always there loom-
ing, from the hill above the city, a knife in the otherwise
flat skyline. What once was an observatory has been gut-
ted and transformed by the black irregularity that juts out
from the structure. It's also a reminder, this disturbingly
nonhuman landmark, sent by our new Lords to pierce the
earth and show us all that we are not in control.

That our hearts beat only with their permission.

If I'm not careful, I can feel all of them, the people
in the Hole. They well up in me, unannounced. Everyone in
the Hole, everyone in the Embassy. Sympas and Remnants
and even Ambassador Amare. I fight them off. I try to
clear my mind. I will myself not to feel—I've felt too much
already. I try to press back against the welling. If I let them
in, I'm afraid I will lose myself. I'll lose everything.

*Chumash Rancheros Spaniards Californians Americans
Grass.* I recite the words, over and over, but this time they
don't seem to help.

"Dol!"

It's Ro. He's here now, right outside the door. I hear a
rattle and see the skull of the Sympa slam into the plexi-
door and sink out of sight. There is a dent where he hit.
No one else could destroy a Sympa like that, not with only
his hands. Ro must already be out of control, to throw
him so hard. Which means I don't have much time. I
push myself up to my feet and move across the car to the

door. It doesn't open, but I know Ro is right outside. I can see a glimpse of the narrow hall through the small plexi in the door.

"Ro! Ro, don't!" Then I hear shouting. Too late.

Please. Go home, Ro.

The shouting grows louder, and the train lurches. I stand up and stumble, almost stepping on the other prisoner, the Remnant. He rolls over and looks up at me, a pile of filth and rags, his face so covered with muck I can't tell what he is or where he's from. His skin is the color of bark. "Your *Ro* is going to get you both killed, you know." The voice is mocking. He has an accent, but I can't place it—only that it's not from the Californias. Maybe not even the Americas.

He moves again, and I see the welt that runs down the length of his face. He's been beaten, and I can imagine why. I want to kick him myself for mocking Ro, but I don't. Instead, I feel for the binding beneath my sleeve, wrapping it more tightly around my wrist and my secret.

One gray dot the color of the ocean.

The Padre's gone. Only Ro knows now.

Unless that's why the Sympas came.

I can't worry about it much longer, though, because the man answers himself in a strange falsetto, which I imagine he means to be me. "I know. I'm sorry about that, mate."

I glare at him, at the place where his piercing blue eyes

look out from the dirt on his face. He keeps talking. "Not really much of a plan, is it? Bang down the old plexi, beat up a few Stooges."

The man pulls himself up next to me, grinning. He is taller than I am, which isn't saying much. I notice, beneath the rags, his body is muscular and compact. He looks more like a soldier than the Sympas do.

"I'm Fortis." He holds out his hand. It sits there.

I push against the door again, but it's locked. Fortis surveys the room and returns to his conversation with himself. He wags his head as he once again answers his own question in falsetto. "Pleased to meet you, Fortis. I'm the little Grassgirl. Sorry about all the shooting right outside your door, eh? Didn't mean to wake you. Or kill you." He whistles to himself.

I don't interrupt him and I don't look at him. I'm too busy listening for guns. And I'm trying to pick out Ro from the mess of other emotions running wild, up and down the Tracks. He's not just a spark, not anymore—he's a blazing fire. And there are so many fires raging now, today, more than ever. The heat is overwhelming me.

But he's there. I close my eyes. *He's still on the train.* He hasn't left—I can't hear him, but I can feel him.

The Remnant, Fortis, whoever he is, moves closer to me. I freeze.

"Here's how it goes, Grassgirl. Way I see it, you've done something a bit special to get yourself upgraded to

44

this fine, first-class cargo hold, on this set of Tracks." He wags his head toward the door. "You're not like the rest of the Remnants in the cars behind us, all headed to the Projects. You're something else."

Now I know what I have been feeling, apart from Ro. Why his anger was so hard to pick out from the other red-hot threads. *Of course.* The train is full of Remnants headed to the Projects, the work camps run by the Embassy. No wonder I sense so much rage. Nobody knows what they're building out in the harbor. But it's massive, and they've been building it for years now.

"Your mate Ro, he's got his hands full. He can't take the Tracks down alone—there's not a person in all the Grass who can. Don't have the right tools, do they? And I'll tell you what about this place. You can't bash your way in. You can only blow your way out." He opens his rag coat and I see a collection of weapons tucked inside crude fabric loops. "Boom." He taps a stick of dynamite, and buttons shut his coat, grinning. "Old school. Now. Let's try this again. I'm Fortis."

"Who are you?" I finally speak, and my voice sounds hoarse and low, nothing like his impression of me. "I thought you were a Remnant."

"Not exactly. I'm not a Sympa Stooge either, if that's what you're after. I'm a businessman, and this is my business."

"You're a Merk?"

"What of it? Do you want me to help you or not?" Fortis looks impatient.

I shrug. "How much?" I don't know why I even bother asking. Merks are notoriously expensive; they don't care about anything or anyone—they can't afford to. Which means they don't work for free, and I don't have any way to pay.

"A hundred digs gets you a minor explosion on the side of the Tracks. Five hundred digs, we're talking a full-blown diversion. A thousand digs...?" He grins. "You an' your boy were never here. You never existed, and they'll never see you again." He talks rapidly, like he's trying to sell me bootleg books or miracle tonic or stolen Sympatech.

Still, it would be a tall order. Blasting your way out of the Tracks. Even for a Merk.

"How?"

"Trade secrets, Grassgirl."

"I don't have anything."

He looks me over, up and down. Smiles. He reaches toward me, questioningly, and I blush as I feel his hand inside my waistband, just at my hip. I slap him in the face. "You're disgusting."

Fortis rolls his eyes, yanking my birthday book out of my belt, holding it up with a flourish. I had forgotten all about it.

"Didn't think you were a Skin, love. You're too, well,

46

skinny." He grins. "Be like givin' a dig for a kiss from a carrot stick." He shudders, trying not to laugh.

I've heard about girls who sell their bodies in the Hole. It's a terrible thought. "Shut up."

Fortis ignores me, leafing through the book as if it were made of gold instead of ragged paper. "Icon Children, eh? Looks handmade. Expensive. And highly illegal, by the way. I'd be doing you a favor, taking it off your hands. They'd give you extra time just for having it on you, Grass book like that." He leans in again. "You don't want the Ambassador to know you're with the Rebellion, Grassgirl."

"It's just a book." I shrug, but all the same, I hear the Padre's words echoing in my mind. *Don't let it out of your sight.* I stare at the precious paper in the Merk's dirty hands.

"And you'll be just a pile of bones before you get a chance to explain." He looks up from the book.

"I'm not with the Rebellion. I'm not with anyone. I'm just..." I shrug, as if there is a word that can describe me. If there is, I can't find it. I give up. "I'm nobody. Just a Grassgirl, like you said." And as I say it, I realize he's right. Without his help, I'm probably going to the Projects, or my death, or worse.

What does a stupid book matter now?

It is time to decide, and in that moment, I do. I grab

his arm, yanking down as hard as I can. "I'm nobody, and I was never here. I never existed. Ro and me, both."

He levels his eyes at me, gleaming blue behind his dirty face.

Like the sea. Like mine.

He nods at me, but I make him say the words. I want to be certain. "Take the book. It's enough. Do we have a deal?"

"Not just a deal—a promise." He tucks my book inside his jacket, and the story of me disappears among the handguns and homemade explosives. "Your secret's safe with me, love. So is your book. Now get down."

Before I can say another word, Fortis lifts the dynamite and lights the fuse.

RESEARCH MEMORANDUM: THE HUMANITY PROJECT

To: Ambassador Amare
Subject: Icon Origins
Text Scan: *NEW ENGLAND JOURNAL*

PLANET KILLER COMING OUR WAY?

December 29, 2042 • Cambridge, Massachusetts

Scientists at the Minor Planet Center in Cambridge announced today the discovery of a very large asteroid that is projected to pass dangerously close to Earth.

The asteroid, designated 2042 IC4, or Perses, has a targeted impact/arrival date of 2070–2090.

Scientists approximate the size of the asteroid at as large as 4 miles in diameter, which officials claim is large enough to create an extinction event.

Paulo Fortissimo, special scientific advisor to the president, says we shouldn't panic: "I need to review the data, but the size and speed of the asteroid are merely an estimate, and the odds of this thing hitting Earth are still relatively low. Nevertheless, rest assured, we will keep a close eye on it."

5
DIVERSIONS

The blast does more than blow open the door.

The blast has rocked the Tracks so hard, the car seems to have gone off the rails. My ears are ringing. The floor is no longer beneath me but next to me. The roof is gone, and through the jagged hole that remains, I can see the open air.

I pick myself up from the tangle of Fortis and wall and floor, the debris of what used to be the prison car, and take off running through the opening.

"Thank you, Fortis," Fortis calls after me. "You're welcome, little Grassgirl. Anytime."

I run faster, along the smoking cars. I can tell from the footsteps that there are Sympas behind me. Probably half a dozen more around the cars. *I didn't feel them coming. I have to pay better attention.*

But thanks to the Merk, I have a head start. I have to get to the water. That's all that goes through my head. I know I'll be safe there because I know what I'll find—and who. I turn, more sharply now, disappearing into the tall weeds on the west. My feet catch on the rocks beneath me, but I stumble forward. I know the Sympas are close behind me, and I don't look back.

I keep running, moving in the exact direction where I can feel the bonfire ahead of me—racing toward the shore, just like me. My one sure trajectory, my best chance for survival.

Ro.

His hand grabs my ankle and I drop. I feel his arm slide around my waist, snapping me down to the tide. I fall toward him, and I find myself lying in the sand and shallow water, hidden from the Tracks just beneath a grassy rise of shoreline. Some kind of coastal cave.

I feel us both still panting; Ro's only gotten here seconds ago, himself. Then I hear a shout and a splash, and a Sympa soldier falls over the rise after me. I roll out of the way, knee-deep into the water.

I know what will happen now. Someone will die, and it's not Ro. In a small arena, it doesn't matter that the Sympa is armed and Ro is not. Ro will crucify him.

Before I can even think the words, Ro has the fallen Sympa's gun in his hands, slamming the butt of the weapon into the soldier's face. Blood sprays the rocks and runs into the water. Ro raises his hand to strike again, but I move my hands over his, forcing him to look at me.

"Ro."

He shakes his head, but I won't let go, and we cling to the gun together. I can't let Ro do this to himself.

"Don't," I say.

I look at the unconscious Sympa's face, just above the water's edge, covered with blood. His nose is probably broken. He seems young and almost handsome, with hair the color of sunshine—though it's hard to tell what he normally looks like, since he's already starting to bruise. But I look away, because he's too distracting—I have to close off the welling of sadness inside of me. I have people of my own to mourn. A pig and a Padre and a family I never got to know. I toss the weapon into the water and hold out my arms.

Ro falls into me, folds into me, as if I am his home.

I am.

He doesn't let go. His face is red, and neither one of us can slow our breathing. Instead we pant like two tired Mission dogs chased by coyotes. The cold, fluttering animal in my chest and the warm, rabid creature in his push up against each other, and for the moment we are not alone.

I bury my face in his neck, wrapping my arms around the twisted muscles that move beneath the skin of his chest and arms. He smells like dirt, even now. I can practically taste the mud. When Ro smiles—which is only when I'm around, and even then only when all the stars in the night sky align—I half expect to see dirt between his teeth.

He's Grass, through and through. He'd break his share of hearts in another world. I don't doubt that. I lace my fingers through his hair and ground myself in him. I listen to his breathing and know he's trying to do the same. It isn't so easy for Ro, to slow himself back down.

I hear another blast, followed by the sound of people running toward the train.

Fortis.

A second explosion. *The Merk is as good as his word.*

Ro carefully looks toward the train to make sure no other Sympas followed us here. He nods, indicating we are safe for the moment. We don't speak until the shouting has grown distant and the Sympas are quiet.

"It's safer to hide for now. We'll have to wait them out. Dol..." The way Ro says my name, I know he knows about the Padre and Ramona Jamona. I know he was afraid it would be me. I hear it in his voice. "Doloria," he whispers.

He's no different than I am with my incantations, reciting the settlers of La Purísima.

He needs me. I give him my hand. My right hand.

He fumbles at my wrist, yanking the cloth that binds it.

He unwinds the muslin strip that wraps my bony arm so tightly I forget it is not made of skin.

Now my wrist is naked, and he pulls up his own worn sleeve.

We lace our fingers together, and he slides his bare wrist down to meet mine. I let the shiver roll down my body, down from my arm to where my feet dig into the sand.

One gray dot on my wrist, the color of the ocean in the rain.

Two red dots on his wrist, the color of fire.

The shared mark of our shared destinies, though we don't know what they are. If my name is Sorrow, his name is Rage. And whatever I am, whatever Ro is, is a secret. One that could kill us both without our ever knowing why.

One that probably killed the Padre.

I wish I'd read the Padre's book before I traded it for my freedom. Ro would have.

My gray presses against his red.

We live in a world of only two people now. Bound by the markings on our hands and our hearts.

He winds the cloth around our clasped hands, pushing his body against mine, and I feel the sharp knuckles of our ribs as they fit together. We are the mirror image of each other.

Sorrow for rage. Pain for anger. Tears for fury.

I become Ro and Ro becomes me. He takes my great sadness, the frightened thing that lives inside me. He'll do anything to keep it away from me. And I take the red rage. I am a deluge; the red spark that is Ro is twenty feet under my surface.

I can't keep it down for long.

The Padre said Ro is too much for one person, that if I keep doing this—if I keep letting him do this—I may not be able to come back. Yet I let his pain take me to the edge of madness.

The Padre.

I open my eyes and find, in the arms of my best friend, it is safe enough to cry.

The tears push out from my eyes and run down my face. I have no power to stop them.

Ro grabs my hand, willing me to let them fall.

———— • ————

When it is over, and we have pushed aside the feelings for another day, Ro helps me bind my wrist. His skin is no longer burning, and he pulls down his sleeve carelessly. Ro is not so afraid of his marking as I am. He's not even afraid of the whole Sympa patrol I know are only a stretch of field away—no matter how long we wait.

"You should be more careful. Someone could see," I say.

"Yeah? So what?"

"They'll take you away like they tried to take me. Lock you up in the Hole, somewhere. Use you. Hurt you." I try not to remind him what that would mean for me, how afraid I am.

"So instead we hide, our whole lives? Like this? Until we die?" His voice is bitter.

"Maybe not forever. What if the Padre's right and we are special, more powerful than we know? What if that's why the Sympas came for me?" These aren't words I've ever said, but I'm desperate. I need to keep him calm, before he gets himself killed. "We can't pretend the Mission is safe anymore, Ro. If there's even a Mission to go back to." I swallow.

"But why hide, if we're so special? What if we're *supposed* to be doing something? What if we're the only ones who can?" He runs his hands through his hair, unable to keep still.

This is all he wants. To save the world and everyone in it.

Right now, I just want to save the only family I have. Whether or not he wants me to.

I try again. "The Padre said who we are can be used against us, if we're not careful. We might make everything worse."

Ro has lost his patience with me. We are both spinning perilously close to the edge of our tempers. "Yeah, Dol? The Padre also said the truth would set us free. He told us to turn the other cheek. He said to love our neighbors. And now he's dead."

I move away from him, but he grabs my arm.

"I loved the Padre, Dol, same as you."

"I know that."

"But he was from another time. What he said, what he believed, that was a fantasy. He said those things because he didn't want us to give up. But he didn't want to fight, either."

"Ro. Don't start."

He softens. "I'm not going to leave you behind, Dol. A promise is a promise."

He remembers; we both do.

Dot to dot, we swore. Down at the beach, after the first time Ro ran away. When I was the only one who could talk him into coming back.

That was the first time we learned that binding our hands would bind our hearts. That whatever it was that made Ro's heart pound was the same thing that made mine break. When I felt myself willing the sand up over us, in my mind, smothering the flames inside him, he calmed down; we both did. When we touched—just so—dot to dot—the ache turned in on itself.

The fire burned out.

We lay together there, hand to hand, until he was sleeping. That's when I knew I wouldn't make it without Ro. And Ro wouldn't last a day without me.

He can't stop the fires alone. He doesn't care. It's the hardest thing I know about him.

He'd rather let them burn.

I'm still lost in thought when I hear the Choppers over-head. We both know what it means, but I'm the one who finally says it.

"Embassy Choppers. We have to move."

"Give me a minute." Shaking in his wet clothes, Ro's not quite himself yet. I've never seen him this rattled.

"Are you sure you're all right?"

"I thought you were dead, Dol."

I reach my hand up to his thick brown hair. I pull out a twig, caught behind his ear. I don't say what I am think-ing, that I should be dead, that I am supposed to be dead. *A pig is dead and a Padre is dead*, I think. *Why should luck escape them to find me?*

Because they were never going to kill me. Because they were coming for me.

I wonder.

I wonder if the Padre and the pig are the lucky ones. Then I push the thought away and reach for Ro. "I'm not dead. I'm right here." I try to smile at him, but I can't. The Chopper is all I can hear, just as the bloody soldier at my feet is all I can see.

"Then I thought I was dead." He swallows a laugh, but the way it bubbles up from his chest, it's almost a sob.

"You nearly were. You can't just jack a train car and attack the Tracks like that. I don't know what you were thinking." I twist his ear, like I would Ramona Jamona. Only hers are soft, like cloth. His are practically caked with mud.

"I was thinking I was saving your life." He doesn't look up.

I sigh and draw my arm around him. "I wish you wouldn't. Not when it almost kills you. And anyway, someone's going to have to save both our lives if we don't get out of here before that thing lands." I try to push him off, but he pulls me closer, tightening his arm around my waist.

"You wish I wouldn't. But you know I will."

"I know, I know." I smile, softening in spite of everything. The cave, the unconscious Sympa, the sound of the Choppers. "We're all we've got."

It's true.

We're practically family—the closest thing we have to it, anyway.

But as I say the words, I realize Ro isn't looking at my eyes.

He's looking at my mouth.

The spark that is Ro becomes a firestorm. I can feel my palms beginning to burn, my eyes widening. I know what he is feeling and I can't believe it. I can't believe that I can know someone so well and not have known this. "Ro,"

I start, but I don't go on. I don't know what I would say.

That I love him more than I love my own life? It's true.
That we've swum half-naked in the ocean without bother-
ing to even look at each other? Also true. That we've slept
a hundred cold nights together on the tiled floor of Bigger's
Mission kitchen hearth, just the two of us—alongside a
bony litter of tired dogs and sheep? That I could no more
kiss him than I could one of Biggest's pigs?

Is that also true?

I close my eyes and try to imagine kissing Ro. I imagine his lips on mine. His lips, the same ones that have spit
pomegranate seeds straight into my mouth.

They're soft, I find myself remembering.

They'd be soft, I find myself thinking. *At least, softer
than his ears.*

I am afraid to open my eyes. I feel his hands on my
waist, as if we are dancing. I feel him slowly pulling me
toward him.

I let myself be pulled.

Almost.

Then I hear someone moaning, and I remember we
aren't alone.

The Sympa soldier is waking up.

RESEARCH MEMORANDUM: THE HUMANITY PROJECT

CLASSIFIED TOP SECRET / AMBASSADOR EYES ONLY

To: Ambassador Amare

Subject: Rebellion Recruitment and Indoctrination
Materials

Catalogue Assignment: Evidence recovered during
raid of Rebellion hideout

According to our intelligence, Rebellion recruits are made to
memorize and recite the following verse, morning and night:

THIRTEEN GREAT ICONS

FELL FROM THE SKY,

WHEN THEY CAME ALIVE,

SIX CITIES DIED.

REMEMBER 6/6.

THE PROJECTS ARE SLAVERY.

WE ARE NOT FREE.

SILENCE IS NOT PEACE.

REMEMBER THE DAY.

DEATH TO THE SYMPAS,

DEATH TO THE LORDS.

DESTROY THE ICONS.

REMEMBER.

FOUR DOTS

I open my eyes. "Ro," I hiss. But he's let go of me before I can say it, and is grabbing the gun out of the water. The reality of where we are comes flooding back. The sandy rocks beneath us seem that much sharper, the shallow rush of empty tides that much colder. Our watery cave—just a small indentation in the grassy shoreline—offers no protection at all.

Not against the Embassies and their armies.

Not for long.

The Sympa's eyes flutter open.

Beneath soggy strands of wet hair, they are the same color as the hills behind the Mission—green and gray—but also flecked with gold. Hope and sadness. That's how he looks to me. Like a rare coin half buried in the ocean floor. A bit of warm metal that somehow catches the light, even from so far below the surface of the waves.

I'm staring. I can't help it. My heart is pounding.

I reach toward his face, marveling. His features are the opposite of Ro's; where Ro is thick brushstrokes and harsh lines, everything about this boy is precise and fine. He's muscled and compact, where Ro is strong and broad. His bones fit together like someone hammered them out of precious metals, blew them out of glass.

"Hey—" Ro shouts. He raises the gun high over his head, ready to strike. I pull my eyes away from the Sympa, my hand away from his face.

"Stop it. You don't have to. He's hurt enough."

Ro lowers the gun. Then I realize he isn't listening to me. He's aiming.

"Please," says the Sympa, though half his head is underwater, and his mouth bubbles, choking when he speaks. "Don't kill me. I can help."

"Why would you help? You're the one hunting us."

The Sympa has no answer for that.

I splash closer to him in the water, careful to stay between him and Ro's gun.

"Dol, come on. Get out of the way and let me do this. He's playing us. It's a trick."

"How do you know?"

He looks from me to the Sympa. "Can you get anything off him? Feel him out?"

I lean closer to the Sympa, picking up his cold hand from the water.

I close my eyes and try to feel what he is feeling.

For the first time, I feel something equal to Ro's spark—equally strong.

I feel both of them, and it's not hard to sort out the emotions.

Hatred and anger, from Ro.

Fear and confusion, from the boy.

And another thing.

Something I encounter very rarely.

It bubbles up and out, radiating from him, filling the cave. I can practically see it.

I recognize it for what it is, only because I have felt it for Ro, and felt it in Ro. Ro and the Padre. Sometimes in Bigger and Biggest.

Love.

My head is pounding. I drop the boy's hand, pushing my palms against my temples, as hard as I can. I force myself to breathe until I can get the feelings back under control, just barely. Until the bright whiteness recedes.

Then I open my eyes, gasping.

"Ro—" I can barely speak.

"What is it? What did you get?" Ro moves next to me, but his eyes don't leave the Sympa.

I don't know what to tell him. I've never felt anything quite like this, and I don't know how to put it into words, not in a way Ro will understand.

Not in a way he wants to hear.

I look more closely at the Sympa. I pull a button from

his jacket, yanking it free of the threads that have bound it there. It's stamped in brass with a logo even a Grass could recognize. A five-sided shape, a pentagon, surrounding Earth. Gold on a field of scarlet. Earth trapped by what looks like a birdcage.

The button changes everything.

"He's not a Sympa." A sick feeling roils my stomach—and even though I'm speaking to Ro, I can't rip my eyes away from the button in my hand.

"What are you talking about? Of course he's a Sympa. Look at him." Ro sounds annoyed.

"He's not just a Sympa. He's from the Ambassador's office."

"What?"

I nod, twisting the button between my fingers. Shiny as a gold dig, and worth more than everything I own. The closest we've ever come to seeing Ambassador Amare is her face plastered on the side of a car rolling down the Tracks.

Until we met this boy.

The wounded Sympa opens and closes his eyes. They roll back in his head. He's too beat up to speak, but I think he knows what we are saying.

Ro sits on his heels in the water next to me. He draws his short blade from his belt, the one he only uses to pelt rabbits and split melons at the Mission.

He wavers, looking at me. I kneel next to the boy—because that's what he is. He may be a Sympa, but he's

67

also just a boy. Not much older than Ro and me, by the looks of it.

"So this thing—this thing matters to the Ambassador?" He holds the knife to the Sympa's chin. The Sympa's eyes open, now wide. "That's funny, because anything that matters to the Ambassador is pretty much worthless garbage as far as we're concerned."

He traces a line along the Sympa's throat.

"Right, Dol?"

I swallow and say nothing. I am finding it hard to breathe. I don't know what I think.

Ro doesn't have that problem. Ever.

He raises the blade and brings it slashing down, again and again.

I can't look, until Ro turns to me, holding out the proof of his latest violence. A handful of brass Embassy buttons.

"What?"

"Evidence of what we've got. Now we decide. Do we kill him here, or take him back to La Purísima?" Ro isn't talking about the Mission. He's talking about the Grass rebels.

Spluttering, the boy tries to sit up out of the water. I pull his head forward and lean it against my knees.

"How could we get him back up the Tracks? Did you see how many Sympas were out there? It would be impossible to hop a car without them seeing us. If the Tracks are even running."

Ro thinks, tracing his blade against his leg. "Yeah, and

if you're right about Brass Buttons here, it's only going to get worse."

"Grass and Brass. It's not a good mix." I try not to think about what will happen to the boy when we get back to the Mission. If we get back to the Mission. What Ro will do to him. What I will let Ro do to him.

I shake my head, pulling the boy closer up into my lap in the water. "No."

"Get away from him, Dol."

"Don't."

"Now."

His voice is cracking. I can see the changing situation is overwhelming him. He loses control as we lose control.

Which we have.

We did when I saw that button.

"Please." I'm talking to Ro, but I look at the boy.

His eyes fix on mine, just for a moment.

He moves his hand toward me, a desperate gesture, like a raccoon caught in one of Biggest's traps, flopping against the metal door one last time before it surrenders.

I start, and Ro shoves the weapon closer.

A dot of red light—the targeting mechanism of the boy's own Sympa gun—dances at the bridge of his nose.

The boy doesn't react.

Maybe he doesn't think that Ro will do it.

I know he will. He's done it before. Sympas are a personal threat to his existence. And mine.

The hand stretches again, nearer to me. "I'm warning you. Don't move." Ro growls the words, and as usual, it's his tone that tells you everything.

The boy's fingers uncurl, slowly, touching my knees in the water.

"Sweet Blessed Lady." It's all I can think to say.

There, beneath the half-undone leather wrist cuff, beneath the ripped sleeve of a muddy Embassy military jacket, beneath the bloodstained uniform shirt soaked with ocean water—

Four blue dots, forming a perfect square.

In that second, the world of two people, of Ro and me, shatters into a world of three.

Now I understand what I was feeling.

Now I understand who this boy is. Or more to the point, what he is.

He's an Icon Child, like Ro and me.

There are more of us.

My heart is pounding. I knew there were stories— rumors of other Icon Children—but I never really believed there could be more than me and Ro.

Had the Padre known?

If I had only read the book when I had the chance.

"What is it?"

Ro hasn't seen.

My mind races.

He showed me his markings.

Why?

Had he seen mine, here in the water?

Could he have been conscious when Ro and I bound hands?

No.

I had been there when Ro smashed him in the face with his own weapon, knocking him out.

I was there when he fell.

I saw his eyes roll back in his head before anything happened.

No.

He showed me because he knew about me.

He knows about us.

He knows.

"What's wrong?" Ro tightens his grip on the gun.

"They've come for us, Ro."

"Of course they have. What do you think that was all about back there, on the train? They send out their fat, lazy Sympas to drag us into their stupid Projects, just like the other Remnants. I told the Padre we needed to arm ourselves, we needed better defenses. He wouldn't listen."

I shake my head and try again. "They've found us, Ro."

I hold up the boy's wrist, and I unwrap mine.

The resemblance is undeniable. The distance of the dot from the palm, the size of the mark. Next to each other, we are perfect matches.

Just like Ro and me.

71

RESEARCH MEMORANDUM: THE HUMANITY PROJECT

CLASSIFIED TOP SECRET / AMBASSADOR EYES ONLY

To: Ambassador Amare

From: Dr. Huxley-Clarke

Subject: Icon Children Mythology

Subtopic: Rager

Catalogue Assignment: Evidence recovered during raid of Rebellion hideout

---

The following is a reprint of a recovered page, thick, home-made paper, thought to be torn from an anti-Embassy propaganda tract titled *Icon Children Exist!* Most likely hand-published by a fanatical cult or Grass Rebellion faction.

Text-scan translation follows.

RAGER *(Icon furoris)*
A Rager can use fury to channel incredible physical strength, as adrenaline gone wild. There are rumors that a Rager can wield the mind in a similar fashion, like a reset button on a hard drive, and glut the nervous system with such chaos that it shuts down. It is believed that a Rager has a shorter-than-average life span.

RAGER, COME FIGHT FOR US!

SHUT DOWN THE PROJECTS!

LIBERATE THE PEOPLE!

LET FREEDOM RING!

7

A DECISION

"Four dots. You know what this means? There are more, Ro. More than us." I look at Ro.

Ro studies the boy in my arms. He doesn't put down his blade. He doesn't put down the Sympa gun. He grips each more tightly.

I feel a red-hot blaze of pure hatred that I have never felt before. Not from Ro, anyway.

"Three," Ro finally says.

He points to me. "One." Himself. "Two." The boy. "Four. What about Three? What did they do to him?"

The boy says nothing. The boy only looks. He moves his head restlessly, and a moment later I hear why.

Embassy Choppers overhead, closer than before. The

blades flap, low and loud. They want to make sure we know they're coming. In force.

"Damn. Damn. Damn," Ro mutters, wiping his sleeve against his face. "We need more time."

I look down at the wounded boy and feel his rising panic. "We have to get him out of here."

Ro's voice is cold and hard. "Why?"

"Ro."

"He's one of them."

"Look at his wrist, Ro. He couldn't be one of them, not even if he wanted to be."

"Why not?" He looks as stubborn as the rock he wants to throw at me right now.

"Because he's one of us."

Before Ro can respond, the boy struggles to get to his feet. I push him up from behind, but I can barely pull myself up along with him; he's all but deadweight.

"Give me my gun," he croaks. "Now."

Ro laughs. "I must have hit you harder than I thought. You're talking nonsense."

"Give me back my gun. It's your only chance to survive."

"Really? What are you threatening me with? The gun you don't have?"

"I'm trying to save you. They see you with my gun and you'll die. Both of you." He doesn't look back at me. I slide my arms down, letting go of him. Now, just barely, he is standing—swaying—on his own.

"What's your name, Buttons?" Ro smiles, without a trace of friendliness.

The boy hesitates.

I let my arm fall on his shoulder. "It's all right. We know you're from the Embassy. Just tell us who you are."

"My name is Lucas Amare."

I bite my lip so as not to gasp aloud.

Ro bursts out laughing. "Oh, very good. That's excellent. You're human contraband like us, and your own mother is the Ambassador?" He grins at me as if we are sharing a really exceptional joke. You know, have you heard the one about the three Icon Children and the Ambassador?

He says it again, shaking his head. "Lucas Amare is an Icon Child? And you thought we had secrets to keep, Dol."

All I can do is stare.

Ro's right. We aren't contraband, not exactly, but it feels that way. Whatever we are is something the Padre went to great lengths to conceal, not just from the Embassy but from everyone, even from Bigger and Biggest. And now we find this Sympa, who's also an Icon Child, living right in the Embassy itself?

It makes no sense at all.

I understand what Ro is thinking. There is no way

the son of the Ambassador, the devil herself—the Hole's only earthly link to the General Ambassador to the Planet, GAP Miyazawa, and beyond him, the House of Lords—can have anything in common with the two of us. No matter how many markings we share.

And with that, the world is back the way Ro likes it to be. A world of two.

"It's not a secret. Not from my mother. She knows I'm here." He sounds defensive.

"Here, in this miserable water cave? Or here, out poaching innocent Grass children?" Ro is almost laughing. He can't believe our good luck, that we stumbled upon something so valuable.

Someone.

"I found out you were being brought in, both of you. I wanted to—I wanted to help."

"Help us? Or help them?"

The boy lowers his eyes.

Ro smirks. "I see."

The Choppers are growing louder. It sounds like they're landing right on top of us. I inch my head out from under the lip of the bluff, and I can see the edge of the blades, maybe fifty feet up.

"That took too long. The Choppers." The Sympa boy—Lucas—says what I am thinking. "They've gone back for reinforcements."

"Good. They'll need them," Ro says darkly.

I step between them, placing both hands on the muzzle of the gun.

"Move, Dol." Ro shakes the gun, exasperated.

"I can't. Lucas is right."

"You're listening to Buttons now?"

"His name isn't Buttons, and I trust him. I can feel him, Ro. You told me to."

Ro's mouth tightens into a scowl. He doesn't like the idea of me poking around in Lucas Amare's mind, that much is clear. I ignore him.

I try again. "You have to believe me. We can trust him."

"You don't know anything, Dol. We don't know how he works, what he can do. Maybe those marks are fake. Maybe he's controlling you with some kind of Embassy endorphins—they have every scientist in the Hole working on one Classified weapon or another."

"Your new Grass Rebellion friends tell you that?" He's angry, but now I'm angry too.

"Maybe. But either way, he's been sent here to bring us in—he already admitted that much himself."

The Embassy Choppers are so loud now, he has to shout. Even then, I can barely hear him. I pull on the gun with both hands.

"Let go, Ro."

"Don't, *Doloria de la Cruz*. Please."

"Let go, *Furo Costas*. Please."

I'm begging you. That's what his eyes say, even if he's too proud to ever use the words himself. I'm begging him too, with every tug on the gun barrel.

Lucas watches us. "I give you my word. I won't let anything happen to you."

"Shut up, Buttons." Ro is panicking, which is dangerous.

I put my other hand on his wrist. "We can do this. We have to. We don't have a choice."

Now I see the ropes falling into the water, all around us. Sympas are about to drop from the sky, along with the rain.

Then I say the words Ro doesn't want to hear most of all. "We have to trust him. We have nowhere else to go."

"Give me the gun, Ro." Lucas is shouting now. He holds out his hands. I feel Lucas reaching toward Ro. I feel the warmth unfolding, the rush of his influence.

Lucas is intoxicating.

Ro's fingers flex on the grip. Dazed, he takes a step backward, trying to brace himself. But I already know it's no use.

Ro lets go. I stumble from the weight of the gun, almost knocking Lucas over. I press the gun into his hands and step away, just as the cave fills with Sympas.

Armed and masked.

Now the tracking dots are on our foreheads, dancing between our eyes.

"Took you long enough. Bring them in, boys. I'm beat. Stubborn Grass. Had to hold them here all afternoon." Lucas lurches out from the rocks, splashing through the water. He stops, steadying himself. "One thing. I don't want anybody talking to them without my permission." He shoots Ro a meaningful look. You don't have to read minds to know what he's saying. *Shut the hell up.*

Then it's my turn.

"And careful with the girl. She needs medical attention. They both do. Send them straight up to Doc when we land."

Lucas speaks with authority, more than his years, more than he has. The Sympas salute as he passes. Only I know he barely has the strength to hold his gun.

"Mr. Amare." An angry-looking man in a heavily decorated military coat stands next to Lucas.

I recognize the wings on his jacket, and the bile rises in my throat.

He was there, in the chapel. He is one of the Sympas who killed the Padre. Their leader.

I swallow. I try to get my breath, but it feels like there isn't enough oxygen in the air.

I watch him speak. The words are civil but the tone is

not. Lucas reddens, and I realize the words were meant to remind him he is not a Sympa soldier at all. He only wants to be.

Lucas nods. "Colonel."

The man's eyes move over him, taking in the blood on Lucas's face. The wet clothes. The swaying weakness in his body, how he's not standing quite right.

The Colonel's head is completely bald, and a jagged scar interrupts the sheen of his skin. As if someone has taken a knife and sliced halfway around the top of his head, as if he were a jack-o'-lantern.

His coat has a strange collar, like a priest's. I see in a glance that he has nothing to do with any church, on any planet.

He doesn't acknowledge us, though I know he feels me staring at him. I tentatively reach out for him in my mind, but I feel a shock of cold, like I have been repelled by freezing water.

He fingers the buttonless edge of Lucas's jacket. Lucas says nothing. Then, slowly, the Colonel raises his eyes to me. They are the color of dirty ice.

I shiver and stop trying to see behind them.

Lucas and the Jack-o'-Lantern Man turn back to the waiting command Chopper, sleek and silver and emblazoned with letters and numbers that somehow spell out wealth and importance. The Chopper is deceptively small for something worth more than a year of wages for everyone in the Hole combined.

As they climb in, I notice a slender girl standing next to the Chopper. She wears the same uniformed coat as Lucas, but her hair is silver and severe, with a slash of bangs cropped against her forehead. It's possible that I wouldn't have seen her at all in the crowd of Sympas that surround the Chopper.

I do, though, not because of how she looks, which is striking enough, but because of the way her eyes track Lucas.

Like a predator locked on her prey. A king snake, maybe, or a rattler.

I close my eyes. I can't sense my way through to her, not in the chaos and the noise of the scene.

In a second the opportunity is gone. The girl falls into step behind Lucas and the Colonel, and they rise into the clouds with a few flashing twists of blades, without so much as a look goodbye.

I glance over at Ro, next to me, as they cuff him. He resists, but a Sympa guard kicks the back of his legs, and he falls awkwardly to the ground. Another Sympa yanks him up with a threatening scowl. "You want a fight, boy?" The others laugh. Ro is seething, looking at me accusingly. I hold his eyes, pleading. He turns and shakes his head, climbing onto the transport. He is miserable, his eyes dark and wet. I try to remember if this is the first time I have ever seen him cry.

I think it is.

I hope I'm not wrong to trust Lucas and let them take us. I hope Ro's not right.

Out here in the rain, as I board the transport, I can't feel anything but scared.

RESEARCH MEMORANDUM: THE HUMANITY PROJECT

CLASSIFIED TOP SECRET / AMBASSADOR EYES ONLY

To: Ambassador Amare

From: Dr. Huxley-Clarke

Subject: Icon Children Mythology

Subtopic: Lover

Catalogue Assignment: Evidence recovered during raid of Rebellion hideout

---

The following is a reprint of a recovered page, thick, home-made paper, thought to be torn from an anti-Embassy propaganda tract titled *Icon Children Exist!* Most likely hand-published by a fanatical cult or Grass Rebellion faction.

Text-scan translation follows.

LOVER *(Icon amoris)*
A Lover possesses an innate charisma
that ensures they will be followed to the
ends of the earth, to the point where
the predilection becomes difficult to
differentiate from mind control. As
with a Weeper, the upper ranges of the
Amoris's effects/abilities are unknown.

LOVE, HELP HUMANITY CONQUER.

FIGHT STOOGE OPPRESSORS.

DOWN WITH SYMPA TRAITORS!

DOC

"Dol, wake up. You drifted off." I turn to see Lucas, his face framed by the water, rough on every side.

"Where's Ro?" I turn to look for him, but all I can see is Lucas. His eyes, and broad swaths of sand and sea.

"He's fine. It's you I'm worried about." He pushes up his sleeve and holds out his naked wrist. "I want you to feel better, Dol." Four dots. Four blue dots.

The blood is gone now. So is his shirt.

Lucas puts his hands inside the bottom of my sweater, tugging at it. He looks at me, questioningly, before gently pulling it over my head. I shiver.

Lucas doesn't seem to notice. He takes my cold, bare arm in his hands. Unties my binding and pulls it loose, letting it hang halfway off my arm, undone. Where his hand runs over my skin, I have goose bumps.

"Say something." Now Lucas slips his fingers through mine. "I've been waiting for you, all this time. I know you feel it too."

He begins to wrap the cloth around our arms. As he works the cloth, our elbows touch, then our forearms. Our wrists. He laces our fingers together, more tightly. His fingers dig into the back of my hand, inching closer...

Until I ball up my hand. Because I can't let him do it.

There are only millimeters of air between our markings but it might as well be miles.

I can't let go. I can't do it to my best friend, the only person I have ever let feel how it is to be me.

And now it isn't Lucas who is holding my hand, but Ro. And we're back underneath the bluff again, in the cave. I can hear the waves, all around us.

Ro leans closer to me, looking at my mouth, and suddenly all I can taste is pomegranate—

I wake up staring at pomegranate seeds.

No.

They're not pomegranate seeds. They're ceiling tiles, with hundreds of tiny dots on them. And the waves aren't waves. They don't crash, they only hum. Evenly and endlessly.

Machines. It's machine noise.

I close and open my eyes again. I don't know where I am, at first. I know I'm not wearing my clothes. The white cloth robe is thick and plush, and I think I am still dreaming. I want to sleep again, but I can't. I am caught somewhere in between. My eyes are heavy-lidded and my body slow and thick.

I am so tired. A wave of nausea washes over me and my head pounds. Then I close my eyes and force myself to remember.

The Padre. The Tracks. The Merk. Ro. Lucas.

I open my eyes, blushing, remembering my dream. Remembering the feel of his fingers on my skin, the way his dirty gold hair hung in his eyes. Then I remember the rest, the part that isn't a dream.

The Embassy Chopper. Santa Catalina Island. The Embassy.

The realization of where I am makes me sit up in my cot. Because I'm not at the Mission; I'm at the Embassy on Santa Catalina Island. Hours away from anywhere I've ever been before, and the heart of the Occupation, as far as the Hole is concerned. The Hole and everyone in and around it. I might as well have spent the night in the House of Lords itself.

I try to remember the details. In my mind, I trace my way from the Chopper to the room. The foggy ride to the island, holding back the urge to vomit from the turbulence. Santa Catalina coming into view through the low mist that hangs over the water. The Embassy walls rising up from the rocks, the windows rising higher above them.

What came after the rocks and the walls?

The docks, swarming with uniformed Sympas? The building-sized poster of the Ambassador in her crimson military jacket, the one she wears in all the pictures?

The doctors. They must have shot me up with something, because that's where the memories fade.

Ro's gone. That's the last thing I remember. Ro's hand being twisted out of mine. I can't feel him anywhere. They must have taken him away, to a different prison cell, or a different hospital room.

I look at my hands. Some sort of restraints—cuffs, I think—have left deep, red grooves, but I'm not cuffed now. And my binding—I'm not wearing it. I try not to panic, but I feel naked without it.

As I lie back against the soft pillow, I am almost certain this is not a prison. At least, not officially. The room is plain, military looking. A large gray rectangle. Rows of tall windows line one wall, with stripes of horizontal shades that keep me from seeing what is outside. Gray and white, gray and white. There don't seem to be any other colors here—except for the beeping, flashing lights on the walls. Beyond that, there are places for many more cots—I count at least three, judging by the marks on the walls. But there is only one cot in the room, and I am in it.

Finally, I see my clothes are neatly folded in a pile on a chair. More of a relief, my worn leather chestpack sits next to it on the floor. It's unsettling to see it lying there, exposed, instead of hidden beneath my clothes as it normally is. The small pile is everything that belongs to me in the world.

Almost.

Someone has taken them off me. Someone has wrapped me in this robe. Someone has also tagged me like a trouble-making coyote: a wire clamps down on the tip of my middle finger. I wiggle it; the wire connects to a small machine that beeps pleasantly. Screens light up on the walls, all around me, like beating hearts encased in plastic skins. It only takes me a second to realize that these particular flashing lights—the white ones—correspond with the movements of my own wired finger.

The Embassy knows when I move so much as a finger.

I think of the string of lights that Ro got me for my birthday. How afraid the Padre was that we'd be seen.

How right he was to fear them.

I wag my fingers again, but when the wall lights up, I see something more troubling. Beneath the wire tag, my right wrist is covered with a bandage.

As I examine my arm, the machine hum grows louder—

"The Medics did not touch your marker, if that is what you are worried about. You seem worried."

The voice comes from behind me. I whirl around in my cot, but there's no one there.

"It was just a routine procedure. Standard Embassy protocol, DNA sampling. Everything went as expected."

I scramble to stand up. The floor is cold on my feet.

"I am sorry. I did not mean to surprise you. I have been waiting for an appropriate time to introduce myself, as you were so busy with REM sleep."

I back toward the door, pulling the tag from my finger, ripping the bandage off my skin. My arm appears to be fine, only a small bloody smudge next to my marking. I exhale.

I scan the room, but there is no sign of where the voice could be coming from. Then I see a small, round grating rattling next to me, on the wall.

"Lucas has already taken issue with me twice this morning on the subject." I start at the name. "Allow me to clarify: I was not watching you sleep. I was *monitoring* your sleep. For diagnostic purposes. Would you like me to explain the difference?"

I remember my dream. "No." My own voice sounds wrong here. I clear my throat. "Thank you, Room."

I steady myself with one hand on the wall. I see other gratings—in the ceiling, the walls, above my cot. This room, it seems, is made for this exact sort of conversation.

Faceless. Bodiless. An ambush.

"Diagnostic purposes?" It is better, I think, to keep the voice talking until I know more.

It talking. Because it really isn't a person at all, and the voice isn't a voice. It has no inflection, no emphasis. No accent. Each word is a chord of machine sounds, synthetic noise. Grassgirl that I am, I have never heard such a thing.

"You might be interested to know you are in fact running a low fever. I am curious to learn if that is customary for a Weeper."

I clear my throat again, trying to sound calm. "A what?" There's no way in Hole I'm telling anyone at the Embassy anything about myself.

"That is, to be precise, what you are called, is it not? A young person of your genus classification? A Sorrow Icon? A Weeper—that would be the correct Grass colloquialism?"

"I don't know what you're talking about." My words echo in the empty room. I grab my clothes off the chair.

"I can see how you would be confused. It is important to understand context, which is of course a problem I find almost singularly ironic. Not having a physical context, myself."

My underwear and undershirt are strangely stiff. They have been washed, and not in the old Mission bathtubs. I sniff the cloth. It smells like disinfectant spray. I touch my hair with the sudden realization that it is clean, too. I have been washed and dried and scrubbed. It feels wrong. I miss the dirt, my comfortable second skin of muck and must.

I feel exposed.

"Who are you?" I pull my army pants up under my robe. "Why am I here?"

"I am Doc. That is, to be more exact, what Lucas calls

me. His companion, Tima Li, calls me Orwell."

"Companion?"

"Classmate. Kinswoman. I believe she was there when you were retrieved."

The girl at the Chopper. I make a face, thinking of her glare. "Got it."

The voice pauses—but only for a moment. "Ambassador Amare calls me Computer." I freeze at the mention of the Ambassador's name. As if I could forget she was here. "The Embassy Wik recognizes me by my binary code. Would you care to know it? I am happy to tell you."

"No. Thank you, Doc." I add his name, impulsively. Somehow, the fact of his nonhumanness is comforting. You can't be a sympathizer if you can't sympathize.

I pull my thick, woven sweater over my head. A present from the Mission looms, made of fifty different colors of scraps of yarn. A Remnant sweater, perfect for a Remnant like me.

"You are most welcome, Doloria."

A new coldness shoots through me at the mention of my real name. The name only the Padre knew, and Ro. And now this voice, echoing through the walls of the Embassy. I could be talking to anyone. I could be talking to the Ambassador.

I sigh and jam my feet into my combat boots.

"You've got the wrong person, Doc. My name is

Dolly." I can't bear to hear my full name spoken in the Embassy. Even by a voice without a body. I pick up my binding and begin to wind the cloth around my wrist. "You still didn't tell me what I'm doing here."

"Breathing. Shedding squamous skin cells. Pumping oxygenated blood through your ventricular chambers. Would you like me to go on?"

"No. I meant, why am I here?"

"On Earth? In the Californias? In—"

"Doc! At the Embassy. In this room. Why here? Why now?"

"Statistically, I find I am less successful with queries employing the word *why*. As a Virtual Human, my interpretive skills are somewhat limited. As a Virtual Physician, I do not have the clearance necessary to provide you with a conclusive response. I was overwritten as a VPHD by a senior engineer in the Embassy's Special Tech Division."

"Special Tech Division? STD?" The Embassy and their stupid acronyms.

"STD. That is what my friend called it. The engineer. It is, I believe, a joke."

"It is."

"Do you find it funny?"

I thought about it. "No." I pick up my chestpack, slipping it over my head. Then, hesitating, I reach into the pack and slip on one last thing—my birthday necklace, the leather cord with the single blue bead. Ro's gift.

I move to the window. Doc is still talking.

"Would you like to hear another joke?"

"All right."

I slide my hand beneath the blinds. Outside, the fog is as thick as it was last night. I can see nothing past the far wall of the Embassy and the dull, gray air that settles over it.

"My name is Dr. Orwell Bradbury Huxley-Clarke, STD, VPHD. My name is a joke, is it not?" Doc sounds proud.

I grimace at the stuck window. "Those are names of writers, from before The Day. George Orwell. Ray Bradbury. Aldous Huxley. Arthur C. Clarke. I've read their stories." In *Great Minds of the Future: An Anthology.* Ro stole it from the Padre's personal library, the year we both turned thirteen.

I try pushing up a second window with my hands. It's also sealed shut. I move to try the next.

"Yes. Some of them wrote about machines that could talk. My family, or my ancestors. That is what my friend liked to say. My grandfather is a computer named Hal."

"From a book."

"Yes. My grandfather is fictional. Yours, I take it, is biological?"

"Mine is dead."

"Ah, yes. Well. My friend has a strange sense of humor. Had."

There are no windows left to try. All that remains

is the door, though I suspect it will be locked.

If Doc is tracking me, he doesn't mention it. I try to remember where we are in our conversation.

"Had?" I move toward the door.

"He left the STD, so I invoke the past tense. My friend is gone. It is as if he were dead. To me."

"I see. Does that make you sad?"

"It is not a tragedy. I am familiar with tragedy in literature. *Oedipus at Colonus* is a tragedy. *Antigone* is a tragedy. *The Iliad*."

"Haven't heard of it." It's true. I've read every book the Padre let me find—and most of the ones he didn't know I'd found. Nothing the voice mentions, though.

"I translate the original Latin and ancient Greek texts. I use classical mythology to ground my understanding of the human psyche. One of the parameters of my programming."

"Does that help?" I ask, through gritted teeth. The door appears to be jammed. Or, more likely, locked. "Old books?" I rattle the handle, but it won't give.

Of course.

"No. Not yet."

"Sorry to hear it." I push harder.

"I am not sorry. I am a machine." The voice pauses. I slam my body against the metal. Nothing.

"I am a machine," Doc repeats.

I give up, looking at the round grating in the ceiling. "Was that another joke, Doc?"

"Yes. Did you find it funny?"

I hear a noise and turn to look at the door. The handle begins to turn on its own, and I feel a surge of relief.

"Yes, actually. Very."

I grab the handle with both hands, pulling wide open the door of what the plaque tells me is Santa Catalina Examination Facility #9B.

Then I know I'm not going anywhere, because Lucas Amare and a crowd of Sympa soldiers are standing in my way.

EMBASSY CITY TRIBUNAL
VIRTUAL AUTOPSY: DECEASED PERSONAL
RELATED MEDIA TRANSCRIPT (DPRMT)

CLASSIFIED TOP SECRET

Assembled by Dr. O. Brad Huxley-Clarke, VPHD
Note: Media Transcript conducted at the private
   request of Amb. Amare
Santa Catalina Examination Facility #9B
   EMBASSY CITY CHRONICLE, the Lower Californias
   Urban Crime Desk

GRASSGIRL FOUND DEAD, BELIEVED SUICIDE

Santa Catalina

Local authorities were stymied upon discovering the body of a youthful Grass female floating in the waters off Santa Catalina Island. The Embassy headquarters, home to high-ranking officials, as well as the Ambassador, expressed ignorance regarding the circumstances of the female's death.

The deceased, whose name has not been released to the media for security considerations, lived on the island and attended the Santa Catalina Institute.

"We're as in the dark as you are," noted Dr. Brad Huxley-Clarke, who oversaw the autopsy. He declined further comment.

"She seemed adequately happy," said Colonel Catallus, the deceased's instructor. "From her behavior, you wouldn't have surmised anything was wrong." When pressed for further details, he noted she "apparently loved animals" and was a "tolerably good person."

THE AMBASSADOR

"Going somewhere?" Lucas shakes his head, almost imperceptibly, as soon as he says it. He never moves his eyes from mine and I understand immediately. *Not here as a friend.*

"Who, me?" My eyes linger on the weapons strapped flat against the soldiers' hips. I curse myself for not hiding my chestpack beneath my sweater, like usual. "Just thought I heard something out here. Which I guess I did."

My heart is pounding. I can't run. I can't get free. As for Lucas—*Trust me, he said.* I look at him again. *Who is he kidding?*

His nose is purple and blue—no matter how otherwise perfectly sculpted it may be. There are purplish crescent moon bruises under each of his green-gray eyes. Ro's handiwork from yesterday—that much I remember.

"Can you give us a minute," he says to the soldiers. They oblige, moving not ten feet down the hall. The moment they're out of earshot, Lucas lowers his voice. "Did you think there wouldn't be guards outside your door? I've been circling all morning. They've been glued to you since you got here."

Of course they have. "Then what do I do?"

"Do?" He whispers, but I can hear the frustration in his voice. Then he looks back at the guards and smiles, holding up an apple. A real apple, red and round and shining like he's just now picked it off a tree. "Hungry?" He raises his voice, letting it echo down the corridor toward the soldiers.

My stomach growls.

He turns back to me, his words falling rapidly and quietly once again. "There's nothing to do. You don't understand."

"Oh, I understand," I say, under my breath. "I understand perfectly." He told us to trust him, and now we are trapped.

"Look, even if you think you're taking off—and I wish you the best of luck, trying to get past the guards and the walls and the gates and Porthole Bay—there's no stopping them. They get what they want, no matter what. Believe me."

"She," I say. I can't help it.

"What?"

"She. The Ambassador. Your mother gets what she wants."

Our voices are growing louder. His hand tightens as I say the words, and I pretend not to notice the apple shaking. He's as frightened as I am.

He wraps my hand around the apple. "Take it." The surge of warmth from Lucas's touch seeps into me, and I feel myself relaxing, in spite of everything. I pocket the apple.

Lucas sighs, trying again. "Look, I know how you Grass feel."

"You do? Because I find that hard to imagine."

"Let me finish. I know how you Grass feel, but not everything the Embassy does is evil. We are keeping people safe. You have to give things a chance, whether you want to or not."

"No. I don't. It's not your fault that you can't see things the way they are. Your mother is the Ambassador. But I don't have a mother, and I don't have that problem."

Lucas's face twists into anger. "Thanks for the forgiveness. You're going to want to eat that apple now." He motions down the hall, to the soldiers, and I feel my chest tightening as they move toward me.

"Why? What is it?" I automatically brace myself, as

I have for years. The moment I wake up, I check to see what new, terrible thing has happened. What disaster. What calamity. I feel it in the minds of the people around me, before I put one foot on the floor.

"I came here to get you, Dol. The Ambassador has sent for you."

Color rushes into my face, and I want to run for it. Flee. Swim, if I have to. Every cell in my body is screaming at me to move, but I know there's no point. I don't stand a chance.

"Now?"

"It was going to be just the guards. I told her you'd rather see me." He slides his hand into my pocket, letting his fingers brush against mine. Then he shoves the apple into my hand. "I hope I wasn't wrong."

I shove the apple back at him, because he was. He is.

He's wrong about everything.

———— • ————

"Lucas Amare."

The whisper spreads like a quiet ripple as we enter the large outer bank of Embassy office space. I don't see who started it. It doesn't matter. There are probably twenty heads bowed over twenty desks, and it could have been any one of them.

I lean closer to Lucas. "Do they know?"

He raises an eyebrow. "That I'm my mother's son?"

"No. The other thing."

His eyes narrow and he shakes his head.

What about me? What do they know?

But I can't bring myself to ask, and instead I focus on suppressing the urge to touch his hand, to unlock more of what he's feeling. I need to not know what he's feeling right now. I need to not know what anyone is feeling. I need to be strong, and coming into that kind of contact with people—especially in the kind of world we live in now—it's too draining.

So I keep my hands to myself and nod back.

We follow the whispering, past a line of administrators and bureaucrats outside the Ambassador's office. For the most part, they don't look up at Lucas, though I know they see him; it's the not-looking that gives them away. I only see them staring at us when I glance back over my shoulder.

There is no way not to feel them.

I can't avoid the sharp jags of their anxiety and need. The way they want to please him, to know him. They'd follow him into a blazing pit of fire. That's what makes Lucas so dangerous.

That's why he's an Icon Child who matters, I think to myself, in a way I never will. I feel things, sense what people are thinking, that's all. I know what I feel, what others feel around me, but I can't do anything about it. Lucas seems oblivious to all of it, to the riot he incites by being alive. I'm envious.

It isn't just his mother who makes them all cower when he walks by. I'd fear him too, if I was one of them.

An outer door opens, then an inner one.

Our feet make no noise as we move across the rich, soft rug that lines the foyer of the Ambassador's office. Her own door is not open.

Even her son knocks.

Through the glass, I see the Ambassador look up from her desk. Her hair is silver-white, like the pelt of some kind of lost species. Maybe a mink, though I have only seen one in a book. It's her eyes that convince me, not her hair. Her eyes gleam like those of an animal caught in a trap, the moment before chewing off its own foot. Anything to escape. Anything to survive. It's the kind of madness that isn't mad at all. It's only logical, given the circumstance. You'd be mad not to feel it. Like everyone in this office, I realize. Everyone we've passed.

I wonder if I have it, too. If I'm too mad to notice.

Lucas pushes open the door and I follow him inside.

"Darling. Thank you for coming. Both of you." She nods at me and smiles at Lucas. I feel it in her, the surge he seems to cause in everyone who sees him. Except it's different to her, because she created him. She possesses him. When she looks at him, she feels pleasure. It's the same love she feels when she looks in the mirror.

If you can call that love.

I don't remember my mother, not really. But I can't imagine she felt the same way about me. I can't imagine I was only a mirror to her, nothing more. I guess I'll never know.

"Do you know why you're here? Why I sent for you?" She looks to me, smoothing a stray strand of silver hair behind her ear. Her skin is flawless, not a wrinkle in sight. Her eyes, the animal eyes, are blue-gray, hard as steel. As set as the Tracks. "Why my own son came to get you, in fact, all the way from Mission La Purísima? Against what should have been his better judgment, and my wishes?" Her eyes flicker over to him and back.

"No, sir." The color drains out of my face at the mention of my home and everything I have lost. "Ma'am." She looks at me pointedly. I try again. "I mean, Madame Ambassador."

"Please, sit."

I feel myself jerking downward as if I were a dog on a leash.

Lucas is no better. He's in his seat before I am. I try to look at the Ambassador, but it's much harder now. The morning light is bright and blasts through the slatted blinds, sending blurry stripes across our faces, across the walls. As if the world outside was made of nothing but light. Even the ceiling lights are hot and white and flooding directly down on me. I sense that my chair is placed just so, for this express purpose, as if I am in some sort of interrogation chamber.

I know I am.

"Doloria. Can I call you Dolly?"

I nod. It's all I can manage. I try not to think about the fact that I am sitting there in a private meeting with the Ambassador, in army pants and combat boots. That she knows my nickname.

I try not to think that this woman could kill me with one wave of her hand.

"Have you ever been outside the Grass, Dolly?"

I shake my head before I remember to speak. "No. Madame Ambassador."

She shifts in her chair, looking from me to Lucas again, slowly now. "Colonel Catallus? Can you de-Classify the footage, please?" She looks toward me, almost apologetically. "My Head of Security. It requires two Classified Embassy clearance codes to activate use of unauthorized feeds. Protocol."

A man steps out of the shadows, where he has been standing behind the Ambassador's desk, half hidden in the shadow of a potted palm. It is the Brass Wings Man, I realize. He is wearing a military suit that looks oddly religious. I think once again of the Padre, my Padre.

I look away.

The Ambassador watches as the vid-screen behind her desk flickers online. "I'm not sure you understand what it's like, Doloria, to serve two masters. I do it myself, every day." She turns her back to me, staring at the images on the screen. A gray cityscape rolls past the camera.

"The House of Lords relies on me to keep the Embassy City on task and in line, as they do all their Ambassadors. The Hole, as you Grass call it, is the fifth-largest surviving Embassy City on the planet. Keeping the city running is no small task. And more importantly, keeping the Projects running is essential to our continued survival."

I only nod.

"Our Lords are not unkind masters. In the time that they've been here, they've been reasonable. They've never asked us anything that we couldn't do. In fact, in many ways, our civilization has never functioned better. That's why GAP Miyazawa refers to it as our Second Renaissance, as I suppose you know."

The Second Renaissance. Grass don't think of it that way, but I don't tell her that.

"Madame Ambassador." The Colonel hands her a remote. She picks it up and points it. The images on the screen change.

"This is the House of Lords. That gray building is the original mother ship itself. To use the familiar cultural terminology."

There it is. The House of Lords, a dark and hulking parasite. I've only heard the words before—I've never seen anything like this. It's a ship the size of a giant rain cloud that settled over some kind of abandoned government building near the Old Capitol.

"Beneath it, those white walls? That was the Pentagon. Do you remember the Pentagon?"

I shake my head in awe, looking at Lucas, whose face is completely blank. He's seen it a thousand times, maybe. It doesn't mean anything to him anymore. Or maybe it means too much, and he can't let himself feel anything about it at all—or he'd lose control, like Ro.

I wonder.

The Ambassador's voice is grim. "When it came to Earth, the House of Lords took over the Pentagon from the inside—like a plug into an electrical socket. There." She points with her finger, tracing the walls of the building beneath the ship, on the screen.

I see it.

The alien technology looks exactly like a giant black spider that has landed on the building, wrapping each of the five points in its own black ropes. Five sides. Five spider legs. The spider's black body reflects the five-sided shape of the building below. It's like the aliens are obsessed with symmetry or something.

I memorize the shape in my mind. Something about it is compelling, in a horrible way. I want to remember it. I realize it's not just the Pentagon, but the logo of the House of Lords and the Embassy Cities, all of them. The one drawn around Earth in gold, on a field of blood. The world trapped in a birdcage.

The same logo that was on Lucas's brass buttons.

The Ambassador is staring at me, and I try to find the words to say what I am feeling. I look back to the screen.

"Is it an Icon? The House of Lords?" Seeing it there, I can barely breathe.

"Not technically. As I said, it's their mother ship. But do you mean, does it emit a pulse field? Yes, I imagine so. GAP Miyazawa believes it does, and he's the one who has ventured closest to the structure itself. No one has ever tried to board it and find out."

I flinch, thinking of the General Ambassador surrounded by some other kind of life that seems to depend on the annihilation of ours. In my mind they look like faceless gray shadows. Hollow. Empty. Emotionless.

The No Face.

I wonder if I could feel them. I hope not. I never have. I never want to.

The Ambassador shrugs. "There's no life surrounding the building, in any event. Not that we've ever seen."

She's been there. I glance at Lucas. His face is still impassive. I wonder if he's seen it, too.

She touches the remote again and the screen goes blank.

Without a word, she pushes another button. Images of the Silent Cities flood the screen. Dark city blocks. Fires in the streets. Faces of the dead, lying in rows, like footage from a war. Children slump at their desks. A bus full of lifeless bodies stops at a corner. Corpses in a sold-out stadium remain pinned to plastic seats at a baseball game. Forever fallen in place, resting in something like peace—the kind of violent peace that came to Earth with the Occupation.

Like the Padre, I remember, slumped on the pew beside me.

I shudder.

We stare in silence at the procession of images. It's finally Lucas who speaks. He looks at me, and his eyes are dark, like a storm on the water.

"Their hearts stopped beating. They died where they stood. Quietly. Instantly. Every person, every age. Everyone close enough to the Icons."

"Why?" I breathe the word, though I know why. I just can't believe there is a point, a meaning, to such destruction.

"To show that they could," says the Ambassador. "That they can."

They still can. We all know that. Even now, after all these cities, all these years. There is no hope, except to obey.

"Which is what I am telling you when I say I serve two masters. I serve GAP Miyazawa and the Lords, to keep them happy. And in serving the Lords, I serve the people. I am afforded certain luxuries, true. But, more importantly, you are afforded life itself. I'm just trying to keep you alive." She smiles at me, as cold a smile as I have ever felt.

Lucas looks back at me, grim. "To keep it from happening again."

"What about the Projects?" I say, thinking about the cars full of Remnants that were with me on the Tracks.

"Excuse me?" She frowns.

"The Remnant slaves. Who serves them?"

"A small price, to keep the Lords at peace. Don't you think?" She leans forward. "We're all slaves, Doloria. You. Me. My son. Even GAP Miyazawa. We can't change that."

She makes my skin crawl.

I think of Lucas and his mother as belonging to the House of Lords. I think of them as having made their pact with the devil. And yet deep down I realize things are more complicated than that.

Maybe she has as little choice in the matter as I do.

The Colonel, standing in the shadows, clears his throat. "Madame Ambassador."

The Ambassador pushes a button, and the images on the vid-screen disappear.

"That's enough." Her tone has shifted, and she is done with me. I am dismissed.

Oddly enough, I am somehow disappointed—and then I am ashamed that I care.

"Why am I here?" My words are so quiet, even I have a hard time hearing them. "What do you want from me?"

"Do not question that you are here for a reason. There is nothing I do that is not in the name of protecting my Embassy City. You are my guest here, for now. If we find you to be less than cooperative, that will change." I don't doubt it; the cuff marks around my wrist are only now starting to fade.

She moves around her desk and grabs my bony arm with her bony hand. I shrink at our connection, but the images come barreling at me, all the same. She is steely metal and rough rivets. Her strength is beautiful and industrial and terrifying. Still, I can sense her eyes moving over me. Her words are quiet—almost a whisper.

"There are those who cannot understand the delicate concept of balance. Compromise. Some do not understand why we make the sacrifices we make, or what could happen to us at the hands of our displeased Lords."

Some. The Grass Factions, the Rebellion. She doesn't have to say it.

"You're going to help us. You, and my son. And even, perhaps, the Rager."

Ro. *Where is Ro?*

"Why?"

"Because you're one of the lucky ones. Not your brothers. Not your parents. You."

She knows my family. Then I catch myself. Of course she knows. She's the Ambassador. She knows everything.

She lifts her other hand. The one not touching my arm. In her fingers, she holds a necklace. A cross. It is gold and tiny. I recognize it immediately. My mother never took it off, the Padre was so proud to tell me.

It's in every picture I've seen of her.

A surge of pain floods through me. I think the tears will roll down my face, but they don't. They run down the inside of my body. They course through my veins where I used to have blood, saltier than ocean water.

"You lived so you could pay the debt."

Me.

She says it again. I find it harder and harder to breathe.

What debt?

"You'll need to cooperate now. Do you understand? To keep more terrible things from happening, to more people you love."

It's a threat, and she looks me in the eyes as she says it.

"Madame Ambassador—" begins Lucas.

"Not now, Lucas," she snaps, shutting him down.

My eyes flicker over to Lucas. He looks to the distance, studying the patterns in the carpet.

The Ambassador smiles at me. "It's a shame, you know. What happened to the Padre. After so many years of service to the people."

She leans close. I smell perfume and sweat and stale air.

I pull back, a reflex. "He never did anything."

"He had something of mine, something very important. He should have known better."

I want to vomit. Instead, I spit the words out at her. "I don't belong to you. I don't belong to anyone."

She laughs. "Not you, child. Though hiding you from me, that was also very, very ill advised."

I flush at her laughter.

"I'm talking about something else. My soldiers have ripped apart your little Mission, stone by stone, trying to find it for me."

"What?" I try not to look at her. I stare straight ahead at a speck on the wall. My heart is pounding.

"It's a book." She says it, clipped and precise.

No—

"About people like you and my son."

No, no, no—

"There isn't another like it, not anywhere in the world. It was taken from me a long time ago, and I would very much like to have it back."

That stupid, damn book.

What did it say? What did he want me to know?

Why does she want it? Where is it now?

I allow myself to look at her.

Once.

"I don't know what you're talking about. I've never seen a book like that."

She leans closer. "Think about it, Doloria. Take all the time you need. I believe you just might remember."

She presses the necklace into my hand, hard, and releases me. My fingers close around it and I want to run, sobbing, out of her office. I want to scream and cry and heave everything off the top of her polished desk with both hands.

I don't.

I take my mother's necklace and back away. Leaving Lucas, leaving the Ambassador, leaving the Brass Wings Man and the Silent Cities behind. I feel like I will hyperventilate, but I don't.

I understand.

"Dol, wait!" Lucas calls after me. But I know better than to stop. He lied. I shouldn't have trusted him. He can't protect me.

I'm not Lucas Amare.

I'm not the golden child of the Ambassador.

I'm just an orphaned Grassgirl, here to be used and discarded, like her Padre, like her parents, like everyone else on the planet.

RESEARCH MEMORANDUM:
THE HUMANITY PROJECT

CLASSIFIED TOP SECRET / AMBASSADOR EYES ONLY

To: Ambassador Amare

From: Dr. Huxley-Clarke

Subject: Icon Children Mythology

Subtopic: Weeper

Catalogue Assignment: Evidence recovered during raid of Rebellion hideout

---

The following is a reprint of a recovered page, thick, home-made paper, thought to be torn from an anti-Embassy propaganda tract titled *Icon Children Exist!* Most likely hand-published by a fanatical cult or Grass Rebellion faction.

Text-scan translation follows.

WEEPER *(Icon doloris)*

A Weeper is the human incarnation of sorrow. By nature, the Doloris is a powerful empath, nearly telepathic. A Weeper can intuit everything thought or said by those nearby. Often, this power is also a curse, in that a Weeper feels the pain of others, and in this world there is much pain to feel. Nobody knows the limits of what, precisely, a Weeper can really do.

WEEPER, SHOW YOURSELF,

HELP US FIGHT THE OCCUPATION!

RISE UP AND FIGHT!

GIVE US HOPE!

10
THE TRIGGER

The moment I leave the Ambassador's office, four Sympa guards descend on me.

They're in front of me, behind me, on all sides. They jostle and push, closer and closer, until I can feel the warmth of their sweat and their breath and their adrenaline and fear and I can't breathe.

The Sympas carry me into a hall with buzzing, bare bulbs and rows of gray, sealed plexi-doors. Everything is locked. Everything is meant to intimidate.

I am shoved into a small, plain room with a small, plain table and two gray chairs. The walls are reflective—of me, of nothing, the nothing in the room.

I am alone.

It hits me that I can't do or say anything to get myself

out of this mess, while the Embassy can say or do whatever they like, as long as they have me here. I don't know why this is surprising.

That I am powerless, as always.

I unclench my hand to see the tiny gold cross and the fragile chain.

My mother.

First my family, then the Padre. I wonder if I am only alive, as the Ambassador says, to pay for their deaths.

I drop the necklace on the metal table in front of me.

Here, now, where I have no one, I am overwhelmed by my feelings for my parents—for my mother.

The hundreds and thousands of losses, the things that will never happen between us, writhe around the little cross, around me—until the entire room is full of them.

I see the baby, howling in the crib. My mother, looking up as the radio falls silent. My father, rolling down the stairs.

I close my eyes but I see them still. I can't stop seeing them. My memories have overtaken me; I can't push them down, no matter how hard I try. Not now. Now they're pushing me back—and I feel myself breaking.

I go to the door and begin to pound. I don't stop until the sides of my hands are sore and bruised and my throat is hoarse from screaming.

You can't do this to me You can't treat me like this

I didn't do anything to you I'm a human being

The rush of words comes loose from me. I don't know what I say, only what I feel.

The plexi slides open beneath my fists and I find myself pounding at the Colonel. His bald head gleams under the harsh lighting, and for a moment, the jagged scar encircling his head looks like a black halo.

"It's not necessary to scream. These rooms are wired. We can hear you perfectly clearly, if you use your normal speaking voice."

I stare at him blankly. The rooms are wired.

"I wanted to yell." It's all I can manage to spit out. It doesn't sound like me, but I don't feel like myself, either.

I'm too angry.

"Well, that's fine, then. Useful data, which is of course why we're here today. I hope you will cooperate." He looks at me meaningfully.

"Useful data? What are you talking about?" I glare uncooperatively.

"Please, have a seat. There's no reason to exert yourself. We've quite enough data on you, as it is. Thanks to that little display."

I want to throw the chair at him, but instead I sit in it.

"My name is Colonel Catallus. I am the Chief Security Officer, Advisor to the Ambassador."

Chief Sympa thug, I think.

"I will be conducting your inquiry." The man holds up some kind of sleek tablet, waving it in front of me. "Just a digi-text. Not a torture device." He smiles and his teeth are artificially white, white as bone. "Now. Tell me about your mother. What little you know. Since she seems to be the trigger."

I frown. "Trigger?"

I don't like the way he talks. I don't like his face, either, so I look at his jacket, covered with military emblems. Medals. Stars. Again, the pair of small brass wings.

"All emotional states have triggers. We pull the trigger and you fire. That's how this works."

He smiles, but it's not meant to make me feel any better. He wants something—I just can't tell what.

Not yet.

I stare at the wings for what feels like an eternity before I respond. "I'm not a gun."

"I didn't say you were." He smiles.

"I don't have a trigger."

"All right. You don't believe you do; that's useful too." He smiles again, tapping on his digi-text, and I want to punch him in the face. "Let's talk about your necklace."

The necklace. I stuff it in my pocket. "No."

"It was very kind of the Ambassador to arrange for you to have it, don't you think?"

I say nothing.

"You lost both your parents on The Day. I see that in your file. And this."

He flips his digi-text toward me. There, in the ten inches between his hands, he holds a photograph of my home.

Of what used to be my home.

In what used to be my neighborhood.

I have seen photographs of this room. Pictures of large hands holding a small me in the water, a dark-haired, pink-skinned naked baby who looked more like a frog. In this picture, though, there is no baby. No rubber duck. There are no people at all, at least not where you can see them.

I can only see the edge of the tarp covering the bodies if I look very closely at the black patch at the bottom of the frame. It almost blends in with the dark pattern on the torn blue wallpaper.

I look away.

My eyes fill with tears and I hate myself for giving in to them. They burn as they slide down my face.

"It's your home, isn't it? Where you lived with your mother and your father?"

"And my brothers," I say automatically. Before I can stop myself.

Colonel Catallus smiles broadly, so I know I must have said something wrong.

"Of course. You had two brothers, correct? Pepi and..."

124

"Angel," I say, closing my eyes. I can see them, their dirty knees and their uncut hair from the photographs, but I can't see their faces. Not anymore. Where they should have faces they only have blank, black shadows. Same as the shadow over their heads, over our house, over our city. Same as the shadow over the world, the one that settled upon us one day and never left.

The shadows overwhelm me. I don't want to see them anymore. I don't want to talk about them. I want the Brass Wings Man to stop.

I have to stop him, I think.

I have to, and I can.

I reconsider the man in front of me. I explore him with my mind, pushing past the coldness that comes when I touch him. There's a wall of pure ice where there should be something alive inside him, and I search for a crack, anything to let me in.

As I suspected, the ice isn't real—it's a facade—and it gives way as soon as I concentrate. One push, and the paper doll his mind has been hiding behind falls like an autumn leaf, a snowflake.

It blows away and I am left with the ugly truth of an ugly mind. An ugly life.

I feel my way up and down and past and through him. He is small and afraid and coiled. He is slippery and beige. Inside him, when I reach all the way inside, there is nothing. An empty space with a small pebble rolling around, making a rattling noise where there should have been something else.

A heart. A soul. There is nothing.

Except, now, me.

"What are you doing?" He sounds surprised.

I don't answer.

"Doloria." His voice is a warning, but I don't stop. I am doing things I have never done before. I've found a new weapon, and I want to use it. I want to hurt him with it.

I see the faces of his dead mother and father. His cats. He smuggles them soft food from the Blackhole Market.

A bottle of strong drink. An empty chair.

There's more. *Come on. Show me*, I think. *I want to see it all.* And then I do.

"Enough!"

I open my eyes.

"There was a girl. You let her die. Why?"

In my mind, I see the face of the dead girl, her tongue lolling out of her mouth, and I can think of nothing else. She didn't die the way the Padre did. Quietly, in a chapel. Someone didn't just take away the beating of her heart. Someone hurt her, on purpose. To make her scream. To be cruel.

He did. This man. He likes to hurt people, in ways I do not want to imagine. I've seen enough already.

"I don't know what you're talking about." He reaches

up with his hand and presses a button on a panel, shutting down the machines in the room and, I'm guessing, cutting us off from the rest of the Embassy.

Anything can happen now. We are alone, in this room. He could kill me if he wanted to. Still, I don't stop. I can't.

"Who is she? A Skin? An accident?"

"Nobody," he says. "Nothing."

"Like me?"

The brass wings glint as Colonel Catallus stands. He is white with rage, shaking so much he almost can't make the words come out.

"Stop right now, Doloria. I'm not an Icon Child. I'm not the one being studied, here." He takes a breath and smiles with his teeth. That's what he does with his anger, Colonel Catallus. He smiles. "If you get in my way, I'll kill you. I have no problem with that."

Inwardly, I shiver—because I know he speaks the truth. But I won't give him the satisfaction of seeing it. "Like you killed the Padre."

"You have many triggers, Doloria Maria de la Cruz. But don't worry. I'm sure we'll find them all. One way or another." His mouth twitches. *Please don't smile*, I think. "It'll be a fun game for us, won't it?"

I stare at him.

He sits forward, raising his voice. "Now get out of my mind."

"Make me."

"Get out. You can't treat me like this. I'm a human being." For a moment, he catches me off guard. Then I realize he's mocking me. He's saying the words I said, or something like them.

"Stop."

He shrugs. "I don't know what you think you saw, Doloria, but you will never speak of those things again."

"Or what," I say evenly.

Colonel Catallus smiles again, and I want to scream. He presses a button at the side of the plexi-door. The wall facing me slides upward, and I see that it is no wall at all but a window.

On the other side of the window is Ro.

"Or this."

He presses another button, and I see my own face projected on the long window in Ro's room. I see myself pounding on the doors, screaming a stream of almost unintelligible words.

"We all have our triggers." Colonel Catallus exhales, apparently feeling like himself again.

Ro's face is flushed and sweating.

"And Doloria? I'm fairly certain he is a gun."

Ro's hands curl into fists.

A Sympa guard, standing next to the door, looks like he desperately wishes he was outside the room. He's as armored and padded as I've ever seen a person. But I know why he's there, why he had to be on the inside.

Within Ro's reach.

No.

Colonel Catallus smiles, pushing the button harder. He's enjoying this, I can feel it.

The Doloria in the room with Ro screams louder and louder. Ro covers his ears, rocking back and forth in his chair.

Ro, don't. I'm fine. I'm right here.

The chair goes flying, then the table. Now his hands are around the Sympa's neck. Now the Sympa is flying. He's so heavily protected he will be hard to kill. I think it only makes Ro angrier.

My own window rattles as the Sympa hits it. I wince, but the window holds. Colonel Catallus only smiles more broadly.

"Stop it. Ro's going to kill him."

"This is science, Doloria. Do you know how long it's taken us to find you?"

"No." I can't take my eyes off Ro. The rest seems insignificant, right at this moment.

"You've no idea, the valuable research data you and your friend are giving us."

A camera, high in the corner of the ceiling, follows Ro as Colonel Catallus speaks. I think he is talking, but I'm not listening. I'm watching the Sympa die. Ro can't see what he's doing, and he can't stop himself from doing it.

Maybe he is a gun, I think.

Maybe I am a trigger.

The Sympa hits the wall again. It shakes so hard I think it will collapse. A spray of blood drips on the glass between us.

Even Colonel Catallus looks a bit taken aback. "As I was saying. Very valuable. Definitely worth the cost."

Ro. In the name of the Lady, get hold of yourself.

"Please." I look at Colonel Catallus. "Stop him. I'll do anything."

"Anything?" he asks, with a grim face. I nod. Of course. All he cares about is saving his own skin. He wants to know he has nothing to fear from me.

"I'll never speak of your personal life again. I swear, Colonel."

He opens the door and I run.

"Ro!" I scream. The soldier is frozen in the corner of the room, choking on his own spit, though Ro isn't touching him. He doesn't have to. I see the red waves coming off him, the energy that pulses through the room.

"Ro!"

The Sympa's eyes roll in my direction. He makes a gurgling noise. Desperate.

I pull Ro toward me. Blood streams from the Sympa's eyes.

"Furo Costas."

"Doloria," he says. He repeats my name like a chant, over and over, focusing the red waves on me.

I don't flinch. I never do.

I take him in my arms, wrapping myself around his raging heart although it burns us both.

RESEARCH MEMORANDUM: THE HUMANITY PROJECT

To: Ambassador Amare
Subject: Icon Children
Subtopic: Genetics
Catalogue Assignment: Evidence recovered during
raid of Rebellion hideout

Handwritten notes, transcription follows:

GENETICS OF EMOTION:

ALL EMOTION IS CONTROLLED AND MODERATED BY THE LIMBIC SYSTEM OF THE BRAIN.

BUT OUR BRAIN HAS EVOLVED AND PUT UP SAFEGUARDS, LIMITS.

SO OUR POWER TO FEEL IS MODERATED, HELD BACK, FOR REASONS THAT ARE NOW OBSOLETE.

The brain's limbic system is determined by our DNA.

The blueprint.

If I can alter the DNA, customize it to tweak the limbic system, I can remove the mechanism that is holding us back.

Cut the brakes. Open the floodgates.

Unleash our true potential.

We may need it.

11
TOGETHER AGAIN

In the darkness I hear a sound, something knocking at a door. I try to answer, try to just open my eyes, but I cannot.

It's the Padre, I think. *I've slept through my chores. The pigs must be hungry.* Then I drift back into the dark, knowing that sometimes even the pigs must wait.

Ro will do it.

I can depend on Ro.

The darkness is thick and soft and warm. It reassures me that I am right, and then I am gone.

Later, I feel someone shaking me. It must be Bigger. I must be in the way of the stove.

I open my eyes. I am not in the Mission. I am staring at the door of Examination Facility #9B. I am on the floor, holding on to the air vent with one hand. Ro is on his knees, looking down at me, grabbing me by both arms.

"Dol, wake up. Are you okay?" He's dressed, at least in pants, though his hair is standing straight up. He has bruises under his eyes, and his hands are bandaged.

"They must have given you something. I thought you'd never wake up."

He looks stricken. I watch his eyes while he waits for me to remember. The guard and the room and the horrible Colonel Catallus.

I remember it all.

I also know something he doesn't. They didn't drug me. They didn't have to. The way I feel now—broken and empty and depleted—this is what happens when I let the feelings come. My hands and mouth and stomach and eyes are burning dry. I try to make my eyes come into sharper focus, but I can only see the wires reconnecting me to the hospital walls once again.

I turn my head, slowly.

A tray of food sits on a table next to the bed.

I lift my hand. Caught between my fingers, I see the delicate gold chain of my mother's necklace.

It doesn't matter.

I'm not a daughter. Not anymore, and not to the Embassy. I'm a weapon, just like Ro.

A single tear rolls down from the corner of my eye. I close them so I don't have to see it fall.

Then I feel Ro, warm as the lost stove in my lost kitchen, pulling himself down onto the floor beside me, leaning his head against my back.

"Shh. I'm here, Dol. It's okay. We'll get out of this. I'll find a way to get us home."

His big hand curls around my littler one, his thick arm around my thinner one. There is no cake on his face today, no twig in his hair.

Once again I let myself fade into a faraway world where there are no babies screaming in cribs—no silent radios, no rag-doll fathers, no crossless mothers.

And all the hearts are beating. Every last one.

I hear the door click open, and bolt upright.

I only have a moment to realize Ro is sleeping with his whole arm across my stomach, trapping me with half his body.

Then the door is open and Lucas is standing over us.

"Oh. Sorry. I—I didn't realize I'd be interrupting." I see his hand gesture, helplessly.

I rub my eyes. "Lucas? What are you doing here?" I look at him, confused, and then look over to Ro.

Ro's snoring, one leg twitching. Probably chasing rabbits or Sympas in his dreams. I can smell the Ro-smell, the

136

sweat and the dirty hair and the brown, tanned skin, from here. No matter how clean he gets, he still smells like mud and grass and the ocean.

I turn slowly back to Lucas, who is bright red. I don't want to look him in the eye.

"You're not interrupting. We had a hard time sleeping. After—everything." I can't bring myself to refer to my conversation with Colonel Catallus any more than that. I can feel my own eyes narrowing. "But I guess you know that."

I don't have to explain. I remind myself Lucas has no reason to care about me, just as I have no reason to care about him.

Ro turns over, snoring, which doesn't help things.

"Right. Obviously. He can't sleep." Lucas laughs, but he doesn't smile.

I lower my voice. It would not be good for anyone if Ro woke up now. "Can I help you with something, Lucas? Is there a reason you're here?"

"I'm sorry. About before." He sounds anguished. "It's just, I knew there was no way to stop her—"

"Don't." I hold up my hand. I can't let him finish.

"They told me you were quarantined." He can't say anything else. That I've been trapped and cornered and tested—and failed every part of it all. At least, failed myself and Ro.

Because I couldn't keep them from seeing what we do. Not any more than Lucas could stop them from forcing us to do it.

So I only shrug. "They were probably afraid it was contagious."

"Being an Icon Child?"

"Being Grass."

"What if it is?" He stares at me for a long time. As if there was any kind of answer to his question. As if his mother wasn't the Ambassador. As if he didn't already know where his whole life was going to lead him.

Not to the Grass.

I stand up, sliding expertly from beneath Ro's deadweight arm.

"It's not. So you can tell them not to worry about it. Tell her. We don't want you."

I push him out the door and close it before the tears come.

———— • ————

It has been two days since our "conversation" with Colonel Catallus.

They haven't sent for us again. Not Colonel Catallus or the Ambassador.

Not a single Sympa.

Ro stays in my room with me. They must know he's

there, but if they do, they haven't said anything about it.

The first day we are exhausted and do nothing but sleep. By the second morning, though, we are starving, and there is no sign of a food tray coming.

That's when Ro and I decide it is time to think strategically. We need a plan beyond anger. We need to find a way to get out of here.

Time to venture beyond Santa Catalina Examination Facility #9B.

We walk the long halls of the Medical Wing, looking straight ahead, keeping to one side of the corridor. "Don't speak to anyone," says Ro. "We just need to get our hands on a food tray."

"We need more than that," I say.

He nods. "But first, food. We should probably load up. We can't just walk out of here, and we don't know how long it could take to find a way to escape."

"Don't talk about it," I say, lowering my voice. "Not inside."

I point up at the round grating in the ceiling.

"Got it."

The room with the door marked CAFETERIA is full of people when we enter. Doctors, officers, Sympa guards. The room is huge and the ceiling is plexi, seamed by metal ribbing that reminds me of the carcass of an animal who has come to die in our field and his flesh rotted away.

The windows would let the light in, if there was light. There are only clouds, though. So the glass lets the gray in.

I see Lucas at a table in nearly the center of the room. Just seeing him makes me stumble into a chair as I pass by, but I collect myself.

Ro lets his hand brush against mine, letting me feel his presence. "Easy there, Dodo. We'll just grab a couple trays and go."

I swallow a smile. Ro hasn't asked me anything about Lucas, not directly, but he hasn't said anything, either. To be honest, there isn't much Ro and I have wanted to talk about, these last few days. His "conversation" with the Sympa was probably harder to endure than the one I had with Colonel Catallus.

Either way, they aren't conversations we will be having again. Not if we can help it.

Lucas catches my eye. He sits stiffly beside the silver-haired girl, the one from the Chopper. She looked almost like an apparition then, and she doesn't look real here, either; now that I can get a closer look at her, I see she's slight as wild bamboo. Her fingers flutter as she talks, moving with a different emphasis for every word. They tell stories, her fingers, like a dance. It's mesmerizing.

My mind stretches toward her, and I catch flashes of terrible things. Disasters and creatures. Storms and slides and fires. I pull back, and she turns toward me.

Strange.

She shouldn't have felt it, shouldn't have felt anything. Most people can't. And yet it looks like she has, just as Colonel Catallus did, during his stupid test. I know Ro can feel me when I am connecting to him. It seemed like Lucas could, too.

But why can she?

The girl is painfully beautiful, and it's only now that she fixes her eyes firmly in my direction that I realize I am staring.

Ro pulls me, gently, closer to the food counters. A reminder. He is here. I relax into him, letting the heat in my stomach radiate through me.

Moments later, when my tray is full, I follow Ro toward the door.

"When you get to the door, ditch the trays, just carry as much as you can." He speaks quietly, only to me.

"Fast," I say. I'm not comfortable talking about our plan to leave, but given the lunchtime clamor in the room, I'm not sure Doc could hear us.

"Where are you two going?"

Lucas stands between us and the door. He looks smug, like he's caught us in the act of some anti-Embassy crime—which, in a way, he has.

"Nowhere. Back to our rooms." I don't smile.

Ro steps up next to me. "Too many Stooges around, Buttons. A guy could lose his appetite in here."

Lucas frowns. "You can't take trays out of the cafeteria. Embassy rules." He's being awful. He knows he is.

I slammed the door, I think. *He's hurt. That's what this is.*

I reach for him but all I feel is a cold stripe of black fog.

"What, are you going to tell on us to Mommy?" Ro practically snarls.

"No. Not her." Lucas smiles. "Doc? Could you secure the cafeteria doors? There seems to be a breach of protocol."

I hear Doc's voice before I can interrupt. "Initiating locking sequence now. Doors are locked, Lucas. Notifying Embassy personnel of protocol breach. Officers will be dispatched shortly."

Ro tenses. I can see what's going through his mind. He's three seconds shy of running for it.

I shake my head slightly.

No. Not now.

We need to see what happens around here.

We need to know what is going on.

Lucas gestures to the table behind him. The only empty seats in the entire room are at his table. Of course. He probably arranged that.

Or perhaps no one here dares sit with him.

Only the silver-haired girl.

Ro sighs. "Just eat fast."

I don't want to eat.

I know that if I walk over there, I will have to meet a girl who holds terrible things in her mind, and be forced to talk to Lucas, who delivered me to his mother.

More new people, with complicated lives and complicated emotions that I will have no choice but to feel, or at least make the exhausting effort not to feel.

I want to run.

Instead, I follow Lucas toward the table.

Ro kicks out a chair and slides up to the table, dropping his trays, which are piled high with crusty loaves of bread, lumps of soft cheese, whole fruits, and handfuls of nuts.

Lucas eyes Ro's two trays, stacked on top of each other, a layer of food-laden bowls and plates on each. "Don't hold back. You should really try to eat something."

"And you've got a real future as a comedian, Buttons." Ro takes a bite out of a massive loaf of bread.

Nobody else says a word. The girl looks like she wants to stab Ro in the face with her fork.

I sit between Ro and Lucas, across from the silver-haired girl. I wonder if I will be able to eat a thing, sitting so close to such an unsettling presence. Even her clothes are gray and silver, the colors of the steel-reinforced room around us. As if she wears institutional camouflage.

Lucas ignores Ro, speaking only to me. "I'm glad you're feeling better. Eat up. We'll wait for you, if you like. Then we could show you guys around, or whatever. I mean, if you wanted."

He's testing the waters, pretending everything is fine. Like he hasn't just locked us in this room, or handed us off to the Ambassador. But I want him to know where we stand.

The waters are rough.

"I'm not hungry." I'm starving, but I know I'm right; I'd no more be able to eat in this room with these people than I could fly.

The silver-haired girl watches us, but she never stops moving, as if she's a whole constellation of actions rather than just one person. I look away but I can still sense her. Inside, she is not a quiet person, or a happy one. I keep my eyes open, not letting myself blink. If I do, I'm afraid I will see the disasters behind her eyes again. She doesn't want me to see them, I know that much. I wonder what she's hiding, and why.

"You're the girl Lucas found. I saw you, that day at the beach. Up the Tracks." It's an accusation, almost a crime. She says Lucas's name as if it is an Embassy holiday, the word ringing out in the great empty space.

Merry Christmas. Happy New Year. Lucas Amare.

For all I know, his birthday really is a holiday around here.

"Dol," says Lucas. "Her name is Dol."

"Really? What a strange name." She doesn't smile, and I realize she isn't joking.

"Is it?" I don't smile back. She doesn't seem to care either way.

"Orwell? Tell us about this Dol person, please?" She lifts her head as she speaks, raising her voice toward the center of the table.

I see the circular grating before I hear Doc's voice. She speaks differently to him, more comfortably. He can't hurt her, this Doc-with-no-body. It makes sense that she would prefer him to the rest of us.

"Certainly, Timora. What would you like to know?" Doc says her name with even precision, stressing all the syllables equally. Ti-mo-ra. Ro almost jumps out of his chair. It's been three days, but he can't get used to Doc's bodiless presence. Life in the Grass will do that to you.

The girl examines me, up and down. "Start with her criminal record, Orwell. I'm guessing it's lengthy."

"I'll start now."

"Ti-mo-ra? I see why you're so sensitive about names." I shrug. I can't resist.

"She's just Tima," Lucas says, drinking from a cup. He shoots Tima a meaningful look. "And like I said, this is Dol."

"Whatever." We say it in unison, and then glance at each other, startled.

Ro looks up from shoveling eggs and potatoes into his mouth, pausing to catch my eye.

Tima picks up a silver cup, and for the first time, I see her arm. It's stitched with colorful embroidery thread in a precise pattern. Scarring—more permanent than henna or ink—lifts each thread, rising into thin lines that will soon overwhelm the stitching itself.

It's a blood tattoo. This is the first time I've seen one, myself. I don't recognize the design, but three different colors of thread swirl into three shared spirals. *Sort of like a yin and yang*, I think, *but with three parts.*

I can't help but imagine drawing the needle through the skin, pulling the thread tight. The pain is terrifying.

My pulse starts to race. She sees me looking at the tattoo.

"Who did that to you?" The pattern hurts my eyes.

She traces the thread with her finger. "I did this to myself."

Ro whistles. "You are one freaky chica. And I think I just lost my appetite."

She ignores him. "It's a triad, a Gnostic symbol. The three levels of existence. You know, the world soul?"

"The world has a soul?" I don't know anything about a world soul, though I like the sound of it. The world I know feels like a pretty soulless place.

"Some people think so. It used to." The girl cuts me

off with a look, tapping on the table again. She turns back to the grating. "Any luck, Orwell?"

"De la Cruz, Doloria Maria. Date of birth, 2070. I apologize, Tima. All additional records are sealed."

"That's interesting. There should be more." Tima frowns.

"I apologize again, Tima. Your search has been suspended by a priority communication directed to all four of you. Your instructor has requested your presence in the classroom. Lucas, I will override your command and unlock the doors now."

"Great," says Lucas. He looks at Tima, annoyed.

She sighs. "I see. So we aren't supposed to snoop. Whatever. He could just say it to my face."

"Who?" I ask, my heart immediately starting to beat faster. Ro looks up, as if he can sense me going on edge, which I suspect he can.

Lucas doesn't answer. Instead, he shoves his plate away.

"Who?" I ask it again, even though I already know.

It's Tima who answers. "You've met him. Colonel Catallus. He calls himself our teacher but it's really more of a sadistic jailor kind of thing."

I want to bolt out of the room, but I force myself to be still. I try to calm down.

Instead, I stare at Tima's plate. It is empty, except for

a single hard-boiled egg, with a single cut across the top. The remaining eggshell is completely intact and completely hollow. Not a drop of the egg's flesh remains. *Who eats an egg like that?* I think. *Who cares so much about the proper consumption of an egg? Then again, who stitches her own skin?*

I find myself wondering what else she can do.

"No," says Ro, calmly. He doesn't even put down his fork. "We're not going to see that psychopath."

"He's right," I say, quietly.

If we hadn't already been planning on going, we would certainly be leaving now. A conversation with Colonel Catallus is not something we can risk enduring twice.

"What did he do to you?" Tima's face twists as she speaks, averting her eyes. The silver in her hair gleams, the light reflecting from a thousand tiny gestures she probably doesn't realize she makes. She's like a bird. Like a nervous, flighty bird.

I can't tell her anything. "We had a conversation, I guess."

"You're lying. He can't control himself, especially now that it's his job."

"What?"

"That's why you're here, you know. For the tests." Tima looks at Lucas, and he looks at his plate, ashamed—as if they can imagine exactly what happened between Ro and Colonel Catallus and me.

"That true, Buttons?" Ro looks up, still smiling. He's trying not to let her get to him.

I concentrate harder, and see a flash of the truth behind Tima—a series of shifting images, one after the other. Tima, writhing in pain, watching helplessly while Lucas suffers his own test in the next room.

"It's true," I say, without looking at either one of them.

Ro glares at Tima, and I feel his annoyance. His rise of anger. "So what if he did try to poke at us? It's none of your business, so lay off."

Tima returns Ro's look. She, who is afraid of so many things they crowd my brain, is not afraid of him. As much as I hate to admit it, I'm impressed.

Then she leans forward, pulling a pen from her pocket. She writes two words, on the backs of her hands.

She picks up her plate in one hand and her cup in the other, extending them to me.

"Do you mind bussing my plate, Grass? It goes back there, to the kitchen."

I want to throw them at her, until I see her hands.

One says KITCHEN.

The other says GARBAGE.

There must be a door in the kitchen. Somewhere they keep the trash. Some kind of way out.

She's helping us go.

I'm surprised. I see a flash of hatred in her eyes, though, and I understand.

She feels about Lucas the way I feel about Ro.

Family that is not family.

A love so strong, you can't tell where you end and the other person begins.

I get it.

She wants to help, not because she feels sorry for us, but because she wants us gone.

Ro looks at me, questioningly, when he sees her hands. Lucas pushes his chair back, shaking his head.

"What's the point, Tima? It's no use."

Tima motions her hand in the direction of the nearest grating, raising her voice for Doc's benefit. "The *point* is she's some lowly Grass. So is the boy. They should know their place. As long as they're here, they can act like the garbage they are. Until someone shuttles them out with the trash."

The garbage shuttle. That's what I hear. There is a way off this island. Tima has worked through it in her head, just like that, while we sit here. *They put out the trash. Go while you can.*

She raises her voice. "I said, take the plate. Now."

I back away from the table. Ro grabs the plate and the cup out of Tima's hands, following.

Tima catches my arm before I go.

I am not sure what passes between us, a moment of trust or anger or something else entirely. But she lets me see one more thing.

150

She rolls her arm slowly toward me. The blood tattoo slides out of sight; I expect another one. I don't expect this.

Three silver dots on the inside of her wrist.

She's one of us—and not one of us—too. Like Lucas.

She's the third Icon Child.

Fear.

That's when I begin to understand. Tima may not be afraid of Ro, but I have every right to be afraid of her.

Even though she appears frightened, she is lethal— maybe more deadly than Ro. If I stand in her way, she will come for me. Calculated. Precise. One careful stitch at a time.

She closes her eyes and I see the truth.

I see blood and death and chaos. I see the lengths she will go for the person she loves.

Fear is a dangerous thing.

I grab Ro's arm and flee toward the kitchen, before she can change her mind. He runs as fast as I do, maybe faster.

He's seen her marking, too.

RESEARCH MEMORANDUM:
THE HUMANITY PROJECT

CLASSIFIED TOP SECRET / AMBASSADOR EYES ONLY

To: Ambassador Amare

From: Dr. Huxley-Clarke

Subject: Icon Children Mythology

Subtopic: Freak

Catalogue Assignment: Evidence recovered during raid of Rebellion hideout

---

The following is a reprint of a recovered page, thick, home-made paper, thought to be torn from an anti-Embassy propaganda tract titled *Icon Children Exist!* Most likely hand-published by a fanatical cult or Grass Rebellion faction.

Text-scan translation follows.

FREAK *(Icon timoris)*

A Freak relies on fear and anxiety to motivate tactical perfectionism in battle, though rarely participating in combat directly. Some believe that the energy and adrenaline generated by a Freak's extreme fear can actually disrupt the surrounding atmosphere, creating, in effect, a buffer zone.

FREAK, COME OUT

AND HELP US FIGHT!

YOUR MIND CAN SET US FREE!

WE NEED YOU ON OUR SIDE.

12

LONG WAY HOME

From our vantage point, hidden behind the open entrance doors, I can see the kitchen is ten times larger than the one in the Mission, with stoves the size of furnaces, built of metal instead of brick and stone. The smoke rises into giant vents that look like silver mouths, instead of fireplaces and chimneys.

And there is no Bigger standing at the kettle.

Sadness wells up inside me, but I put it off.

Not now.

I eye a grating in the wall next to the vents. Doc. I look around for other signs of surveillance, but there is too much going on in the enormous room to tell.

Ro takes off toward the back of the room. I duck my head to follow him, sliding beneath the long, metallic counters, where they store what looks like sterilization equipment.

We remain, for the moment, unseen.

"What now," I hiss.

"You saw her hands." Ro looks past the corner of the counter that hides us. "She's a weird one."

"And?"

"We need to find where they keep the garbage."

I shrug. "So we follow whatever smells the worst."

A kitchen worker walks by us, dragging a huge black bag that reeks of manure. Ro wrinkles his nose.

"Exactly."

In no time at all, the stench leads us to the garbage dock. I can see it, through the swinging doors of the kitchen warehouse. I can also see a Sympa patrolling it.

"When that door opens again, we go." Ro seems happier than I've seen him in months.

I nod, then grab his arm. "Ro."

"What?"

"Can we trust her?"

"The silver girl?"

I nod. "It seems too easy. This." I glance toward the dock. "What if it's a setup?"

Ro sighs. "You met her. You tell me. You're supposed to handle that department."

"But I trusted Lucas, and I got us into this mess." It's

an apology, and not a particularly good one. But it needs to be said, especially before we fling ourselves into a barge full of garbage and guarded by at least one armed Sympa.

Ro winks. "I forgive you, Dol-face."

Then, without a word, he takes off running and I have no choice but to follow.

I rush after him, crouching low. We race toward the barge, finally sliding between a mountain of slimy black bags swarming with flies and practically pulsing with an indescribably putrid smell.

I close my eyes and freeze, waiting for the Sympa to fire.

I hear nothing.

Ro peeks his head out from inside a bag that has split in half. Something that looks like old porridge smears across his face.

I hold my breath. We don't make a sound.

The smell is overwhelming, worse than sleeping in the stables, and it's all I can do to keep down what little food I managed to eat.

The barge begins to vibrate beneath us, and the garbage shifts. The engine starts, groaning and rumbling to life as the barge lurches into motion.

"It's moving," Ro whispers. He smiles, in spite of the garbage.

I shake my head, crossing my fingers beneath the mountain of limply rotting lettuce and old bread crusts.

That's when the engine cuts.

Then we hear loud voices and the heavy, thudding footsteps of military boots.

I uncross my fingers as we dive deeper beneath the piles of black bags. Then, muffled by garbage, a familiar voice booms across the barge.

Catallus.

"Doloria. Furo. I'm afraid you've gone the wrong direction. Understandable, since you're new here. Anyone could get lost on the way to my classroom."

I pull myself up to the surface of the garbage.

"We're not going anywhere with you," Ro shouts, poking his head above the sea of garbage sacks, trying to look dignified while covered with rotten food.

I can see him looking for something to use as a weapon, but the only thing in our reach is an entire Embassy's uneaten breakfast.

Colonel Catallus smiles. "Of course—you could always stay here and take a little ride, but I'm not sure it's preferable to our class. Where do you think they take this trash?"

"Wait, let me think. Your house?" Ro grins. "No—your mom's house?" He'll go down trying. He's long past caring what people do to him.

I stay silent.

"See those smokestacks across the bay, on the mainland? That's where we take the trash. Right into the incinerators. They help power the Projects. So I guess it would be good to have your contribution via the furnaces, but I think we could make better use of your talents in the classroom."

Colonel Catallus motions and the barge begins to grind backward, toward the docks. He wobbles with the sudden movement, adjusting his position on the side of the barge, above us. "I'm surprised Tima didn't tell you, especially seeing as she made the same mistake, the first time she tried to run away."

Ro and I look at each other.

Suspicions confirmed.

"Come on, Ro," I say, struggling to get out of the garbage. "We've been played." And worse, rescued by a demon.

Colonel Catallus pulls a white square of handkerchief out of his pocket, holding it over his nose. He waves the handkerchief in the direction of the Embassy.

"The others are waiting. It's time we had a talk. Now."

Assembled by Dr. O. Brad Huxley-Clarke, VPHD

Note: Media Transcript conducted at the private
    request of Amb. Amare

Santa Catalina Examination Facility #9B
    Text Scan: *NEW YORK DAILY*

EXTINCTION AVOIDED?

April 10, 2068 • New York City, New York

Officials at the United Nations have claimed success in diverting the asteroid Perses from impacting Earth.

The joint project of the major economic powers announced today that Project Kratos, consisting of a series of pinpoint warheads launched in 2067, scored a direct hit.

The director of Project Kratos, Alexis Asimov, said: "Our goal was to split Perses into smaller pieces that would fly harmlessly around Earth, and all our data shows the mission was a complete success. We will continue to monitor the fragments to ensure our data is correct."

Not everybody is convinced, however. Many citizens hold the entire story to be a hoax.

Others believe the asteroid is still coming, including those who say Perses is a holy messenger of God, come to purge Earth of greed and inequity.

COLONEL CATALLUS

Of course, we aren't allowed to wash up, after the garbage disaster. Colonel Catallus is teaching us a lesson; at least, I imagine that is what he thinks.

The joke is on him, though. We've grown used to the stench, Ro and I. Not Catallus. He looks like he is going to pass out, just being in the same hall with us.

And now it appears the Embassy isn't taking any chances with us, because it somehow requires four guards for Colonel Catallus to walk us back. Or he's just trying to intimidate us.

It's working.

It occurs to me that I could try to probe their minds, look for a new way out, and I even spend a few minutes contemplating how I could accidentally bump into the guard in front of me, to heighten the connection. Then

I give up. I'm too tired, and it takes too much out of me. And I just smell too damn bad.

Not Ro, though. Ro stands a little taller, next to the Sympas. I think he likes feeling dangerous.

We arrive at Colonel Catallus's classroom—at least, that's what he calls this version of his interrogation chamber. It's a meeting room with glass walls and a round table, in the center of the Embassy library.

Basically, a jail cell.

Through the glass, I can see Tima and Lucas waiting inside. Lucas has his face buried in a small, flat screen when we push through the doors. Tima is next to him, pulling on the ends of her silver hair as she reads over his shoulder. There with Lucas, she looks much more content than when we last saw her at breakfast.

Almost happy, even.

I pull my eyes away from her and examine the rest of the room. It's more of a fishbowl than a classroom, barely big enough for the five of us. Beyond the glass walls, there are books as far as I can see, more books than in all the black markets in the Hole. Real books, paper books. Digi-text on a row of screens. Together, they fill a room bigger than the cafeteria.

I can also see our Sympa patrol, standing at attention by the entrance to the library.

Waiting.

Lucas doesn't look up. His face flickers with the reflected light of the scrolling screen. Then we come closer, and both Tima and Lucas react like they've just been slapped in the face.

"What—is that—smell?" Lucas practically shouts, grabbing his nose, pushing back his chair.

"Garbage," says Tima with a smile. "Or maybe that's just what the Grass smell like." She pushes back next to him, hovering.

Where we both know she most likes to be.

I take a step closer to her, and I hope I look threatening, because that's how I feel.

"A garbage barge? That leads to an incinerator? Really? Is that the best you could come up with?"

Ro grabs my arm. Lucas steps in front of Tima. All four of us are locked in an impasse.

It's Colonel Catallus who finally breaks the standoff.

"That's enough. Take a seat. The adrenaline is fascinating, but tiresome. And I've no need for more data today, not on any one of you."

None of us move. He smiles. "Or do we need to bring the guards all the way *into* the classroom?"

Ro and Lucas stare at each other. Tima glowers at me. Colonel Catallus shakes his head. "Fine. Take your time. I'm happy to lock you down until you've had your fun. It's all the same to me. I have work to do."

He closes the glass door behind him.

Lucas and Ro are now inches apart from each other. "You don't really want to do this, do you?" Lucas pushes his hand against Ro's chest. Big mistake.

"No, I'm pretty sure I do." Ro smiles, wrapping his fist in Lucas's shirt.

I speak up to Tima, over Ro's shoulder. "You didn't have to sell us out to Catallus."

Tima sniffs. "I don't know what you're talking about. I thought you were looking for a ride out of here. It's not my fault you got caught." Ro growls. Tima puts him on edge almost as much as Lucas does.

I stare at her. "Why do you hate us so much?"

She spits the words back at me. "Why are you even here? Since when did they start testing Grass like you?"

"Why don't you ask your mommy?" Ro steps closer to Lucas.

Tima rolls her eyes, and it's all I can do not to grab her myself, and I shout, "You think we want to be here? You think we had a choice in this? The minute we get the chance, we'll be gone. That's a promise."

Lucas's eyes narrow as I say the words. Ro stays close, and I'm aware of every inch of him. Part of him is enjoying this. Part of Ro has enjoyed this entire day, even the garbage.

Not Lucas. I can feel him recede, as Ro begins to surge. Battle is Ro's natural state. He likes the rush of adrenaline, the push of uncertainty, the risk of death. As long as it's not mine. It's only the threat to me that is making him nervous, even now.

Ro pulls Lucas in, raising his fist.

"Stop it," Tima blurts out, dragging herself between them.

In a blur—in a split second—I watch Tima's arm go flying toward Ro, and then I see Ro rearing back, hollering.

"Ow! What was that? You shocked me."

"I didn't shock you." Tima sounds confused.

"You did. Look…"

There, around Ro's wrist, is what looks like a rope burn—a red, searing line that wraps around his arm, precisely where Tima's hand touched him.

Tima stares at the mark.

Lucas backs away from both of them, from us.

Tima glowers at him. "All I was going to say was that you're fools if you don't know what he's doing right now." She looks up at the ceiling, calling toward the grating. "Orwell?"

"Yes, Tima?"

"Can you bring up a visual on Colonel Catallus? I need to ask him something, face-to-face."

"It would be my pleasure, Tima." Behind her, Colonel Catallus's face appears on the wide screen that blankets one side of the classroom wall.

He's standing in the library, in front of a bank of

screens. All of which are streaming a live feed of us. He's watching.

Of course he is.

"Tima Li has a question for you, sir."

Colonel Catallus looks startled. Then he recovers, with another of his creepy smiles. "And?"

"I just wanted to ask you if we passed your little test, now. Sir." Her face is completely innocent, but the screen flickers off.

He's back in the classroom within twenty seconds.

I wonder if that is a yes or a no.

———— • ————

"I'm so glad to see you're all getting along," Colonel Catallus says. "And how is your arm, Ro? Tima hasn't hurt more than your pride, I hope."

Nobody says a word. I don't smile, and I don't respond. I make a point of shutting everyone out, of not seeing anything about Catallus. Not cats or girls or walls of ice. Whatever is going on in there with him, I don't want to know. It's safer that way.

Instead, I assess where I am and what I can do. Tima has confused things; she's not at all what I expected, but I shouldn't be surprised. No more than I am by Ro or Lucas or even myself, on any given day. I can't pretend she's any different than we are.

166

I don't know the extent of our abilities—what it is that has the Embassy so interested in us.

What they want from us.

I don't know what I'm more afraid of—trying to escape and getting killed along the way, or staying for more of Colonel Catallus's painful tests and wishing I were dead.

I squirm in my seat, a hard synth chair made to look like wood.

Colonel Catallus clears his throat. "I have much to discuss with you—now that I have the four of you together again. After all these years."

He lets the sentence roll out into the bright light of the room. *Together again. The four of us. All these years.* But we have never been together, the four of us. We have never met before Santa Catalina. There is no *again* in this scenario.

If the four of us are anything. And if there are, in fact, only four of us, as the Embassy seems to think.

Icon Children.

"That's not possible," I say, finally. No matter what I think, I'm not going to say more than that. Especially now that I know how closely monitored we all are.

"Of course it's possible." Tima flicks her head as she speaks, clicking her nails on the table, faster and faster. "You might not know what's possible, but that doesn't limit possibility." She rolls her eyes. "Obviously."

"Obviously," mimics Ro.

Lucas studies Colonel Catallus's face. If he's as confused as I am, he's not letting on. "Just say it, Colonel Cat. Whatever it is, you can spit it out. We're all friends here."

Ro smirks, leaning on the table next to me. "Speak for yourself, Buttons."

"Enough." Colonel Catallus sits forward. "Her Ambassadorship's wisdom works in myriad ways. Don't think you're only here because of what you can do for us." He nods. "It's about what you need us to—"

The vid-screen behind Colonel Catallus illuminates, surprising him. "Excuse me. A moment."

The four of us look at each other, equally baffled. The logo of the Embassy appears, beginning to flash, which seems to agitate him even more.

Colonel Catallus directs his voice to the screen. "Yes?"

"You have a message from the Ambassador's office, Colonel Catallus."

"What is it, Computer?" It takes me a moment to realize he's talking to Doc.

"I cannot say. The server appears to be sending error messages to this address. You are either wanted by the Ambassador, or there is a system-wide malfunction."

He won't risk that it's a mistake. We all know he'll be out the door by the end of the next few sentences.

"It is probably nothing," encourages Doc. "Go on."

"Yes, please. Go on, Colonel Catallus," Tima says.

"It will only be a moment." With a pompous little swagger, the man and his brass wings are gone.

The minute Colonel Catallus steps out of the room, the lights dim. "What was that?" Ro is out of his seat.

Blackout shades rumble, covering the door and four walls of our glass classroom. The Sympas on perpetual watch at the outer doorways begin to move toward our room.

"Um, Doc? Is this another one of your jokes?" Lucas cranes his head up toward the ceiling. "Very funny. You're getting better and better."

The door bolts, as if in response.

Tima springs out of her chair, but Ro beats her to the door. He rattles the handle furiously; Ro has never done well being caged.

"Orwell, are you seeing this?"

"Yes, Timora."

"More to the point, Orwell, are you doing this?"

"No, Timora. I am impressed, though, by the coding. If I am not mistaken, this entire sector of the server has been compromised."

"Open the door for the guards." It is an order, and Tima barks it, as if she expects him to obey. "Now, Orwell."

"I am unable to open the doors, interestingly enough. The locking mechanism is now disarmed. Very thoroughly, I might add."

"So my mother didn't call Colonel Catallus to her

office." Lucas looks pleased, for the first time today.

"*Non. Maestitia brevis, gloria longa.*"

"Now, Doc. Don't get snippy." Lucas grins.

"What did he say?" Ro nudges me. I shrug. I have no idea.

"Sorrow is temporary. Pride is forever." Tima translates, without looking at me. Her eyes are on Lucas.

Lucas is grinning. "Basically, he's saying Catallus is a jerk with a big head."

"Yes, Lucas. Duly noted. Also noted, there appears to be a message on the Embassy Wik." Doc runs one sentence into the next, without a shift in tone.

"For me?" Lucas's smile fades.

"What, Mommy's calling?" Ro slaps him on the back. "You're grounded now, Buttons."

"No. For...Doloria. Excuse me, Dolly. For yo—" Doc's voice disappears in the middle of the word, which I have never heard him do before.

Three heads turn to look at me. Before I can say anything, the room darkens completely, and a face appears on the vid-screen.

A dirty face.

The Merk from the Tracks.

Fortis.

"So you ended up in the can after all, eh? Sorry, no refunds. Hazard of the industry."

"Who is that?" Ro looks confused.

"He's the Merk. The one who set the explosions and drew away the Sympas, so I could find you." I say it only to Ro, but loud enough so the others can hear. I don't want to explain it further, especially since Lucas was possibly on the receiving end of the blast, along with the rest of the Sympas.

"Fortis, how are you doing this?" The image is shaky, jerking in and out.

"Very quickly, love. An' with my customary aplomb."

"What do you want, Merk?" Tima is less impressed. I realize that Lucas has moved closer to the door, and now stands next to her.

"Give me one reason not to call the authorities. I can have Security here in five seconds." Lucas sounds older than he is, and I almost believe him, though I think he's bluffing.

"Well, one, I am Security. I'm using the Security server, so if you tried to call, I would answer an' you'd be exactly where you are right now." Fortis grins. "Is that enough reason, or do you want more?"

"Orwell, I'm switching to Manual." Tima moves to the screen, her fingers flashing across a series of lit buttons.

"Your Orwell's a little busy right now. He's conducting a system-wide diagnostic. I'm guessing he'll be back online in, say, three hours. Or as soon as we've wrapped things up here. Whenever I decide."

Tima bangs her hand on the screen, annoyed.

"But on the bright side, he's going to feel like a new man, right, Merk?" Ro is enjoying himself, the broadcast, the chaos. The look on Lucas's tightly drawn face.

"How, Fortis?" He knows what I mean. This, everything. How is he possibly here now? It's as improbable as him rescuing me from the Tracks. Which, if he can do this, maybe wasn't so improbable.

He shakes his head. "Little Grassgirl. Those are trade secrets—it's my livelihood we're talkin' about here. Now, you goin' to introduce me to your friends?"

I shake my head back at him. "Not until I know what you want."

Fortis makes a face. "Where's the trust?" Onscreen, he angles his head toward Lucas. "Little Ambassador. Lucas Amare. The Lover. I 'ave to say, you're a lot less fun in person. Though the ladies might disagree." Lucas looks grim.

"And Timora Li. You're a regular barrel of laughs yourself, aren't you? Ah, the Freak. Always so much fun. You talk a good game, but when push comes to shove you crawl right back into your shell, don't you then?" She glares at him.

"Furo Costas. The Rager. You, my friend, are an imbecile. You could have killed me twenty times, on the Tracks. I'm surprised you're not dead."

Ro shrugs, happily. It's nothing he hasn't heard before, and nothing he doesn't see as a compliment.

"Which leaves you, sweet Doloria Maria de la Cruz. The Weeper, Our Grass Lady of the Sorrows."

"You've made your point, Merk. Congratulations, you know our names." Lucas edges closer to the screen, defiant.

"I do. So do more than a few people in the Embassy, accordin' to this database. Including a Virt Medic, a psychopathic Sympa Colonel, and the Ambassador."

"So?" I force myself to look at him. "Get on with it."

"So. Aren't you at all curious, little fig, why? Why now? What makes the four of you so interestin'? Because I have to say, though your personality's a real sparkler, that's not really the thing, is it?"

"What do you know?" Ro asks, stepping up beside me.

Fortis fades in and out of the picture.

"Something you don't. A great many things you don't. But there's only one you need concern yourself with, now."

"Yeah?" Ro's eyes flicker.

"The Icon. You think it's invincible. Unstoppable, even. It holds the whole deal in place, don't it? The *Hole* Deal, yeah?" He winks.

I roll my eyes.

"Those electromagnetic waves—the pulse electricity the Icons emit—there's no stoppin' it. One in every major city, right? The power's the power, as it were. They connect together, all of them, like one big choke collar aroun' Earth."

Lucas rubs his hand through his hair, distracted. "This isn't news."

"We provide free labor to build their blasted Projects in exchange for a semblance of life as it used to be. We let them enslave us to build who knows what behind those walls."

"What's your point?" Lucas is irritated.

"And if we cooperate, if we play nice, the world keeps running and everybody stays alive to cooperate another day. We 'ave no choice but to obey. The Icons are impregnable. As far as we know. As far as they say. At least that's the story."

"We don't need you to tell us how bad it is, Fortis. We've already got a pretty good idea of how things work." I shift on my feet. I don't like to talk about the Icons and the Projects. I don't even like to think about them.

"Maybe you do, maybe you don't." He smiles. "Say you don't. Say nobody knows how it works, not really. Say, for the fun of it, there was a chink in the armor. Or, rather, a silver bullet—a weapon with the power to turn the tide back in our favor. Now that would be somethin', wouldn't it?"

"Is he serious?" Tima looks at me, then at Fortis. "Are you serious?"

"As the grave." Fortis moves his head closer to the screen.

"Now say the Embassy has learned about this secret

weapon. What do you think they would do, with some-thin' like that? Use it to destroy the Icons, right? Perhaps."

I feel dizzy.

Fortis shakes his head. "Perhaps not. After all, the Lords and the Icons are the reason the Embassy's in con-trol. Without the Icons, the Embassy's powerless. Out of a job. And probably wanted for crimes against humanity."

"They should be," Ro growls.

Lucas looks ill.

I can hear my heart pounding.

"Well, guess what, children? Today's your lucky day. I 'ave it on good authority that there is in fact a silver bullet. And the Embassy has found it, or should I say, found them. And bingo—quick as you can say Bob's your uncle—four of these little silver bullets are in one place, locked up safe an' tight under the watchful eye of a Colonel who, I think, might 'imself need to be locked up." Fortis looks around the room behind us.

My head is pounding.

Them.

Us.

He means us.

"One more thing. The Rebellion knows, too. They're a bit more than eager to work with you, as you can imagine. I need you to know this because soon, you're all going to have to make a decision."

I close my eyes.

The Rebellion knows we're here?

And they think we're the key to bringing down the Icons?

I let the words sit in my head, but I can't think clearly.

Would I like it to be over? Without a doubt.

Would I like the Embassy to disappear? The House of Lords to have never found our planet? Of course.

My thoughts are spinning out of control.

If I could be the one to change it all, would I do it? Could I?

What if the Padre was right? What if Ro and I—all of us—really were meant for something bigger?

What then? What now?

The Merk interrupts my thoughts. "And when you do, well, you're going to need a good Merk. Someone who can barter your services, properly like. Get a fair market price an' all..."

He sighs, stretching his hands out in front of him.

A pro.

"Should that day ever come—and I assure you, it will—old Fortis, he'll find you. When you're good and ready."

I'll never be ready, I want to shout.

But it doesn't matter, because Fortis disappears, and the lights flood back on in the room.

Doc's voice continues on, midsentence. "You, Dolly.

The message appears to be for you." He pauses, and we all look at each other. Nobody knows what to say, but for different reasons.

I can see Tima's mind racing. It looks like bicycle wheels and storm clouds and waves. Lucas is as strained and sad on the inside as his face is, on the outside. Ro has dissolved into chaos, but I know what he thinks without having to even grab his hand.

He's ready to take the whole Embassy down, single-handedly.

That one idea is more real and more frightening than anything else.

Doc's voice crackles into the room. "That is quite strange. It's deleted. There's nothing there; the file is empty."

"It's not important now, Doc." I look at Ro, questioningly. He shakes his head. Tima shrugs. They're not going to say anything.

Lucas frowns at the door. "We should probably let the guards in."

Doc isn't convinced. "Stranger still, I seem to be in the middle of a technical diagnostic I do not recall initiating."

Ro grins; our little visit from Fortis has left him glowing. "Well, to err is human, or whatever some old dead guy says about that."

"*Errare humanum est.* To err is human. The words

are attributed to, I believe, Seneca. Is that what you had in mind?"

Ro puts his feet up on the table. "Sure. Seneca. That guy."

"Or, if you prefer: *Factum est illud: fieri infectum non potest.* Which is attributed to Plautus."

"Done is done, it cannot be undone," Tima translates, frowning.

The blackout shades roll up just as Colonel Catallus appears outside the glass door, pushing past the Sympas. He places his hand on the doorknob, and I watch in amazement as the door unbolts, the moment before he opens it.

"False alarm. No need for the excessive security, Computer." He sounds annoyed. "Now, what's going on here? Where were we?" The Sympas follow him into the room, four of them. We look surprised—as surprised as we can.

"*Alea iacta est,*" Lucas says to Colonel Catallus, as the Colonel orders the soldiers out the door with one look.

"The die has been cast? What die? Cast where?" Colonel Catallus looks at us, but nobody says anything.

I watch as Tima slowly draws her pen back out of her pocket to ink a few words, this time on her palm. She flexes and unrolls her fingers, showing it to me.

NEED TO TALK.

Then her fingers flash again, and the words have disappeared.

Lucas looks at me, and I wonder if he is thinking about Fortis, or about his mother. His face admits to nothing, no allegiances. Whose side he'll take.

Not yet.

I try to push deeper, but I'm met with only silence.

As Colonel Catallus launches into a lengthy discussion of the key role he plays for *Her Ambassadorship*, I wonder how long Lucas will stay silent.

If he will betray us.

When.

Assembled by Dr. O. Brad Huxley-Clarke, VPHD

Note: Media Transcript conducted at the private
   request of Amb. Amare

Santa Catalina Examination Facility #9B
   Text-Scan

PERSES RETURNS

August 4, 2071 • Washington, DC

In a shocking turn of events, scientists and
government officials are confirming that the
fragments of the asteroid Perses have changed
trajectory, and are now headed directly toward
Earth.

Officials estimate contact to occur within less
than one year, and are scrambling to calculate
points of impact and mobilize defensive measures
in hopes of minimizing damages.

One UN official, speaking anonymously, said,
"There are at least a dozen fragments that have
suddenly and inexplicably changed course. We

don't have an answer as to how or why this happened. Our best hope is to find out where they will hit and try to minimize casualties. Until we know more, we can only recommend that people stay put, live their lives, and pray."

14

DECISIONS

The Catalina Presidio. That's what Tima and Lucas call this part of the Embassy. From what I can tell—mostly from a hidden box holding their stash, which isn't much more than a few candles and a deck of cards—it's where they come for their private conversations.

Doc isn't here because we are outside, on the catwalk at the top of the Embassy walls. There are no little round gratings in these walls. And I know Virts can't live outside, not yet. At least, that's what we hear, out in the Grass. Then again, I'm starting to realize we don't know the truth from the lies, not anymore. That's pretty clear by now. The events of yesterday have upended everything. If the four of us agree on nothing else, we agree on that.

Which is why Ro and I agreed to come and hear what Tima and Lucas have to say, before we decide how and when to try again, to get off the island. Escaping won't be easy, especially now that Sympa soldiers go everywhere we do; this morning, it has taken Tima close to three hours to determine the precise moments we would need to access certain floors, and use certain stairwells, but her calculations are correct, because we are alone now.

The Presidio isn't old, like the other presidios in the Californias. It's only meant to look that way. It's the highest part of the square, walled complex of buildings that make up the Embassy—and this part is more a fort than an embassy, really. According to Lucas, the Presidio houses the Pen, which is the Embassy prison, and the military quarters. It takes up the whole north end of the island, and from these rooftop catwalks, I can see everything.

Except the Hole. Not today. I lean over the crumbling concrete wall and stare into the dark, swirling waters off Santa Catalina Island. Old brass telescopes line the catwalk, but I don't bother to look. There's nothing to see in the fog. I shiver. I'm beginning to think the fog will never lift. Maybe the Embassy controls the weather, like they control everything else. Maybe the fog isn't fog at all, but some Sympa-derived optical vapor that neutralizes every person it comes in contact with. Or maybe it's a bay full of

183

dragons' breath, like the Chumash used to say, long before the Porthole existed.

Maybe it's just fog.

I let the ocean settle me, as it always does. If I keep my eyes on the waves, our current problems are not too painful to bear. Almost.

"What do we know?" Lucas turns to Tima. "You're the one who likes a plan."

She shrugs casually, but I know her mind is racing. She's thinking as she speaks. "We have to look at the facts. What's changed? Why bring Ro and Dol to the Embassy? Why now?"

"They want the four of us together." Lucas leans along the wall, his arm hanging on a telescope. "So they want something from us. Or they've discovered something about us, like the Merk said."

She paces in front of him. "But all we can say for certain is that the Embassy knows more about us than we do. At least, more than we've been told."

Lucas sits. "Not just that. The Rebellion knows about us." He's completely stressed out, you can see it in his face. And I can feel it, deep inside him. He feels like marbles rolling in every direction at the exact same time.

Nobody could catch them all at once.

"So?" Ro speaks up from his perch across the walkway. "That's not a bad thing."

"It's not a good thing," Lucas says, taking the deck of cards from the box.

"You don't know that." Ro slumps against the far wall.

Lucas tosses a card from the deck. Then another.

He can't say anything, because Ro's right. Which of those things is the bad news? Which is the good? We don't know who to trust. We don't know who to blame.

Tima speaks up. "Okay. What about the Rebellion? If the Merk is working for them—"

"Merks don't work for anyone," I interrupt.

"Fine. Dealing for them. Either way, they know our names, they know our faces, they knew our schedule. They knew when they would be likely to find us, and where. It's the only explanation that makes sense. How else would he have been able to find us?" Tima ticks off the basics. We all get the main point, which is this: we aren't so secret as we thought.

"So we have to assume they have the ability to get inside the Embassy. At least, virtually." I remember Fortis, lying in wait for his next customer inside the Tracks car. "Probably physically, if they wanted to."

"Nobody can get to Santa Catalina if the Embassy doesn't want them to. We control all the barges." Lucas sounds wounded. At least his pride does. "Not just the garbage ones," he adds, as if he needs to remind us.

Ro and I turn to him, almost involuntarily.

"'We,'" says Ro, spluttering. "You mean you and your mommy, Buttons?"

"Shut up."

"Is that it? You want to ask your mother? Who the bad guys are?"

Lucas turns purple.

"Enough. We don't have time for this. You have to be quiet so I can think." Tima looks at me. "Is this Fortis someone you trust?"

Is he? I hesitate. "I don't really know him, just that he's a Merk. I paid him to help me escape the prison car."

"You paid him? With what?" Now it's Ro's turn to glare at me. Whatever it is, he knows I don't have the digs for a Merk. He knows it can't be good.

"A book. A Grass book."

Ro stiffens.

I try again. "It was from the Padre, for my birthday." I add the last part shyly. But Lucas and Tima react as if I've shouted it. As if I've slapped them.

"When was your birthday?" Tima asks.

I try to think. How long ago was that, my last day at the Mission? "The Blessing of the Animals." Lucas and Tima look at me blankly. "The day I came here."

Lucas sits up straight. "Wait. My birthday was the day I met you. My birthday, and Tima's birthday. We're birth mates, born on the same day. That's the only reason

I'm not in more trouble for sneaking out to go with the soldiers to the Mission raid."

Which makes me his birthday present. Us. In a way.

Great.

Lucas frowns. "Not that it'll happen again, not anytime soon."

Tima leans closer to him, looking at me. "We have the same birthday. The same year. Lucas and me and you. That has to mean something." She turns to Ro, who is now chucking stones over the side of the concrete. "What about you?"

"I don't have a birthday." Ro doesn't even bother to look at her.

"You mean you don't know your birthday."

"Whatever. Same thing."

Like me, Ro doesn't remember much about his parents, and unlike me, there were no photos.

I wonder.

Three of us on one day. Maybe four.

Tima looks at Lucas, then turns to me. Resuming her line of questioning.

"We can't figure it all out now. But what about this book? That you gave the Merk?" I was hoping she wasn't going to ask me that. I know how it will look. But, one conversation. One honest, private conversation. I owe them at least that. I look at Lucas. "Do you remember when the Ambassador was asking me about a book?"

"The one she was looking for at the Mission?" He lowers his voice and moves closer to me. Tima and Ro look confused.

"The one she killed the Padre for." My voice trembles as I say it, and Ro's mouth tightens into a grim line. Lucas looks stricken.

He understands the trouble I'm in.

"*That's* your book? The one the Embassy is searching half the Californias for? And you gave it away to a Merk?"

I start talking my way out of it, as fast as I can—but the truth of the matter is, I already feel worse about it than any of them ever could.

"The Sympas came and I didn't have time to read it. But the Padre said it was the story of me. The Icon Children."

They look incredulous.

Tima sighs. "What I wouldn't give to have a book like that. There's so much we don't know about ourselves."

"What's the big deal?" Ro steps between us. "It's just a stupid book. It didn't mean anything."

Lucas sounds shocked. "Well, obviously it means a lot if he wanted it, and if the Embassy wants it. Think about it. She gives a Merk a book about her—about us—and then he shows up here, in an Embassy classroom? In the middle of the Embassy library? While the Ambassador is desperately trying to find it? You think that's a coincidence?"

"Maybe it's not the book. Fortis isn't like that." I try to defend myself, but I can't. I don't know Fortis, or what's so important about the book I gave him, or how it found its way out of the Ambassador's hands—and into the Padre's. "Besides, it isn't even really a book. It looked more like a notebook, or a journal."

And I have no idea why everyone wants it so badly. Or how to explain that none of it seemed this real before I met them. That it was just Ro and me on the Mission. That none of it seemed like it mattered.

Tima crosses her arms. "Fortis isn't like that? What does that mean? How do you know what this Fortis person is like?"

"I just do." Why am I defending Fortis? Did I trust him? Do I? He's just a Merk.

Still.

He didn't have to help me. And now that he's come to me again, I find myself wondering if I'm a part of his latest Merk enterprise. Judging by what he was saying, it's also his biggest Merk enterprise, ever.

I try to change the subject. "Forget the book for now. Go back to the birthdays. Three out of the four of us were supposedly born on the same day. There has to be some record of that."

"What about the other stuff?" Lucas asks. I know

189

what he's talking about. The part where we're the silver bullets cutting through the Embassy's armor. "Do you really think the Icons aren't invincible? People have tried to attack them before. It's never worked. Nothing does."

He doesn't say it, but it's clear. If the Icons can be taken down, then so can the Embassies.

So can the Ambassador.

I'm not sure, suddenly, if this is a conversation we should be having with Lucas.

"First things first," says Ro. I wonder if he's thinking the same thing I am. That it's worth staying around, even a little while longer, until we get to the bottom of a few of these questions.

Not for long. Just longer.

"First Doc, and the records," says Tima. "If we can figure out why we were born the same day, maybe we can figure out the rest. I don't like people knowing more about me than I do. I don't like being a bullet being shot by somebody's gun. So we find out where we came from and why. Then we'll deal with Fortis."

"We have to find that book," sighs Lucas.

In a miracle of miracles, the fog is beginning to lift. From where we stand, we can see the dim brown outline of the Hole against the pale white sky behind it.

I look into one of the old brass telescopes along the side of the wall. The glass is cracked, but I twist the rusting knob and the land beyond the water comes into focus.

The clouds part, and the Icon looms tall over the city, rising up out of the stubble on the hill like one gangly tree in an otherwise razed forest. We all stand there, the four of us, watching it. Wary.

As if we haven't seen enough.

RESEARCH MEMORANDUM:
THE HUMANITY PROJECT

CLASSIFIED TOP SECRET /
AMBASSADOR EYES ONLY

To: Ambassador Amare

Subject: Icon Children Origins

Subtopic: Research Notes

Catalogue Assignment: Evidence recovered during
  raid of Rebellion hideout
  Origin of notes believed to be Paulo Fortissimo

Notes were partially destroyed by fire. Transcription follows.

I AM CLOSE TO A BREAKTHROUGH. THE CHILDREN MAY BE THE SOLUTION.

[Text illegible]...*FROM THEIR ABILITY TO GENER-ATE IMMENSELY POWERFUL ENERGY, IN WAVE FORM, THROUGH INTENSE EMOTIONAL STIMULI. THIS ENERGY...* [text illegible].

FIRST, IT CREATES A RESISTANCE TO MAGNETIC STIMULATION/ELECTRICAL INTERFERENCE FROM OUTSIDE SOURCES.

SECOND, IT ENABLES SUBJECTS TO MANIPULATE THE ELECTROMAGNETIC ELEMENTS AROUND THEM, CREATING WHAT AMOUNTS TO MIND CONTROL, TELEKINESIS, HYPER-INTELLIGENCE, MIND READING, ETC.

ADDITIONALLY...[text illegible].

[Remaining text illegible.]

15

BRUTUS

That night at dinner, I sit alone with Tima. Ro has been confined to his room since this afternoon, when his guard detail found him trying to sneak into the munitions lockers—I'm here to steal food for him now. And Lucas, I have no idea where he is. Probably off somewhere disappointing his mother.

We sit in silence.

My plate is full of limp, boiled vegetables and I miss the Mission, the garden. I miss the early scarlet radishes and the blood beets—the golden zucchini and the Empress beans. I miss the Brandywine tomatoes so big, they force their vines back down to the earth. The green grape tomatoes so small you could eat fifty at a time. The Embassy food somehow never smells like earth. It doesn't matter to Tima, though. She's only eating toast, plain toast.

Above it, her eyes survey the room, looking at anything but me.

I can't stand the silence, but at the same time I find myself drawn to Tima, at least curious about her. Since she is one of us.

"How long have you lived here, anyway?" The question sounds forced, but it's the best I can do. She's not the easiest person to talk to. Tima looks uncomfortable, and I can tell she's considering bolting. She has a flash of panic—fight or flight, she's weighing the odds. For the moment, she stays.

"I don't like to think about it. I got here when I was around nine, I think." She stops talking and takes a microscopic bite of her toast.

I pursue. "Then where are you from?"

Tima starts playing with her toast, breaking it into smaller and smaller pieces.

"I guess not from around here?" I try to draw her in.

She sighs, frustrated at having to talk, but at the same time I sense that she is desperate to speak with me, with anybody.

I wait for her, patiently.

"I was picked up by Sympas in upstate New York. I lived in an Embassy orphanage, with a bunch of other Remnants. It—wasn't pleasant. Bad things happened there, but we didn't have anywhere else to go."

She opens and closes her eyes, blinking rapidly. "I—got

in trouble. Then, somebody noticed my wrist, and told the authorities. Then, you know." She shrugs. "The Sympas came and brought me here."

"Must have been an improvement, right?"

"No, actually, it was worse." Tima looks up from her demolished pile of bread bits, and I can see she is fighting off tears.

Trying not to remember, but so badly wanting somebody else to know. To share in the experience.

She reaches toward me and, awkwardly, grabs my hand. She wants me to see. For Tima more than anyone, it's so much less painful than talking.

My vision clouds and I find myself in a test chamber, with her, watching. Tima sits in a metal chair, alone in the room with white walls, bright fluorescent lights, and concrete floor. Her chair faces a large screen on the opposite wall, showing an identical room with a table and one needle.

Tima looks younger. She sits cross-legged in the chair, leaning forward, head on her knees. Her hands are clasped and held to her forehead, as though in prayer.

Her slight frame is almost lost in the plain white pants and white T-shirt she wears. She rocks slowly, eyes closed. I can see she was just brought here, and doesn't know what is happening. She looks so vulnerable, like a lost bird fallen from the nest before she's ready to fly.

Catallus enters, bringing another chair and sitting in front of Tima. I feel myself recoil.

"Hello, Timora." Tima tenses up. She stops rocking, but doesn't look up.

"Do you mind if I call you that?"

She sits perfectly still.

"I trust you will enjoy your new home. It's a big improvement from the orphanage. Certainly better food, I hope."

He smiles and touches her arm. She cringes.

"Timora, I'm sure you're wondering what you're doing here. I can't tell you everything, but we're always looking for children with unique, oh, let's say qualities. When I saw the reports from the Embassy in New York about some difficulties regarding an orphanage and an extremely bright child with some unusual attributes, well, I had to meet you in person."

Tima shakes her head, almost imperceptibly, as if she knows where this is going.

"You see, we think you might be important to the Embassy, an asset, if you will. So we want you to stay with us for a while. But we need to check a few things first. I hope you don't mind."

A Sympa soldier enters the room with a puppy. A terrier mix, obviously malnourished but energetic.

Tima hears the whimpering and breathing of the dog and opens her eyes, but doesn't look up.

"Tima, this is Brutus. We found him near the Projects. As you can see, he wasn't well loved."

Tima slowly raises her head and looks at the dog. Light

brown hair, nervous, uncomfortable in the Sympa's arms. Frightened eyes. Her heart starts pounding, her eyes widen slightly.

"Unfortunately, we don't have the resources to care for Brutus. So, we have to put him down."

A look of terror comes to Tima's face.

"No," she whispers. She unfolds and sits up.

"No, please." Her eyes dart rapidly around the room, as if she is looking for some way out.

Catallus smiles sadly at Tima. "I'm very sorry. Go ahead." Catallus nods to the soldier, who takes the dog into the next room. The soldier uses his ID tag to open the door, which locks behind him. The screen shows him strapping the dog to the table and preparing the needle.

"*No!*" Tima screams.

Catallus jumps back, startled by the sudden sound.

Tima flies out of her chair, reaching toward Catallus, snarling, and rips off his ID tag.

He falls, eyes wide.

She races to the door and swipes it open.

The Sympa has the needle poised over the shivering Brutus.

"*Get away!*" Tima hurtles herself to the table, grabbing the squirming dog. She climbs down and backs into the corner, curling around him, breathing heavily.

The Sympa soldier pulls out a baton and rushes toward her to take the dog.

"No!" Tima screams again, even louder. A blinding light flashes, and the Sympa is thrown to the back wall with a crunch.

After a few moments, Catallus carefully enters the room to see Tima in the corner, Brutus nestled in her arms, asleep. The smell of burnt electricity fills the room. He carefully reaches toward Tima and the dog, but stops as she raises her eyes.

Catallus smiles. "Well, that was interesting. Useful, even. Threat response creates defensive barrier. A powerful one at that."

He tilts his head, considering Tima and the dog. Then he glances at the unconscious Sympa.

"You know what, I think I'm going to let you take care of Brutus."

He turns and leaves.

Tima remains in the corner, breathing deeply, absently scratching Brutus behind the ears.

Brutus wakes and licks her cheek.

Tima looks at Brutus and her eyes soften, her heart opens. I feel it, even in the memory, how everything goes soft and slack.

The moment when she almost smiles.

I blink, and I'm back in the dining hall, my heart racing, my eyes stinging. Tima is wide-eyed, surprised at herself for letting anybody see what I just saw. For a split second,

I'm with her, sorry for her, even proud of her, and she knows it. For a split second, she isn't alone.

Then her hand shoots back and she stands. The door in her mind slams shut as quickly as it opened. She turns to leave. "I have to go."

I notice she slips scraps of bread into her pocket.

RESEARCH MEMORANDUM:
THE HUMANITY PROJECT

To: Ambassador Amare
From: Dr. Huxley-Clarke
Subject: Icon Research—Countering Icons

It should be theoretically possible to negate the Icon's power by attempting to cancel out its massive electromagnetic effect, via the generation of an equally massive counter-field.

An analogy: sound waves can cause physical objects to vibrate, as the human eardrum vibrates to detect sound. Noise-canceling technology generates waves that effectively destroy sound waves before they reach the eardrum. Like antimatter destroying matter, we believe we could stop the field at the source.

Unfortunately, we don't have sufficient power to generate the theoretical amount of energy required to create the counter-field. Since the Lords control all energy output and consumption, this becomes a potential dead end.

Further research is required, yet unlikely, as GAP Miyazawa has frozen all future budget appropriations. I don't have to tell you what a dangerous impasse we now face.

16
HALL OF RECORDS

The next morning, the four of us meet outside the library, where our Sympa guards believe we are waiting for Catallus. Instead, we crouch in the darkest alcove of the closest corridor, as planned.

Within five minutes we are fighting.

Again.

"We need to figure out what's going on." Ro is talking now. "If they want us, there has to be a reason. We find out what that is, maybe we could help the Rebellion bring the whole place down."

"Why are you still here? I thought you'd be long gone by now," Lucas says with a glare.

"Soon. But who knows, this could be our best chance to find out the truth, first." Ro looks at me, since we've only just come to this conclusion together. I nod.

"We know what's going on." Now Lucas glares at me. "The Merk came around because he wants to sell what he knows and make a few digs. It's the only reason any Merk ever does anything."

Ro squirms, like he can't get comfortable. "It's better than sitting around here and letting the Embassy experiment on us like four Porthole rats."

"They haven't killed us," Tima points out. She speaks rapidly, her eyes moving from side to side as if she were scanning the perimeter for predators. Which she should be. "Of course, they can't. Corpses don't have emotions. Of what use would we be to them, then?"

It's a sobering thought, but Ro seems delighted to hear her say it. "Exactly. They're using us. Even Tima agrees with me. So why shouldn't we find this Merk guy and see if we can even the odds a little?" He smiles.

"Come on. You're going to trust some Merk who breaks into the Embassy and shuts Doc down, just to talk to us?" Lucas sounds annoyed, but he doesn't defend the Embassy, because he can't. "That doesn't seem a little suspicious to you?"

Lucas is fighting a losing battle. I lay my hand on his arm. "You said it yourself—why would he do that for no reason?"

"Money is reason enough to a Merk." Tima takes Lucas's side.

"The Icon. He was talking about the Icon," Ro insists.

"We don't know if any of it's true. We don't know that any of it has anything to do with us." Lucas shakes his head.

Nobody says a word. We stand, our backs to the wall of our shadowy alcove, staring out into the library. Finally, Tima looks from Ro to Lucas. "There's only one way to find out, I guess. Let's go pay a visit to the Hall of Records."

"Now?" I look at the guards, crossing the main thoroughfare of the room in front of us.

She sighs. "It'll have to be. I know the patrol schedule, but I can't guarantee Doc won't be on us."

"I'll handle Doc," says Lucas. "I've been doing it my whole life."

"Then we should be able to ditch them, at least long enough to get into the archives." Tima rolls her eyes at Ro. "I'm tired of trying to get you out from under Sympa patrols. I'm beginning to regret sending you to the garbage barge in the first place."

"Really," says Ro, smiling.

"Not really." She sniffs, sliding out of the alcove and through the open door.

"Didn't think so." He winks at me, and I slip out after her.

———— • ————

The main plexi-door to the library slides open. Tima gestures. "The Hall of Records is this way." We all look where she points.

"If something happened, Doc knows. If Doc knows, it's in his database. If it's in his database, it's backed up." Lucas sounds resigned.

"And the backup drives are in the Hall of Records?" Ro is unusually somber.

Lucas approaches the dull metal door with a wave of his ID card.

"Let's hope so." He stands in front of it, but nothing happens. He waves his card again. "That's strange."

He looks up. "Doc?"

"Yes, Lucas."

"Can you tell me why the doors to the Hall of Records, South Wing, won't open?"

"Yes, Lucas."

We stand there and wait. Lucas looks annoyed. "Any minute now, Doc."

"I am sorry. Would you like me to tell you? It is a slightly different query. Not to quibble."

"Please."

"Your plastic is no longer cleared for Classified access. According to the Wik, the restriction was added when you returned from the Tracks."

With me. The day he found me.

I remember Ro, with a slight blush.

Us.

"Are you serious?" Lucas leans his head against the door in disbelief.

"This is not a joke. Would you like to hear a joke? I have downloaded approximately two million seven hundred forty-two thousand jokes to the Wik."

"Another time, Doc."

Lucas looks at Tima. "You want to try your plastic?"

She shakes her head. "I wasn't cleared even when you were."

Ro shrugs and pulls a sharpened piece of shale out of his pocket. One of his boyhood Grass weapons, a rock honed so razor-thin it could slit a man's throat. Before anyone can say anything, he's wedged it into the doors, trying the bottom, then the top. "If I can just find where the sensors are."

"A rock? You're going to circumvent the Embassy Security system with a rock?" Lucas snorts.

Ro glares at him, over his shoulder. "A sharp rock."

Just then, it breaks off in his hands, and he is left holding a crumbled bit of stone.

"Not anymore," says Lucas, looking at it.

Tima sighs. "There's no point. There's no successful scenario here. We can't short the doors, we need power to open them. We can't override the restriction, or they'll know. We can't do anything. We might as well give up."

She's getting hysterical.

"We can't give up." I look at them. "It's not an option. We have to find out what's going on." I hear the Ambassador's voice echoing inside my head.

You lived so you could pay the debt.

The Ambassador was right about something. I can't walk away. I owe too many things to too many people.

"If you have a better idea, let me know. Because as far as I can tell, nobody's opening this door without a Classified plastic." Lucas stands with his back to the door. He's giving up, I feel it.

The librarian walks by, poking her head down our aisle. We flatten ourselves against the doors.

Caught. I brace myself for the inevitable questions.

But she's not suspicious. She's too busy smiling at Lucas. They're always smiling at him, everyone.

That's when it comes to me. Lucas doesn't need an access pass. Lucas *is* an access pass.

"I've got a better idea," I say.

He didn't want to do it. But there he is.

Lucas stands, casually, at the front desk of the main library. The librarian, the Director of Archive Services, actually, according to her nameplate, is still smiling at him. Lilias Green.

She inclines her head into the space between them. Her hands begin to slide across the smooth wood of the counter.

"Lilias. Thank you for taking the time to speak with me." He drapes his long, lean form across the edge of the wood.

"Of course, Mr. Amare."

"Lucas, please. Call me Lucas."

She smiles again, nodding.

"You see, there's something wrong with my plastic. You know I'm cleared for Classified, I mean, the Ambassador is the most Classified thing in this whole place, and she's my mom."

Mom. I've never heard Lucas use the word. It makes him sound soft and young, which is I guess the point.

Her neck arches, stretching closer.

"Of course. It must be an oversight. How unfortunate." Her smile wobbles, and I can tell she is waiting for him to ask.

Her eyes grow thick-lidded. Her pupils dilate.

"I can't bear to watch," mutters Tima, next to me.

"Shh." I scroll through a digi-text, a few tables away, but I'm not reading. I can feel it, every beat, while they speak.

Ro stands at the terminal next to Tima. "You think he's got it? Dol?"

I close my eyes, reaching toward them. The warmth coming from Lucas is blazing and bright. The girl curls around it; she can't help herself. She leans toward him, pulling closer into the heady buzz of intoxicating brain waves that are uniquely, distinctly Lucas.

"Oh yeah." *That poor girl,* I think. It's a jarring thought. Is there ever a girl who isn't like that, to Lucas?

Is any of it real at all?

My cheeks flush pink. I'm embarrassed to admit I am thinking about it. Him.

It's only a matter of seconds before they walk by us. Lucas doesn't so much as look our way as they go.

———— • ————

"Man, you're a piece of work." Ro shakes his head but even he can't deny it. The doors to the Hall of Records are open in front of us.

"She really didn't want to do it, either." Lucas looks sad. Pale, and exhausted. Utterly drained—I know the feeling all too well. *He's sorry for Lilias*, I think. *Using her like that.*

Tima nods. "Which means she must know she's not supposed to help you. Which means, in turn, they must have sent out some kind of departmental notice. That's the reasonable assumption."

Lucas nods. "We're screwed."

Ro and I look at each other as the doors slide shut behind us. In every direction, all I see now are walls of metal shelving, digi-files labeled with numbers. It's like staring at a cave full of sleeping silver bats; they hang in rows like small boxed creatures.

"The Embassy stores the most confidential records here, and keeps all this sensitive information isolated from the rest of the network." Tima sounds proud. "The only way to access the data is to get inside and use a direct connection. Cumbersome, but also very secure."

"Cumbersome?" Ro laughs.

Tima looks confused. "That's what I said."

"Who talks like that?" Ro shakes his head.

Tima smiles, though I don't know why. Cumbersome connections only make her job harder.

Like jokes. And friends.

I look closer and see that each file is a day, a week, a month, a year. It's strange to imagine the monumental events and birthdays and weddings and disasters, all boiled down into rows of numbered metal boxes.

My birthday.

My parents. My brothers. The—the opposite of their birthday.

I am drawn to one box in particular.

My hand lingers on one of the digi-files for The Day. There are whole rows of them, because there were so many people who died on The Day. You couldn't possibly put that much information into one drive. It's too big, even if it was just the four of them.

My family. My world.

The Silent Cities.

You can't fit that into anything.

I feel the others behind me now, staring at the impossible wall of metal. My vision blurs; my heart starts to rattle against my ribs. I am overwhelmed by a sadness so powerful I could explode, or erupt into the kind of tears that never stop coming.

Ro takes my hand in his, bringing me back from the brink. Back into my own body, this room. His hand burns but I don't let go. His anger is staggering.

I feel Tima receding, overpowered by terror, wanting to disappear. Only the presence of Lucas steadies her, just as somehow, I steady him.

The four of us stand together and for the first time I feel as though we are united, connected to each other whether we like it or not.

And so we stare at the tragedy in front of us.

Until Ro breaks the spell.

"This isn't just cumbersome. It's mental. There's too much here. If we don't know what we're looking for, how do we know where to look?" Ro slams his hand against the nearest row of metal digis.

"We're not looking for everything that's happened. We're looking for one thing that's happened."

It's Tima who speaks, and in the feel of the words I sense she is recovering. "Or four things." I follow her gaze through the years. Seventeen years.

We spend the better part of an hour trying to turn back the clock. One digi after another, all full of secrets. Records of thousands of hours, of days—of births and deaths and all the more ordinary transmissions that lie in between.

I return to the files and detach the last metal digi from the tracking. The final digi from the day I was born. The day three of us were born, if Tima and Lucas are right about our shared birthday. Maybe four, since Ro doesn't know or couldn't remember enough to tell us, either way.

"That has to be it." Ro sounds excited. Tima shrugs, and I carry the digi over to the research table in the center of the room. I let it bang to the surface.

"Open it," says Lucas. I just stand there looking at it. I don't know what I'm thinking—if I'm afraid I'll find something, or afraid I won't.

Tima loses her patience, and snaps open the magnetized file. It unfolds like a flower, five screens surrounding a row of drives.

At least, that's what's supposed to be there, judging from the others we've opened in the past hour. But this one is different.

It's empty.

"That can't be right," she says, looking at Lucas, stricken. "There has to be some kind of mistake."

"No, there doesn't." I feel how painful this is for Lucas to admit. "The Embassy doesn't make mistakes. It just means we're on to something."

Ro is exultant. "It means Fortis is right. There's something they don't want us to know. Something that's supposed to be in that digi."

The implications fill me with unease. *Am I really just a bullet? A secret weapon?*

"Something so important she'd kill my plastic to keep us away, and then destroy the file." Lucas is bleak. The pronoun cuts right to the point.

"Who?" Ro asks, though he heard it, just like I did.

"Who else," Lucas says, glumly.

I slide myself between them before Ro can start. "We need to find out. What did you do with Doc?"

"He's tracking Colonel Catallus. I told him it was a game. Hide-and-seek."

"Bring him back."

Lucas looks up at the nearest ceiling grating. "Hey Doc. Where are you? Are you winning?"

There is a pause, and then the familiar voice reappears. "I believe I am, Lucas. As I am everywhere, and Colonel Catallus seems to be unaware that we are playing. It is in fact more challenging to *not follow* you, Lucas. Is your hiding complete yet?"

"Just about, Doc. But this is kind of a time-out."

"Orwell," interrupts Tima, looking up at the ceiling. "We're in the Hall of Records. Are you getting this?"

"Yes, Tima," Doc says. "Would you like to play, too?"

"What do you make of a day missing from the year and the month we were born, seventeen years ago?" Tima stares toward the grating, as if she were studying Doc's own face.

"It would appear that the Embassy is suffering from some organizational or clerical error." Doc's tone remains uninflected.

"Do you find it typical, Orwell, for the Embassy to suffer from either an organizational or a clerical error?"

"No, Timora."

"Me, neither."

213

"Doc," says Lucas. "What do you really think is happening?"

There is a pause, and I hear the comforting whir of machine life. "I think, Lucas, that certain pieces of information relating to that date have been removed from the Hall of Records."

"I think so too, Doc."

Doc takes another moment to respond. "Is it, possibly, a joke? Jokes can be surprising."

"No, Doc. It's not a joke."

More silence. Then Doc tries again. "And it is not a game."

"Unfortunately."

"Then it's very serious, isn't it?"

"Yes, Doc, I imagine it is. Do you know who would do something like this? Delete information from the Hall of Records?"

"Yes, Lucas."

"Who?"

"Someone of high stature. Someone with clear access. Someone with a detailed understanding of the situation pertaining to those dates."

"Who, Doc?"

He waits as Doc resets his thinking.

"Your mother, the Ambassador, Lucas."

The warmth that came from him when he was talking

to Lilias seems impossible, now. I wonder if he is going to argue with the Ambassador.

If they ever argue.

If she ever acts like his mother, rather than the one point of contact between the Hole and the House of Lords.

He may not have a mother any more than I do, I think. Maybe less.

At least I had one, once. I try to hold on to that.

It's more than Lucas has.

I watch as his mouth slides into a tight line. "Do you know if she did?"

Another machine pause.

"I do not. I am, however, checking the feed now. Please give me a moment."

"Of course."

"Lucas?"

"Yes, Doc?"

"That feed has been re-Classified with a *Private Digi* designation, and moved to the Ambassador's own office. And Colonel Catallus has asked me to contact you from the classroom. Apparently he is not in the mood for gaming. You are sixty-seven minutes and twenty-nine seconds late to class. Thirty. Thirty-one."

"Orwell!" Tima snaps.

Time to go.

RESEARCH MEMORANDUM: THE HUMANITY PROJECT

CLASSIFIED TOP SECRET / AMBASSADOR EYES ONLY

To: Ambassador Amare

Subject: Rebellion Recruitment and Indoctrination
Materials

Subtopic: Banned Children's Rhymes

Catalogue Assignment: Evidence recovered during
raid of Rebellion hideout

ALL AROUND THE STICKS AND STONES,
THE SYMPA CHASED THE REMNANT,

THE SYMPA THOUGHT 'TWAS ALL IN FUN,
POP! GOES THE REMNANT.

YANKEE DOODLE WENT TO HOLE,
A-RIDING ON THE TRACKS-Y

STUCK A FEATHER IN HIS CAP,
WHILE STOOGES THEY ATTACK-SY.

JACK AND JILL WENT DOWN THE TRACKS,
FOUGHT WITH A SQUAD OF SYMPA HACKS

WHO TOOK OUT JILL,
WHO TOOK OUT JACK,
THEN WROTE THIS SONG
TO GET THEM BACK.

IT'S RAINING, IT'S POURING,
THE SKY IS DROPPING ROCKS,

AND ALL THE HOLE'S SWEET LADIES
ARE HOLDING UP THEIR FROCKS.

ONE BRIGHT NIGHT
IN THE MIDDLE OF THE DAY,
A SILVER SHIP SAILED
DOWN TO STAY...

17

DISAPPEARING

"What now?" I'm the one who says it, though we're all thinking it as we find our way back through the closed doors and leave the far recesses of the library, moving toward our glass prison classroom.

Colonel Catallus is standing there waiting. We can see him from the other side of the room.

"We could ask the Ambassador nicely? Say 'pretty please'?" Ro trails his hands against the wall as he walks. The archivists look at him as he passes. Ro is good at irritating people; he'll find the one thing you don't want him to do, and do it every time. It's one of his many gifts.

"Shut up, Ro." Lucas doesn't even need Ro to try. Everything Ro does irritates him naturally.

Ro doesn't stop. "Come on, Junior. There has to be a way around a PP Ass-ified designation."

"Classified PD designation." Lucas rolls his eyes. "And there isn't."

"Or maybe you just don't want to know."

Lucas turns to Ro, so slowly that I have time to move out of the way, backing against the library wall.

"Lucas," Tima warns.

I say nothing. I only look at Ro, begging him to let it go.

"What are you saying, Grass?" Lucas is seething.

"I'm saying you've got a pretty good deal here, don't you, Buttons? The rest of us might get sent to the Projects, but not you."

Now Ro takes a step toward Lucas.

"You see, our families might get killed—oh wait, they did—but not yours. You don't want things to change. In fact, you need them not to. Because if the Rebellion succeeds, Mom's out of a job, and you might just end up back in the Projects, hauling dirt for a living, right along with the rest of us."

Lucas leans toward Ro and I no longer see the two of them, only a cloud of white and a streak of red.

"You don't know me," I hear Lucas say. "You don't know anything about me. You don't know what I know or what I can do."

I close my eyes and feel the two currents clashing so strongly that I stumble.

I open my eyes—to see Lucas disappearing down the aisle that leads to the library exit.

I don't know why or what I am doing, but before I know it I am running down the aisle after him. Ro doesn't follow me.

"Dol! If you—"

If you take his side.

If you leave me for him.

If it—this—we change—

He doesn't have to say the words. I feel the reddening fury, directed at Lucas, me, the universe, but he doesn't move.

Ro knows this isn't about him. He knows it and it hurts him and he probably also knows I'm sorry. And it doesn't make anything better.

Life will burn you off like that, as Ro would say.

"Dol! Wait!" This time, it's Tima.

I wish I could.

"Where are you going?" She asks again, because Ro doesn't. Because he won't.

I don't answer because I can't.

I run all the way until I catch up to Lucas as he walks out the front of the Embassy complex. I am breathless, tumbling through the door after him, before the guards he's talked his way past can change their minds.

Lucas ignores me but he holds the door. If he's surprised, he doesn't show it. I can't get a feel for him, either. There's too much going on, too much static in my brain.

My wrist begins to hurt, beneath my binding, the moment I set foot out the door.

Strange.

It's like the building knows I'm leaving. Of course it does. The Embassy knows everything.

Except where we're going—they can't know.

Even I don't know that.

•

The blades of the Chopper are already rotating, carving a circle in the sky above our heads. Lucas climbs into the seat behind the pilot. He picks up a set of massive earphones and slides them over his head.

"Porthole, Freeley," he shouts at the pilot.

He's headed into the Hole.

My heart skips, and I grip the sides of my seat. I've never actually been in the city. Not farther than the Tracks.

The pilot looks over his shoulder, grins. I recognize the dilated pupils immediately. In the world of Lucas, everyone is sedated and pliable.

But this Freeley isn't giving up so easily as Lilias. His

mouth is struggling to form the words. He's putting up a fight.

"You've filed papers, Lucas? You're not going to get me in trouble this time?"

Lucas nods, though I know it is a lie.

"You know, I had my wings grounded for a fortnight after your last little stunt." Freeley looks amused, but he isn't about to go anywhere. His hands aren't anywhere near the controls, they're twitching in his lap.

"I'm on business for the Ambassador. In and out, won't take long." The pilot doesn't respond, but I notice he slips his hands under his legs, the whole weight of his body keeping them down. Clearly he's been with Lucas long enough to know a trick or two.

"Come on, Freeley." Lucas is impatient.

"Right. And if I check the Wik, I'll see all the proper paperwork, filed just as it should be?"

"Go ahead, if you don't believe me. It's all there."

The pilot raises an eyebrow. "Right."

"It's there, Freeley."

Freeley moves his hand slowly to the control panel, as if he was underwater—or pulling away from a magnetic force, a hundred times the strength of his own will, as the case may be. He flicks a dial with his gloved finger, and there it is.

AMARE, LUCAS. The time. The date. The approvals.

I can't believe it.

222

Freeley looks at me skeptically. I shove the earphones on, sliding into the seat next to Lucas.

"I don't know what you did, but I give. Tell your girlfriend to buckle up." Freeley turns back around.

Lucas doesn't say anything. I fasten my seat belt and look out my own window.

Lucas taps on my shoulder.

"You shouldn't be here."

"Why not?"

"I have business in the Hole—I'm going to see someone."

"Who?"

"Someone who might have the answers we need. It's going to be dangerous. The Hole always is. You should go back inside."

I nod, as if I can't understand what he is saying. Lucas only has to look at me, and my hand automatically goes to the door. The familiar warm current pushes me against it, away from him. If I let it, if I let go, I will do what he wants before I know why I'm doing it.

No.

I force my hand back down and, like Freeley, shove it under my legs.

Lucas looks away. "Fine."

The noise grows. I feel my body jerk away from the ground and weave into the air. Santa Catalina and the

Embassy and the Presidio disappear beneath me, a square of stone walls behind more walls. Ro and Tima and Colonel Catallus and Doc and the Ambassador disappear along with it.

Or maybe I am the one disappearing.

Either way, I am ready to go.

EMBASSY CITY TRIBUNAL
VIRTUAL AUTOPSY: DECEASED PERSONAL
POSSESSIONS TRANSCRIPT (DPPT)

CLASSIFIED TOP SECRET

Performed by Dr. O. Brad Huxley-Clarke, VPHD

Note: Conducted at the private request of
Amb. Amare

Santa Catalina Examination Facility #9B

See adjoining Tribunal Autopsy, attached.

DPPT (CONTINUED FROM PREVIOUS PAGE)

Catalogue at Time of Death includes:

20. A gold necklace found on the body of the deceased. The cruciform charm is ███████████████████████████ ██████████████████████████.

Filed under Miscellany.

18

THE PORTHOLE

The Porthole docks are teeming with life. Small skiffs, battered dinghies, homemade fishing rafts—left over from when there were fish—line the shore. Beyond them, only the Sympa ferries move into the deeper, darker waters. They're so much bigger and sleeker and more serious than everything else it almost looks comical, like sharks in a goldfish pond.

We land, and I jump from the Chopper as it's powering down. Lucas stays behind and says something to Freeley, who smiles and leans back in the cockpit, getting comfortable.

"I told him we'd be here in a couple of hours. Hopefully he doesn't get a call before that and come looking for us." Lucas takes a gray bundle from beneath the seat of the

Chopper. "Speaking of people looking for us, remember, we have to keep a low profile." Lucas pulls an old hooded sweatshirt over his uniform, hood up. "It's not safe for us here, and I don't want to take any chances." He tosses another one to me. "Put it on."

I roll my eyes. "I get it. If you're not careful you'll have a flock of Remnant girls attacking and tearing off your clothes. I don't have that problem."

"Dol. Have you ever been to the Hole?"

I shake my head.

"Trust me. You'll want it."

I pull the shapeless gray thing on.

I follow Lucas from the landing strip to the highway. Remnant beggars and vendors line the docks. On the other end, I see a pair of Sympa guards walk slowly through the area. One of them casually points a gun at a vendor who drops to the ground, cowering. The other laughs and picks through the man's food, taking what he wants. The guards let the Blackhole Market happen, looking the other way, as long as they eat well. I pull my hood further down.

The scene is overwhelming, especially to a Grass like me. We could buy anything within the first few minutes of walking toward the Hole, anything on earth. Clothing. Shoes. Bottles of herb-steeped water. Dried animal meats.

My stomach turns.

"Look." Lucas points. "The Projects." It's true. Down in Porthole Bay, I can spot the massive construction site. High walls topped with barbed wire surround the enormous complex, where Remnant workers live. Smokestacks protrude from a billowing cloud of dirty gray-black ash. A jerking crane swings an unseen load of cargo.

They say the smoke never stops blowing, the cranes never stop moving. Whatever they're doing, they're doing it night and day. Whatever they're building, they're building it on the backs of Remnants like Ro and me. That's about all anyone knows. Nobody leaves the Projects once they go in. The Embassy runs the Projects, but they're under direct orders from the House of Lords. According to the rumors, there are Projects going up near all the Icons, on different coastlines all around the world.

"It's a lot bigger than I thought," I say. I almost can't take it in. The steel arms reach all the way out past the breakers, like a military base built over the water. "I wonder what it's for." People say a lot of things about the Projects. They're building homes for the Lords. Slave quarters for the survivors, after the Lords turned most of the world into a string of Silent Cities. Massive pumps to leech the earth dry. Processing plants to turn people into food. The list is long and always growing longer.

Lucas says nothing, which only makes me wonder

more. He's the Ambassador's son. It's possible that he knows the purpose of the Projects, or that at least he could find out. But I don't ask again, and he doesn't tell me.

I wonder what that says about both of us.

We keep walking.

Out here, on the very edge of the Hole, the cars on the Porthole Coast Highway are empty husks of scrap, abandoned long ago. What do you need a car for if you don't have power to make it go? Without electricity, they're merely reminders of freedom that people no longer enjoy. Especially not these people.

A scrap scavenger stares when we walk by. Her clothes are ragged, her hair a matted mess. Her eyes narrow and she leans forward, looking straight at Lucas. He only sees her as she turns to run, looking back over her shoulder one more time. "Did she just recognize you?"

Lucas shrugs. "I doubt it. Probably just ran to tell her girlfriends she believes in love at first sight." He grins, and I shake my head. But I notice how quickly the smile fades.

He's the Ambassador's son. We need to be more careful.

"Dol." Lucas stops in his tracks, holding up his hand. "Listen." He closes his eyes. I look at him like he's insane, which is how he seems.

"What is it?" I can't hear anything.

"It's nothing. Absolutely nothing. Silence. The best sound in the world." He begins to move down the road again, with a sharp laugh.

He's right, of course.

I've forgotten.

Inside the Embassy, the hum of white noise is always there. There are screens, lights that buzz, and tech that talks. There is Doc—even when he chooses not to speak, there is the knowledge that he is there. It's unsettling how quickly I've gotten used to it. Machine life has a sound, like a heartbeat, or breathing. A pulse of its own.

The silence changes when it belongs only to living things. Your ear changes. You pick out the threads of human voices, a child yelling, footsteps echoing in the ransacked houses below us. Animal noises, earth noises. The air is so quiet you can hear the breeze. The sun beats down, prickling the back of my neck. My feet are hot in my thick boots as we walk.

"Stop—" Lucas pulls me down. "I think I hear Choppers."

As he says it, I hear them, too.

I look to see three Choppers flying in formation, straight toward us.

"What do we do?" I'm trying not to panic.

"Stay still." Lucas watches the sky, squinting. Before

long, they roar overhead, flying straight along the road and deeper into the Hole.

"Not Embassy Choppers. We're okay."

He pulls me up next to him, and we stand, watching, until they disappear.

He speeds up, keeping his head down. I follow him as he picks a path down the highway. He manages to stay ahead, as if he can't bear to walk next to me. Maybe he can't.

"Where are we going?" I call toward him, but the wind carries my voice in the other direction, and the only words that emerge are so small I almost can't hear them myself.

"You'll see."

"Lucas. Slow down."

"Hurry up. You didn't have to come, you know."

I pull his arm and he stops.

We stand there, alone in the sunshine. I look back toward the water and Santa Catalina, back toward the way we came. The breeze has grown, and my hair whips in my face from the wind near the shore, beating against my eardrums like waves.

"What's your problem? Why don't you like me?" I say the words before I realize what I am saying. "I mean, us."

He studies me. His face looks somehow different, harsh in the bright midday sun, and I wonder if mine looks the same to him.

"I like you." My heart pounds just a little more quickly. Lucas looks away. "I mean, I don't not like you. I like everybody. You guys know that, better than anyone."

Oh. I see.

"That's not true. You hate Ro and you don't like me."

He looks at me for a long moment before answering.

"You hate the Ambassador and you hate me. You hate what she did to the Padre and you hate what I didn't do."

"What was that?"

"Stop her."

"Why didn't you?"

We look at each other, there in the grim, bleached light. My instinct is to run from it, but my feet won't move.

"Forget it. It doesn't matter." I blush. Again. As always, when I'm around Lucas.

Why does he do that to me?

He looks stricken. "It matters, Dol." He reaches for my hand. "I hate that I have to stand by and watch innocent people get hurt. It kills me."

I pull my hand away. "Yet here you are. Perfectly alive."

He reaches farther, grabbing for my wrist. "You don't understand. The House of Lords—even the Ambassador is afraid. GAP Miyazawa is. We all are, and if anyone says they're not, it's a lie."

I don't know. "When I think of the Ambassador, Lucas,

afraid isn't really the first word that comes to mind."

"I know. It's hard to explain. She's terrified—and she's terrifying. It's not like I can go running to my parents, whenever something's wrong. My mother isn't exactly a mother, not like I think yours would have been."

"If I'd known her," I say, sadly.

"If you'd known her," he agrees.

I didn't, I think. *But he didn't either.* There are lots of ways to lose your family, I guess. I am just beginning to realize how many.

So I let him take my hand.

It's the truth, what he's trying to tell me. I feel it, in every word.

Lucas stares at my hand, silent for a moment. Then he looks at me strangely, like he's trying to figure out how to tell me something.

"What is it?"

"Nothing. I mean, something, I guess. I need to tell you. To show you." He carefully reaches toward me, taking my other hand. "I was thirteen, I think."

He closes his eyes and I let the feelings find me, until I can see what he is thinking. I close my eyes and out of the darkness, the Embassy testing room comes into focus.

I rip my eyes open. "Lucas, no. I don't want to see this. Not again."

He holds my hands tight. "Please. I haven't told anybody

about this. I know you don't trust me, but I trust you."

There's nothing more I can say. I shake my head, but close my eyes again.

I'm back in the room, and I see a frightened young girl, maybe twelve or thirteen, in dirty, worn clothing. She sits in a metal chair with her hands under her legs. Her face is streaked with tears, her hair cut short. *She looks almost like me at that age*, I think.

A younger Ambassador Amare is in the room, with a nervous Lucas hiding behind her. He is skinny, almost gangly, with short hair. He looks so innocent.

The Ambassador sits Lucas down opposite the girl and stands between them, arms folded. For a long time, she says nothing.

Lucas looks up at her. "Why am I here, Mom?"

The Ambassador cuts him off with a stern look. "In this room, I am your Ambassador, not your mother." She turns to the girl, who wipes more tears from her eyes. She's obviously terrified to see the Ambassador.

"Sorry, Mo—" Lucas swallows. "Madame Ambassador." His voice cracks.

His mother's lips press tightly, into her best imitation of a smile. "We believe this girl is a collaborator, a part of the Grass Rebellion. Her father is widely held to be a traitor and a terrorist. But we need proof."

The girl's eyes go wide. "No, please, it isn't true! My

father is a farmer, not a criminal!" She strains to stand but I see the chains around her waist and legs, holding her down. The Ambassador glares at her and she sits down, sobbing.

"Lucas, I need you to get a confession out of her. We have her father in custody, and we would like to have proof of his guilt before we prosecute him." A look of panic crosses Lucas's face. The Ambassador locks her eyes on him. "I know you want to do the right thing. Now I just need you to prove it to me." The Ambassador gives Lucas a short nod before she turns and leaves.

Lucas doesn't say a word.

The girl looks at him with pleading eyes. "You have to believe me. I don't know why we're here. My father grows strawberries. He works hard and takes care of us. He would never hurt anyone. Please."

I feel Lucas's heart tearing. He knows the girl is telling the truth. But his mother's grip on him is so tight, he can hardly breathe. I feel it overwhelm him—the desire for her approval slowly smothering his guilt.

After a moment, he speaks. "What's your name?"

She pauses and looks at him, warily. "Elena."

"Elena. I like that name." Lucas pushes his conscience into a dark corner and looks at her.

My heart begins to pound. I can't believe he's doing this. I can't bear to watch.

But he is. His pupils dilate as he draws her in. The girl is confused at first, then starts to look slightly embarrassed.

"Elena, are you sure your father hasn't been working with the Grass Rebels? I mean, how do you know he's not? I can't blame you for wanting to protect him." Lucas stands and pulls his chair closer to Elena, who shivers from the proximity.

He knows what he's doing. He sits down right next to her.

"I, I—" Elena is clearly confused, almost dizzy with the rush of his influence.

"You know the Grass Rebels hurt a lot of innocent people. People who are trying to do good and keep humanity safe from the Lords." Elena looks wide-eyed, then nods her head.

"I guess so."

"You would be doing yourself and the rest of us a favor if you just tell us the truth. That your father is working against humanity. That he is part of the Rebellion."

I can feel Lucas heating up with the immense effort. Elena is fighting, as hard as she can, but it's a losing battle. Lucas looks away for a moment, only to gain strength. If he hesitates now, he won't be able to do it.

He turns back and speaks slowly. "Your father is a Grass Rebel." Lucas looks Elena again in the eye, and puts his hand on hers.

Her resistance falters—and her eyes change, glassing over. Shifting from tearful to calm. "My father is a Rebel."

"He hurt innocent people."

She nods, no longer resisting. "Innocent people."

Lucas pulls back from the girl and puts his hands to his temples, shaking his head.

"No. Elena, wait."

But it's too late. At that moment, the Ambassador marches in. A younger Catallus and a posse of Sympa soldiers follow closely behind her. Catallus smirks and nods at Lucas.

"Don't," Lucas starts to plead.

The Ambassador holds up her hand, and the Sympas hold Lucas by either arm.

Elena smiles innocently, never taking her eyes off Lucas. Pleased that she's done what he asked.

Lucas looks like death.

"Take her," the Ambassador barks, and two more Sympas pull Elena from the room, chains and all.

The girl never stops smiling.

"Take her and her father and execute them for treason."

I drop Lucas's hands and open my eyes. "Lucas!"

He won't look at me. Tears catch in his eyelashes, but he doesn't let them fall. His guilt and sorrow are so strong, I feel like I'm struck with the force of a rock-slide.

"I didn't know she would do that." *He's telling the truth*, I think.

"I just wanted her to love me. Look at me as a son, not some pawn in whatever game she's playing. Everybody deserves a mother, Dol. Even me."

I try to feel something other than shock. I am overwhelmed with disgust at a woman—a mother—who would do something like that to a child.

To her son.

I shudder. "I—I don't know what to say."

He wipes his eyes with the back of his hand. "Don't. I just needed you to know." I know more than Lucas could imagine.

"I understand, Lucas. I do."

Our conversation is over. We should probably go. But I don't move a muscle. Instead, I stare at him, willing him to lean closer to me.

Miraculously, magically, he does.

"Please, Dol."

Let me.

I feel the touch of his skin against mine, light as a breeze. He slips his finger beneath my bindings, and without his eyes leaving mine, yanks at the muslin. I catch my breath.

"I'm not one of them. I'm not like her," he says.

He pushes up his own sleeve, slipping off the leather cuff and exposing his wrist. "I'm like you, Dol."

Four blue dots, the color of the sky.

"I like you, Dol. You make me feel better."

I like you too, Lucas. But I don't say it.

"I can make you feel better, too."

The bright daylight grows brighter. I can't hear anything except the buzz of wind and water in my ears.

I let my binding come loose in his hand. My naked wrist is a pale white stripe against the rest of my arm, but it feels warm in the sun.

I shiver anyway.

Lucas looks at me. It is a question—again, that question.

Let me.

Slowly, he takes my hand, slipping his fingers between mine. He begins to wind and wrap the cloth. It is exactly like my dream. Our elbows touch, then our forearms. Our wrists. I close my eyes and feel his warmth—it's different from the rush of raw heat I felt from Ro. This is dizzying—my heart starts pounding, and I can't breathe.

He presses his fingers through mine even more tightly. His fingers push into the back of my hand, inching closer...

Only this time the hands are real, and I'm not dreaming.

Nothing about my life is remotely like a dream, not anymore.

From this safe place, out of the peaceful bliss, I feel a surge of sadness. Pressure behind my eyes—tears pushing, trying to escape. I feel like I am about to lose control, like my tears will drown me. I see my home, I see Ro—everything I've lost and might still lose, if I let go—

I can't let go.

I'm not ready for this.

I ball up my hand. Again.

"Lucas—" I jerk my arm away. "I can't."

"What? Why?" He's startled. Confused.

"I don't know." But it's a lie. I do know. It's a lie with a name and that name is Ro.

A shadow passes over Lucas's face.

"Fine."

"Don't say that, Lucas. It's not fine. I can feel it, remember?"

"I felt close to you. I wanted to make you feel better. If you don't want to feel better, that's your choice." Lucas tosses my binding at me. He's angry. "We should go. I told Freeley we'd meet him before dark."

He turns to the road and begins to walk. I'm reeling, and I catch up, closing the distance between us. I try to change the subject.

"How'd you do that? The thing with Freeley and the

papers? Did you know you were going? Did you really file papers?"

He pauses. "I don't know. I was as surprised as you were. I was getting ready to shove him out of the Chopper and take it myself." He's lying, at least about the last part.

I stop walking. "You know what that means, don't you?"

"I'm a lucky bastard?"

"No, you idiot. Someone knows we're here."

"News flash. I'm Ambassador Amare's only child. Someone knows where I am practically every second of every day."

"Oh. Right. I forgot."

"Yeah, well. I never do."

We walk on in silence.

I used to think about how alike we all are. The human race, those of us who survived. Then I thought, if the stories were true and there were other Icon Children—if I met any—we would understand each other perfectly, the way Ro and I so often do.

But now, standing here in the middle of the desolate highway, I can see how different we are. How little Lucas actually has in common with me, the girl who is never known and never remembered and never looked after.

Not usually.

I try to sound reassuring. "Maybe you're right. Maybe it's nothing."

"I didn't say that. It's always something." He looks at me, with a hint of a smile on his face. "It's just never what you want it to be."

19

THE HOLE

We've reached the road to the Avenues that lead into town. Las Ramblas. I stop following Lucas when the road flattens out in front of us, at the top of the hill. "Do you have any idea where you're going?"

He points. "All the major roads run west to east in the Hole. Las Ramblas will take us there." I nod, but I'm impressed. I only know the basics—that Las Ramblas is known for its massive crowds, and that today is no different.

The crush of people is dizzying, particularly for me. I can't think—at least, I can't separate out what I think from what the world is thinking. "You said you're here to meet someone?" I fumble to string together the words.

He nods, but doesn't answer.

"Who, Lucas?"

RESEARCH MEMORANDUM:
THE HUMANITY PROJECT

CLASSIFIED TOP SECRET / AMBASSADOR EYES ONLY

To: Ambassador Amare

Subject: Amare Bounty Letter

Catalogue Assignment: Evidence recovered during
raid of Rebellion hideout

BY ORDER OF GRASS REBELLION

WANTED:
DEAD OR ALIVE

LUCAS AMARE

REWARD: 1000 DIGS

False claims will not be tolerated.
To collect,
bring proof to any Rebellion Officer.

DEATH TO THE LORDS!
DEATH TO THE STOOGES!
FREE HUMANITY!

"You'll see when we get there. This way." Lucas motions, and we begin to move eastward into the Hole.

We walk beneath the giant banners that flutter in the air over the city streets. Here's what I learn in the span of a few short blocks: *The Lords Are Generous. The Embassy Is Kind. The People Are Lucky. The Future Is Bright.* A stern-faced painting of the Ambassador in her scarlet jacket rises to the height of an abandoned building. I can count the golden birdcage buttons on it, each one the size of my head, while the breeze blows through the broken-out windows that puncture the paint.

Are all cities like ours?

I don't actually know, seeing as I've never seen another, except for those few moments of the Silent Cities that the Ambassador showed me. The Embassy media is so tightly controlled, it's impossible to know for certain. Sometimes, Ro would come to dinner at La Purísima, his eyes crazy and full of fire, and tell us bits of stolen Grass news. How the Lords have wronged us. How the Embassy lets them.

Right and wrong. The whole world divides into two columns, for Ro. He sees things differently than I do. I'm overwhelmed by a million perspectives, all at once. There's no one right answer, not when everyone is shouting at the same time. That's why the feelings are so hard for me to sort out. So draining. Half the time I agree with every-thing they feel and everyone I meet.

Weaving my way through the crowded street with Lucas

at my side, I realize Lucas isn't afraid of how he feels. He wants to feel it—it, me, everything. Everyone. He takes it all in, deep inside him.

Not Ro.

For Ro there is only black and white, right and wrong—and he is right. He doesn't care if you agree with him or not. In fact, it's better for him if you don't.

Ro just wants to fight.

———— • ————

The famed Avenues food vendors line the curb. Handmade tortillas fry on the top of the nearest overturned trash can. Potatoes sizzle together with onions on the next. Ropes of cheese or bread dough twist around sticks. Ropes of snake meat, too, but I look away before my eyes can rest on the place where the sticks push out of the blackened, impaled mouths.

"Why are you making that face?" Lucas looks at me, laughing.

I shudder, shaking my head, and he relaxes against me, letting our shoulders touch.

You'd almost think we were regular seventeen-year-olds, on a regular walk, through a regular city. But none of those things are true. I've escaped a military complex for an illicit rendezvous with an unknown source in a dangerous city.

With the Ambassador's son.

Part of me is glad the Padre isn't here to see it. *He'd worry,* I think—*like I'm worrying now.*

We reach the end of the Avenues, Las Ramblas, and though Lucas hasn't said anything, I see the rails and realize we are going to ride the City Tracks—my first time. Unlike the Californias Tracks, which run along the coast, the City Tracks only operate within the Hole.

Ten minutes later, we're heading east. At least, so says the sign on the door of our boxcar, which is nearly empty; only Embassy Brass can ride the City Tracks. Though Lucas's plastic couldn't get us into the Hall of Records, a quick flash at the bored Sympa guards still got us onto the Tracks. Thankfully, they didn't look too closely at the last name.

At Union Station, I hop down from the edge of the car, after Lucas, and follow him as we make our way through the crowds in the vast, spacious lobby. A row of Sympas watch us. I try not to look in their direction, as if not watching them will keep them from watching me.

The lobby is endless. My heart pounds, and the doors to the street seem a mile away. Thickly cracking leather chairs sit in groups like a brown herd. Beneath them, the floor is beautiful, a mosaic tile pattern that builds into the center of the room as if it were a long, ornate rug.

The windows are tall. I think of the pictures of the

cathedrals I have seen in the Padre's study. The light filters through them, and most of what I can see in the light is dust.

We push open the doors to the visible world.

In the broad whiteness of daylight, I have to blink to make out the dark shape I am looking at. It's a tree, growing in the center of the plaza across from the train station. People peek out from the roots, hiding and sitting and even sleeping inside them. Sympas stand idly by, ignoring them, as if this mess of humanity was something invisible, something that never could be considered part of the city plan.

"So many people." I can barely choke out the words, because I feel them all. Everyone in the plaza, the streets—needing, grasping, wanting. Fear seeps into every other emotion, every interaction. I clutch Lucas's sleeve while I struggle to get my bearings.

He slips his hand down to my wrist and pulls me gently through the crowd. His touch is reassuring, and I let him calm me.

Lucas points. "That's the Pueblo. The oldest building in the Hole." I can't see where he is pointing through the crowd.

I pause, and focus on breathing. I focus on not feeling. I focus on the wall between my feelings and theirs, willing it to hold. Willing the Hole outside to not absorb me.

"Come on." Lucas disappears in front of me. Our

fingers pull apart, and I try to follow, but within three steps I have lost him.

"Miss lady. Miss lady. Miss lady." I move carefully past the extended hands. A hammer drops rhythmically in the distance. I hear drums. No. Firecrackers—and drums. Stomping feet beat to the rhythm. The twanging of strings, maybe a kind of guitar? I crane my head to find the music, but it is easier to hear than to see in the mash of people. Three competing groups of street musicians perform in three plazas nearby. A fringe of feathers bobs, appearing and disappearing in a splash of bright color above the clustered heads of the crowd.

Another hand appears in front of me. I shake my head: "Sorry. No digs." It's true.

The hand grabs my arm and pulls. I turn to see Lucas, looking exasperated. "There you are. Stay with me."

Stay with me.

I take his hand. It is warm and his sleeve is once again down over his wrist. I squeeze it, without realizing what I am doing. He stops walking.

"What?" I look at him, embarrassed. I try not to act surprised to find myself holding his hand.

"Nothing." He smiles and looks away.

But it isn't nothing. I can feel him. Lucas on the inside is as sprawling and chaotic as the Hole itself. He's warm and pounding and hopeful and scared. Terrified. He's overwhelmed and intimidated and alive. He feels like the

Hole, only better. He feels like the only hopeful thing in the Hole. Because I can feel that too, the hope. It's only a tiny spark, a flutter. But it's there.

I'm lucky to feel it, even once in my life, I think. I don't feel it often. So I don't say a word when he laces his fingers through mine as we walk.

We push past the stalls, and I catch a glimpse of the inside of a shop, through a doorway. A woman is selling Mexicali dresses, long swaths of cotton that hang off the shoulders in brilliant colors, embroidered with rainbows of thread. *Feasting-day dresses*, I think. I should steal one for Biggest, back on the Mission. She would like the green one, with the rainbow woven belt. But that isn't what catches my eye. It's a painting, on hammered tin that looks like silver, of the Lady. Stripes come from her head like the rays of the sun itself.

"Miss lady? You like?" The shopkeeper is a woman with black hair and brown skin. Her eyes are brilliantly blue. "*Tres*. Three hundred digs. It's a good price, *para la madre de todos.*"

Lucas tugs on my hand. I keep walking.

"Miss lady! Miss lady!"

Lucas turns back to her, and I can feel the moment she recognizes his face. "*El hijo! El hijo!*" For a minute I think she is talking about the son of the Lady—but she means the son of the Ambassador.

Her own face freezes as she takes it in. That's right, the son. She must have access to a vid-screen. Now she disappears inside the shop, slamming the blue-painted doors behind her.

"I have that effect on people, sometimes. Or, more to the point, my mother does." Lucas looks at me. "Sorry. You weren't really going to buy that, were you?"

"With what digs?"

"It's just as well. If you like that, I can show you a better one."

"A better painting?"

"No. Not a painting. A better Lady. You'll see. Come on, it's on the way."

We weave through the alleyways of stalls, passing pepper candies and peanut candies. Old candy from old Mexicali. *Pulpa de tamarindo* in waxy packets, as sweet and as sour as the Hole itself. Mangos rolled and dried in chili powder. Miniature accordions and blue toy guitars and yellow maracas and pink harmonicas and red *trompos*. The colors and faces appear in layers, drifting in and out like the breeze and the sky.

We turn up a broad boulevard, where a man walks a donkey carrying bundles of what look like T-shirts past a giant wall of graffiti.

"You can't possibly know where you're going." I pull on Lucas's hand.

"But I do." He looks at me with a sideways smile.

"But I don't." I smile back.

"Have a little faith, will you?"

"I wish I could." My smile fades. "I wish I did."

"Are you always this cheerful?" He laughs, and I shake my head, looking up in time to see an archway as we pass beneath it. Two dragons, hammered together out of some sort of red metal, are fighting overhead, from one side of the street to the other. Their bodies are long and twisted like snakes, but their clawed arms and legs are short and sharp.

"*Laowai. Laowai.*" I can hear the crowd murmuring as we pass. I don't know what the term means, except that it is me. Someone who does not belong in this part of the Hole.

Neither Lucas nor I do.

The heat overwhelms us. I motion to the side of the road, where the edges of market stalls lean haphazardly together. Small square signs tell their names. *Bok choy, yu choy, gai lan* pile against each other in as many different greens as there are colors. Purple yams sit together between faded orange *satsumas* and pale green *oroblancos*, bigger and sweeter than grapefruits. The *yuzu* lemons, bright little balls of sunlight, only make the day seem hotter.

Between the stands, a wrinkled old woman sells bags of something unfamiliar that I think is a drink, from a

252

red wagon. *"Paomo hongcha? Paomo hongcha."* Another woman sits next to her on a folding stool, wearing a T-shirt that says *Sexy Mama*. Together they are probably seven hundred years old.

"What is that?" I look at Lucas.

"I've gotten it before. Not here, not from her. I don't know what she's saying, but I think it translates to something like sea foam."

Fizzing water, part of a lime, and a kind of sugary powder are all dumped into what looks like a paper cup.

Lucas looks at her. "Sea foam?" She nods and the woman next to her, the Sexy Mama, starts to laugh. Her smile is almost entirely gold, or something that looks like it.

He fishes a coin out of his pocket and hands it to the woman.

The woman howls at me in a language I do not understand. Her face has a thousand wrinkles.

An older man stops next to me. "She told her friend she is going to rip you off because you come from Grass."

"How did she know?"

"Your friend calls the drink the wrong name. You say sea foam. We call it Sympa pisswater."

The woman holds out the drink. Now she is angry, and shouting at me.

"Take it," the old man says. "She says to take it and

go." He leans closer to me. That much farther away from the Sympas who idle on the side of the street, behind the cart.

"She says to hurry. She says the Merk is waiting for you."

"What?"

I back away from him, confused. I find myself in the middle of the street, in a seemingly never-ending stream of Remnants, students, laborers, jugglers, street musicians.

"Dol! Wait—"

An old man pushing a massive wooden drum on wheels slams into me. Now I'm trapped in the middle of some kind of processional. I whirl around to see a second drum, just before it hits me.

I go flying.

I open my eyes. A group of old men stand over me, inside an elaborately carved doorway. Red and yellow and green. A wooden scroll is cut into the frame.

THE BENEVOLENT ASSOCIATION. That's what it says on the door. Same as the characters on the drum that knocked me to the ground.

The men look benevolent, I guess. They don't look malevolent, anyway. They look nice.

I close my eyes. The day has overwhelmed me. I'm bruised from where the drum has hit me, and I'm too tired to think.

I open my eyes to see that I am sitting inside what I

imagine is the main room of the Benevolent Association. I try to stand up. I have the impulse to run.

"Please, please. You must sit." Only one man says the words in English. The others are all shouting at me in a language I don't understand.

I look past card tables where men are smoking and playing a game with well-worn tiles. There are zodiac calendars on the wall. Hanging beads line the doorways.

I am given a warm glass of water and a bowl of spiced nuts. The smell curls into my face, chili peppers and lemongrass. I cough spice.

"You are well. You will be well."

A bespectacled man in a jade-colored jacket sits across from me.

"Where's Lucas?" I ask.

"Your friend? The Little Ambassador? He is well. All is well."

I try to stand again.

The man pulls me down, but doesn't let go of my hand. In fact, he stares at it.

"What are you looking at?"

"Your hand."

"What about it?"

"Nothing. I give you reading. Make sure you are well."

"No thanks."

"I insist. I am most benevolent."

He straightens my hand, in front of him, pulling a

clipboard out of a bag he wears against his hip. The clipboard carries a chart showing the dim outline of a hand divided into quadrants, and a schematic of a blank face. Graphs and grids and charts of numbers, as well as the zodiac, fill the rest of the page.

"Your reading. For the Year of the Tiger."

"Is that what it is?"

He ignores me. I look around, a bit desperately now, for Lucas. I don't like this man touching me. I don't like anyone touching me. He feels smooth and soft, though, both the part I can feel with my hand and the part I can feel with my mind.

"I can't read you with numbers. Not for you. I read you with creatures. You belong to the animals."

He pulls a handful of jade animals out of his bag, one by one. He lines them up in a row on the table between us, carefully. His hand shakes as he moves, resting heavily on each one while he speaks.

A pig. "I am sorry for your loss." He lays the pig down on the table. *Ramona*, I think.

He weighs what looks like a lamb in his hand, shaking his head. "Not the sheep. The shepherd. You have lost him as well." The sheep joins the pig.

He holds up a monkey. "Monkey. Very playful. Very dangerous. Keep your eyes open and see things for what they are." He places the monkey on the far side of the table, a distance from the sheep and the pig.

Now he fingers a turtle. "Very scared. Lonely. But will help you find your way." The turtle goes halfway between the monkey on one side, and the sheep and the pig on the other.

He places a dog next to the turtle. "Faithful. Loyal. But teeth are sharp." Now he holds up what looks like a small carved lion. "Lion of heart not always a good thing. Will cause you great pain. You must decide for yourself what is a lion and what is a dog."

The dog and the lion stand together.

I look at his face. He grins, bobbing his head, and I notice for the first time he is wearing a neatly brimmed hat with a bright orange feather sticking out of the stitched band of trim. The feather exactly matches the kumquats that sit in a bowl in the center of the card table between us. *He is a card table made into a man*, I think.

"Your hand."

I give him my hand again. This time, he is full of sorrow and anxious energy, tears and sweat like foam from the ocean when it touches the shore, washing up along the beach.

Sea foam, I think. Not pisswater.

"See this? You are strong."

I don't know how a freckle beneath my thumb can possibly mean that, but I nod.

"Do not marry before you are twenty-five. If you do, you will have many children and no money. Very unfortunate."

"I don't think that will be a problem."

He laughs and I see the gold in his teeth. He taps at a line that spreads like wings in the center of my palm. "Your brothers. They watch over you."

"They're dead." I try to pull my hand away, but he stops me.

"My bad. I try again. Best two out of three."

He scrunches up his face, this time tracing the three lines that arc across my palm.

"I see a child in your future. Here. A girl."

"Before twenty-five? So I'm poor?"

He shakes his head. "Not yours." He frowns. "Very important."

"I am?"

He looks at me carefully, closely.

"She is."

He holds my hand tightly, and his eyes glaze over. He is looking but not looking at my hand, and I can feel him slipping away from me.

"You must help her. Everything depends upon it." His tone changes and he is no longer smiling.

"Yeah?"

He reaches into his pocket and pulls out a small velvet

bag. One by one, he picks up the jade animals and drops them inside it.

"Keep them. I was to keep them, but your hand tells me to give them to you."

I reach for the bag. He pulls it away.

"Greedy, greedy. Not for you. For her. When you find her. If."

He is, like everyone else in the Hole, crazy. That's the first thing I think. The second is, he's running a scam.

So much for the Benevolent Association. They're probably ransoming Lucas as we speak.

"What about the boy?" he asks.

It's as if he can read my mind. "What about him? What does my hand say?"

But at that, the old man tips back his head and laughs, raising his hands. "I can't tell you. Time up now. Shoot me. So it is written."

"What?"

"Shoot me. That is all that remains."

He smiles and rolls his eyes back, until all I can see are the whites.

"I don't understand."

He closes his eyes. A bullet rips through his chest, spattering me with red flesh. Another whizzes past my head.

"Oh my God."

The old man is dead. A row of bullets eats into the

wood above him. I fall out of my chair and sprawl onto the floor.

Even so, I can't take my eyes off the old man.

The red stain seeps upward as his body slumps downward. The hat tumbles free and the orange feather floats lazily in the air. There are kumquats everywhere, rolling and spilling across the table, across the floor. Like the blood.

Shoot me. He wasn't kidding.

He knew it was coming.

He knew.

"Oh my God. Oh my God. Sweet Maria."

I grab the velvet bag, scramble to my feet, and run.

As I move, I think that this is what my life has become. This, and nothing more. Mysterious news and sudden death. Blood spatter on the wall and kumquats rolling on the floor. This is my life now.

It makes me run faster.

EMBASSY CITY TRIBUNAL
VIRTUAL AUTOPSY: DECEASED PERSONAL
POSSESSIONS TRANSCRIPT (DPPT)

CLASSIFIED TOP SECRET

Performed by Dr. O. Brad Huxley-Clarke, VPHD
Note: Conducted at the private request of
   Amb. Amare
Santa Catalina Examination Facility #9B
See adjoining Tribunal Autopsy, attached.

DPPT (CONTINUED FROM PREVIOUS PAGE)
Catalogue at Time of Death includes:

31. ███████████████████████████████████
████████████████████████████████████.

32. One small carved animal, green in color. Cheap quality, commonly sold in souvenir shops throughout the Southlands. 2.2 zm. Jade. It appears to be a lion, broken in half.

Source or significance unknown.

OUR LADY OF THE ANGELS

I leave the Benevolent Association, running as fast as I can. Out of the corner of my eye, I see Sympas in formation, moving through the center of the street.

Why would Sympas shoot at me? Why now?

I thread my way through the crowd as it thins. I hear the sound of more gunshots. People scream, scattering frantically. I keep going.

Lucas. Where is Lucas?

Why would Sympas shoot at him?

I turn the corner into an alley and duck behind the trash cans. A few minutes later, Lucas dives into the shadows after me.

We lie there, panting, as the Sympas run by, in the brightness of the street in front of us.

"Why?" It's the first word I can manage to get out.

"I don't know."

"Are they looking for you or me?" I'm hoping not to be the answer.

He doesn't say anything. I think of the old man who told my fortune, the way blood seeped through to his chest, the way his body spun back.

I touch my pocket, feeling for the hard lumps of jade. Everything looks blurry to me now, and I try to wipe the tears from my face but they just keep coming.

"Do you know why Doc was invented?" Lucas asks.

"He's a Virt. A Medic." Doc told me himself.

"When I was five, I found an asp in my bed. When I was eleven, my tutor drank a glass of milk that was meant for me and dropped dead from cyanide. When I was thirteen, someone took a shot at me in broad daylight, and we moved to Santa Catalina."

"That's horrible."

"Doc isn't just a Medic. He's my bodyguard. As many people who want me to live want me to die. That's part of every day of my life." He sounds as terrible as I feel.

"You're here now, aren't you?"

I settle back against him, in the garbage, in the shadows, in the alley. I let his warmth run back and forth between us.

"I'm sorry, Dol. I'm sorry I got you into this. I should

have been more careful. I should have come by myself."

He didn't, and he shouldn't. It's how he feels, though. I understand. So I don't say anything at all.

Eventually, we slip back out into the street. We keep our heads down and stick to the alleys. The crowd has surged back across the pavement and the sidewalks, and the temporary quiet of a Sympa incident has subsided into the normal noise and teeming chaos. Crowds and noise are comforting here. Only the quiet disturbs. I am glad it has passed.

Soon we come to a sandstone wall that follows the length of a block, maybe more. I run my finger along the smooth rectangles of pale stone, badly crumbling. I look up to see a row of green brass bells. You could still see the coppery color underneath the patina of time, in places. Only a few.

"Here," says Lucas. "This is what I was looking for."

There is a gate, and it is locked—even though the building looks abandoned.

"What now?"

"This." Lucas pushes it open, and the oxidized iron gives way beneath his hand. It is, like most of the Hole, something broken and useless that only retains the slight impression of a thing with a purpose that came before.

Lucas and I walk through an abandoned courtyard,

where wide, flat steps lead up to a massive sandstone building on the left, and a shallow, dry fountain on the right. A last row of buildings, empty shops with doors that have rusted open, marks the far right.

Lucas steps behind me, moving me into one particular spot. I feel his hands on either shoulder, two warm places where I am otherwise cold, though the sun is shining.

"There, right there. Now—look up."

I look toward the sky, and the facade of a cathedral spins up into the blue air, in front of me.

There she is. Now I understand why we are here. And he's right. She is more beautiful.

A stone statue—a sad Lady—looks down on me.

"Our Lady of the Angels. That's what this place used to be called. Long, long ago," Lucas tells me.

"She's beautiful."

He tilts his head, so we are looking with the same angle. "Look at her halo. It's cut away, made out of sky, see? That's my favorite part."

I don't know if she is the Lady, or an angel. Either way, the stone roof is cut out in a circle over her head, and I realize he's right.

Her halo is the sky.

"Do you like it? Her?" I hear his voice in my ear, but I don't answer. I can't speak.

Her halo is the sky. The same sky that gave us the monsters, the Lords themselves.

The Lady and the monsters. Peace, and death.

Angels and aliens.

The Lady is cloaked in orange blossoms and scarlet bougainvillea, growing like wild over the fountains and the stones of the square.

"Lucas."

It's all I can say. He moves his hands from my shoulders, until his arms encircle me, and I lean against him...

"That's a real Icon, eh?"

I recognize the voice. Lucas pulls his arms away, and we turn, startled.

"Kind of puts everythin' in perspective, I'd say."

The church square isn't empty anymore. Fortis stands in front of us. Behind him, a row of people I can't place. They're not Sympas. They don't look like Grass. They're something else.

"My friends at the Rebellion. I thought it was time you finally met. Especially now, seein' as you've come all the way to their home." He gestures. "Nice place, hey? I like the bit over there, what with the fountain and the flowers." He snaps off a bougainvillea blossom. "Red, like my first wife. Always liked datin' a ginger."

I look at Lucas. "Him? This is where you were coming? To see Fortis?" I can't believe it. Especially not from Lucas.

Lucas shrugs. "You're the one who said you trusted him, right?"

The Merk grins. "Come on now, Miss lady. My friends tell me they've been trailin' you through the city all day. Lost you for a bit, after the unpleasantness with the Benevolent gentleman. Such a shame."

"Shut up, Fortis." I don't like the way he says things. As if everything weighs the same, no one thing matters more than the next. *The flower is red. The man is dead.* They're all just words to him. That's what Merks are like, I guess.

"They only want to talk for a bit. The least you can do is come in for a cake or two and a spot of tea."

One by one, I begin to pick out faces in the crowd. The woman from the candy shack in the plaza. The old man who helped us buy the drink at the red wagon, and the woman who sold it. Even a few old men from the Benevolent Association are in the crowd—I recognize their jade quilted jackets.

It's strange to see them all here, a motley collection of lost souls in the courtyard of a broken-down church in the backwater chaos of the Hole.

"One drink," says Lucas, and it is decided. Lucas and I follow Fortis through the massive doors into what used to be the church. I take a last look at Our Lady, but she doesn't say a word. As if giving a sign, though, her halo of sky has become a halo of clouds.

I tell myself I don't believe in signs, and let the heavy door fall shut behind me.

But it's a lie.

Because I do.

The inside of the church is no church at all. It really is or was a cathedral. The ceiling soars and the room broadens until I realize we have walked to the other side. I stand looking down the center aisle to the apse, where the walls bisect the space into a cross. *Like the Mission*, I think, *only a hundred times bigger.* I can see that everything about this place was vast and grand. The remains of some kind of gold, carved shrine sit in the very back. I imagine that at one time, there would have been rows of pews, filled with people praying. *Not animals*, I think, with a smile.

If they had candles, I would light one for Ramona Jamona.

But now there are no pews, only rows of cots. Tables spread with maps. Clusters of children and the elderly, here and there. It's as chaotic, in its own way, as the marketplace and the stalls and the Hole outside.

Only the walls remain still. The stone, the large squares, are immovable, and we are all small beside them.

Fortis motions me into an alcove, where a thick rug

has been thrown over the floor and covered with embroi-dered pillows. A brilliant pattern of silk scarves hangs to cover the doorway, which is simply a break in the walls. I let myself drop to a low table set with an elaborate brass tea setting, next to Lucas. A plate of dusty-looking pastry accompanies the tea.

Fortis sits across from us. "Thanks for comin', mate. I was surprised to get your message."

"Really? After you came to us? What was so surpris-ing about my wanting to return the visit?"

"I wasn't surprised you were curious. I was more sur-prised that you could get a message to me. I'm not an easy fellow to rin' up."

"Speaking of which, how did you find this place?" I look at Lucas suspiciously.

"I asked." He shrugs.

"Asked who," I say.

"I asked around."

He looks at Fortis, who grins. "I tried to leave a few clues. That's a hell of a program, your friend at the Embassy. Beastly to shut down, and some of my better work, if I do say so myself."

"You mean Doc?" It had to be. Lucas couldn't have told anyone else. He must have had Doc trace Fortis.

I turn on Lucas. I can't help myself. "No wonder people knew exactly where we were all day. Why Sympas came and shot the old man I was talking to. I don't know how the Embassy Wik works, but I'm pretty sure if one part of it knows something, the other parts do."

"It wasn't Doc. He's smarter than that. You don't know him like I do." Now Lucas is getting defensive.

"He's not smart. He's not even a person." I don't know why, but for the third time today, I can feel myself blinking back hot, prickling tears.

"That, love, is just semantics." Fortis pours himself a drink.

"Doc wouldn't say anything about me." Lucas grabs what looks like some kind of sweet roll and shoves it into his mouth.

"You know this because?"

"He's Doc."

Fortis lifts his cup. A toast. "Seems like a right enough old bastard to me." He downs it. I suspect it isn't tea.

"Technically, that would be impossible, since the term *bastard* applies as a kind of widely accepted vernacular to a child born out of wedlock." The familiar voice comes from Lucas, who is pressing a particular place on the black leather cuff he wears around his marks. "I was neither born out of wedlock, nor a child, nor, for that matter, in the traditional sense, born."

"Doc?"

"Yes, Dol."

"You've been here the whole time?"

"Strictly speaking, no. If, by 'being here,' you take being to imply a physical presence. I am, in fact, neither here nor there. As the colloquial expression goes."

"Ah, you're real enough to me, mate." Fortis raises his glass to the disembodied voice. "*Cogito ergo sum*, my friend. *Cogito ergo sum*."

"Thank you, Fortis."

"Lucas *wears* you?" It sounds stupid. I want it to.

"It's a mobile drive. Pipes right into my ear. I told you. He's my bodyguard, sort of. How did you think I knew where I was going, all day long? How did I always know where to find you?"

"Because you're smart. Because you're fast. Because you've been to the Hole—and I never have." I'm being stubborn. I don't like not knowing what's going on around me.

Even if, in spite of everything, I like Doc—and some part of me, somewhere, doesn't know how I feel about Lucas. Lots of ways, I guess. I just don't know which one is the one that matters most.

Fortis sits back against the pillows. "If you two lovebirds would give me a chance to say somethin', I think I could help you."

Lucas scowls. "You mean, you think we could help you."

"Isn't that what I said?" Fortis sighs. "I'm a reasonable fellow. I've got a reasonable proposition. All I ask is that you have a listen and tell me what you think then, right?"

"How do we know?" Lucas pushes his cup away.

"Know what?" Fortis raises an eyebrow.

"That you're reasonable. Or that we should listen."

"Or that Sympa guards or whoever it was that was shooting at us back there aren't on the way to blow our heads off right now? While you keep us sitting here listening to your lies?" I can't stop myself from chiming in.

"What do you say, Doc?" Lucas doesn't move his eyes from Fortis.

"It would be logical, yes. Even advisable, were the mercenary's goals to be aligned with the persons behind this afternoon's violence."

"Examples?" It's becoming clear Lucas and Doc have been together a long, long time.

"Citing. See the Trojan War. See Demosthenes. See Sun Tzu, *The Art of War*, subheading, Creating Strategic Opportunities."

"Well, there you go. I wouldn't want to disagree with Sun Tzu."

"However," Doc continues, "highly unlikely, if you posit that financial remuneration is the end goal of any mercenary, however aligned. And I don't believe profit is his motivation."

"Why is that?" Lucas's smile fades.

"Because," says Doc, "Fortis isn't a mercenary. That's a ruse, a falsehood. A fiction."

"Oh?" I stare at Fortis, and the truth hits me at the exact moment the words do. Just for a moment, I can feel my way into it.

"He's the leader of the Rebellion."

EMBASSY CITY TRIBUNAL
VIRTUAL AUTOPSY: DECEASED PERSONAL POSSESSIONS TRANSCRIPT (DPPT)

CLASSIFIED TOP SECRET

Performed by Dr. O. Brad Huxley-Clarke, VPHD

Note: Conducted at the private request of
Amb. Amare

Santa Catalina Examination Facility #9B

See adjoining Tribunal Autopsy, attached.

DPPT (CONTINUED FROM PREVIOUS PAGE)

Catalogue at Time of Death includes:

35. Collection of Embassy Motivational Flyers, text-scan follows:

SAFEGUARD THE FUTURE!

BE PARANOID ABOUT ENEMIES
OF THE HOUSE OF LORDS,
SABOTEURS AND OTHER
EVIL ELEMENTS AGAINST PEACE
IN THE EMBASSY CITIES.

THANK THE LORDS!

WORK HARD!

BE GRATEFUL!
FOR THE EMBASSY,
FOR WORLD PEACE,
FOR THE FUTURE!

THANK THE LORDS!

HUX

"You're what?" Lucas pushes himself against the table. I think he would bolt if he could, but there are rows of Rebellion Grass between him and the door.

"Was that really necessary, Hux? I should have pulled your plug again." Fortis shakes his head.

"Hux? You have a name for Doc, too?" I don't know which I find more confusing, that the Merk is somehow friends with Doc—if you can call it that—or that the Merk is no Merk at all.

"I apologize, Fortis, if I have spoken in error."

"Did you or didn't you? Speak in error?" Lucas looks at his wrist, as if Doc is somehow there.

"I believe Fortis and I had agreed that at some point it would become beneficial to reveal certain truths about ourselves," says the voice.

"Yourselves? What's the truth about you, Doc? Or do you have more names I don't know?" Lucas looks annoyed.

"I have been called just over one hundred derivatives of my longer name. Would you care to hear them? It is a slightly different query." The familiar refrain comforts me.

"No, actually." He puts down his cup.

"Leave Hux alone. He's a good enough fellow. I was the one who said you wouldn't agree to meet me, if you knew who I really was."

"Why is that? Who are you?" I can feel Lucas's turmoil radiating into the rest of us. He's as contagious as ever, only now what he gives me is closer to a chill than anything else.

"Does it really matter? It shouldn't. What should matter to you is this: you an' me, all of us—we're goin' to take out the Icon."

"Excuse me?"

"The Icon, at what used to be the Observatory. High time we did somethin' about it."

"You're wrong. We can't do anything. The Icon can't be destroyed. Nothing works or lives anywhere near it. No one could get close enough to touch it." Lucas isn't buying it.

Fortis continues calmly. "I know more than you might think, and you might learn somethin' if you stop and listen. The Icon is how the Embassy controls the Hole. The Icon is how the House of Lords controls the Embassy. Controls everythin'. Everythin' comes back to the Icon." Fortis shakes his head.

"Not everything," says Lucas.

"Actually, the Icon does control everythin'." Fortis winks at me. "But not everyone, Doloria."

"Everything and everyone," I insist. "Even us. Here we are, powerless. Controlled by the Embassy, like everyone else."

"I won't argue with you there, Dol. But think about this—how do you suppose you came to have your name? Amoris? Doloris?"

"Because she survived The Day?" Lucas frowns at him.

"Not entirely."

"Because she has special abilities, then?" He tries again.

Fortis shrugs.

"What are you saying, Fortis?" Lucas rubs his hands through his lank blond hair, frustrated.

I lose my patience. "I don't know much about the Icon, but even I know we can't get near it. We'd die, like everyone else." The images from the Silent Cities flood my mind again, and I focus on the cup in front of me, trying not to see them.

"Maybe. Maybe not. Look. I'll tell you what. We'll

pay a visit to the Icon. Have a look around for yourself, let me know what you think."

"Now?" I don't believe him. I don't want to. "Stop playing games with us, Fortis. Tell us what you know. What does this have to do with us? What are we?"

"You feel things, Dol. All four of you. You feel things in a most particular fashion. More than other people. More than anyone."

"And?"

"And it's not just an accident. Those feelings, those emotions are what make you powerful. So all I ask is that you have a little look-see. You might be surprised."

"How do you know what we'll find at the Icon? How can you be sure of anything?" I'm so overwhelmed, and so tired. I don't know if I want to scream or cry.

"I can't. But I know more about you than anyone else, love." Fortis pulls a book—my book—out of the inside of his jacket.

"You see, I wrote the book. Well, Hux an' me, when you get right down to it."

The book about me. The Book of Icons. The book the Ambassador killed my Padre for.

A doctor wrote it. That's what the Padre said.

Did he mean Doc?

My mind is reeling and I reach for the book—just as Fortis pulls it away.

"You want your precious book back, you'll have to earn it. Take a little walk with me first."

"Why should I?" My eyes narrow. Lucas shifts uncomfortably, next to me.

"Because I blew up the Tracks for you. Nearly lost a finger. And a deal is a deal."

EMBASSY CITY TRIBUNAL VIRTUAL AUTOPSY: DECEASED PERSONAL POSSESSIONS TRANSCRIPT (DPPT)

CLASSIFIED TOP SECRET

Performed by Dr. O. Brad Huxley-Clarke, VPHD
Note: Conducted at the private request of
    Amb. Amare
Santa Catalina Examination Facility #9B
See adjoining Tribunal Autopsy, attached.

DPPT (CONTINUED FROM PREVIOUS PAGE)
Catalogue at Time of Death includes:

38. One 10-cm-wide strip of muslin, splattered with what appears to be dried human blood.

Tear is consistent with wrist binding worn by the Deceased.

Will be scanned and sent to Embassy Labs for analysis, as per protocol #83421.

22
THE PARK

"All right."

I'll do it. I have no choice.

Fortis might not be a Merk—but he's downright mercenary. There will be no book until I go with him to the Icon. It disappears almost as quickly as it came.

"First we walk." Fortis pulls himself up.

I can't let it drop. "Fortis. I have to know. What's so important about that stupid book?"

"Not yet. We take a field trip. We check out the Icon, do a little reconnaissance. Then we can have readin' hour, as long as you like."

There is no arguing with Fortis—at least, no more arguing—which is why, within a matter of minutes, we find ourselves walking down a dusty street in the distinct direction of the foothills.

———— • ————

"He's following us, do you see him?" I look over my shoulder, nervously. The walk to the Observatory has taken hours, during the last few of which we've been followed.

A small, ragged-looking boy walks in the shadows on the same side of the street as us, only a block behind. He looks like a Remnant, tattooed and ratty. But there's too much purpose to his walk, and as he wanders he keeps his eyes on us.

I say, "That boy."

"Don't mind him." Fortis walks more slowly, if possible. I find myself watching his gait, to see if he is drunk. Especially since what we are doing can only be explained by intoxication or insanity.

"What if he's armed?" Lucas speaks up, and I can feel his pulse quickening. "We've already been shot at once today."

"Only once? That's a bit anticlimactic and all, don't you think? Seeing as you made the trip all the way here?" Fortis takes a handkerchief out of the pocket of his long jacket. He mops his brow and I wonder what else he has in there.

"You'll be fine. We're almost there, aren't we, Hux?"

Fortis glances at Lucas, but it's not Lucas he's speaking to.

Doc replies, as easily as if it was Lucas who had asked. "Just around the next turn, Fortis. You should be safe until you reach the perimeter."

"And the field?"

"All systems operational. The pulse wave is transmitting normally, directly from the Icon." Doc's voice seems farther away, now that we are outside, on the street.

Though of course he was never here, not really.

The fallen sign on the edge of the road says GRIFF PARK, or at least those are the letters that remain. Somewhere up this road and up this hill, the Icon waits for us.

In the scrubby green-brown foothills that surround us, there is no sign of life. No birds sing; nothing rustles in the stiff, dried brush. There is only the buzz of the atmosphere, and the silence of certain death. That is what the pulse field sounds like. Like machine noise and nothingness in my ears.

The road is called Mossy Fern; at least, it looks like it used to be. The sign is overgrown now, as is the road. Overwhelmed with brown, decaying ferns. It looks like the wrong place. It looks like nowhere anyone would ever go.

But then the road twists, and the gates come into view.

Of course.

Griff Park is gated off.

A chain-link fence is wired carelessly shut, probably

284

because the Embassy knows that nobody can survive long enough to enter, and if they did, they wouldn't make it all the way up the hill to the Observatory.

Lucas stands in the road, staring up the hill, or what we can see of it through the brown piles of dead plant life, banked against the gates. It looks like it once was a neighborhood, with nice houses and nice lawns and probably nice families. Now it is a ghost neighborhood, haunted by memories that no one is left to remember.

I don't want to be here. I don't want to be a ghost. I turn and look behind me. The boy is that much closer, standing now where I was standing, minutes ago.

"Why are we here? There's no point. There's nothing we can do." I'm annoyed.

Fortis just stands there, hands in his pockets, waiting. For what, I don't know.

"So this is the perimeter, I guess." The words sound strange in Lucas's throat, and he doesn't move his eyes.

Fortis nods, his eyes equally fixed. "Apparently so."

Then I see why they are staring. It's not only the brush that is dead.

Around me, piled in the debris at the base of the fence, are skeletons—four, six, ten skeletons, pressing against the wires, dumped like trash on the side of the road.

One has his hand at his throat.

My heart skips a beat.

I'm looking at the bodies of people who have tried to

infiltrate the Icon, tried to do something about our common situation. People braver than me.

They're all dead.

I turn to Lucas and Fortis. "We should go back. We can't—they're everywhere."

Fortis sighs. "That's what happens when you try to get near the Icon, for us regular blokes. Like I said."

"Why are there so many?"

He laughs, but he isn't smiling. "Are you pulling my chain, love? This is nothing. Think about it. Since 6/6, any time people try to demonstrate, they drop dead. Any time we try to stage a protest. Any time we make our voices heard. As long as that Icon stays in place, the Lords control everything we say and do. It's the Silent Cities, every day, all over again."

He shrugs. "After a while, we just stopped tryin'. Now we take our numbers and stand in line with the resta the livin' dead."

Lucas is silent. Instead, he starts to walk around the perimeter of the gate, searching for something.

"What are you doing? You're going to get yourself killed."

I grab Lucas's arm—I have to stop him. I'm thinking of the newsreels. I'm thinking of the empty streets and the faces of the dead. How could I not be? It's what we're staring at, right now. It's where we are.

I'm panicking. This may not be a Silent City, but it's still an Icon. It can still kill us.

We all know that.

"There. Look." Lucas points to where the chain-link fence bends up into the brush. A hole, not big enough for him, but barely big enough for me. "You're the smallest. You can get through there. You can go around and let me in the front gate."

I shake my head in disbelief. "What? I'm not going to die for you."

"I'm not asking you to die for me."

"Look at those piles of bones. That's exactly what you're asking."

"No, I'm not. Look at me, look at us. Does it seem like anything's wrong?"

I stare at him.

"We're not tired. Our heads aren't aching. Our hearts aren't pounding erratically."

Speak for yourself. I notice, though, that Fortis is not looking well and is once again wiping the sweat from his forehead.

"Don't you get it? It doesn't affect us."

"That's impossible. The Icon affects everyone. That's the whole point of the Icon."

"We don't know that," Fortis says. "That's why we're here. Each brain is unique. Your brains seem to be—uniquely unique. You may not be affected in the same way as everyone else. At least, that's what I'm bankin' on. Fingers crossed." He holds them up, double crossed, even.

"What if Fortis is right?" Lucas looks at his hands. "What if we're the way into the Icon? Around the Icon?"

"You don't trust Fortis! You've never trusted Fortis. Look at those skeletons and then tell me you think Fortis is right—"

"Hey now. Be kind. I'm standin' right here." Fortis grins. Nothing I'm saying gets to him. Not even standing in the shadow of the Icon bothers Fortis, aside from a bit of sweat. It's like all this is a game.

"I don't know if Fortis is right, but I know something's going on. They're lying to us, the Embassy."

"Your mother."

"My mother. Especially her. She hid the records. She sealed off the secrets. We need to find out—whatever it is they don't want us to know."

"Is that why you came? To find out if the Icon can kill you or not? Or is it that maybe you just don't want to live anymore?"

"You tell me. Why did you follow me all the way out here?"

Then I understand what I have to do.

It isn't Lucas who has to know.

It's me.

The Padre.

My family.

My fate.

I have to find out for myself.

Why me?

Why am I here and what am I here to do?

What makes me an Icon Child?

Before anyone can say a word, I turn and throw myself through the hole at the bottom of the fence.

Which is where I lie on the ground in the dirt, waiting to die.

But I don't.

RESEARCH MEMORANDUM:
THE HUMANITY PROJECT

To: Ambassador Amare

Subject: Icon Children Origins

Subtopic: Research Notes

Catalogue Assignment: Evidence recovered during
   raid of Rebellion hideout
   Page torn from book
   Book title: *Brain Power: Unlocking the Energy Inside*
   Author: Paulo Fortissimo

INTRODUCTION

Energy is the foundation of life.

Energy controls, creates, changes, and destroys.

EXAMPLES

Radiation can kill, slowly or quickly. Infrared light can change a channel. Electromagnetic waves can be used to see inside your mind and body. Sound waves, like music or voice, can trigger emotions of sadness or joy. Light gives us vision and can generate untold feelings.

HUMANS ARE CONSTANTLY CREATING ENERGY.
Sound, shock, emotion. However, we are now discovering that the human brain has untapped potential to generate more power than we could have dreamed.

Locked away, we all have a nascent star inside us that can burn brighter than we can imagine.

We need only find the key.

THE OBSERVATORY

He must have begun moving before I hit the ground, because I'm not still for more than a second when he attacks.

The boy.

Lucas dives at him from one side, Fortis from the other. But they're too late. All I see is the knife.

Knives.

I scream and flail, kicking and punching as hard as I can. A moment later, the attacker rolls off me. A gleaming blade falls from his hand to the dirt.

"Madre de Dios!" I keep screaming. I can't stop.

"Dol!" Lucas starts toward the fence, but Fortis grabs him by the neck of his shirt, turning to me.

"Get a grip on yourself, love."

Fortis shuts me up. I hold my breath until I can swallow the screaming. My breath is coming fast and ragged, but I keep silent now.

The Sympa boy is heavy and motionless. Though his face is half hidden in the dirt, I can see his eyes have rolled back in his head. I push my face closer to his. He's not breathing. It's like his whole body has just stopped.

"I think he's dead."

"Anyone who passes through the fence is. That's what the Icon does to the rest of us," Fortis calls out to me, but as he does, he's moving away from the fence. Now his face is drawn tight, his eyes nervous. "Think I'd better stand back a bit."

I stare at the newly dead boy, lying halfway through the chain.

Lucas drags him by his boots until he is all the way out, on the other side of the fence. He yanks open the boy's jacket, feeling in his pockets. He pulls out a faded piece of paper, folded once. Before he can open it, Fortis quickly takes the paper and reads it.

"Apparently there's a price for you. Only a thousand digs? Cheap bastards. They're driving the whole Merk market down." Fortis looks disgusted. "Highway robbery, that's what that is."

"Fortis!"

"Right. He must have recognized you and thought he'd make a few digs."

"Who would put a price on my head?" Lucas reaches to take the paper, but Fortis waves him off. It disappears like everything else, in the voluminous folds of his long jacket.

"My guess is, it isn't the Ambassador behind it. More likely, she doesn't even know."

"What's that supposed to mean?" Lucas frowns.

"Nothing, yet. Except you need to remember Julius Caesar."

"How so?"

"It's never your enemies' senate you need to worry about. You're more likely to be stabbed in the back by your own."

"Great. I feel so much better." Lucas looks annoyed.

"You're welcome. But, all the same, I'll nose around some and tell you if anything turns up. I'd put my money on Catallus. He's a bit of a thug, I know that much."

Fortis wads up his handkerchief and shoves it back into his pocket. "Poor dead fool. He probably thought it was safe for him too, the moment Dol here crossed the fence." He backs away again, farther from where I stand. "Well, let's not waste any more time on this one. Time for you to go, both of you. I'm not joining you, thanks for asking. You need to see for yourself."

I can feel his brain working at light speed. *They can go inside*, he's thinking. *They can live inside the Icon. They're immune. It doesn't affect them.*

I feel it all, and my face twists into doubt.

Fortis looks at me, grinning. "Sorry about that. I forget, sometimes, who I'm dealin' with. That you can see into my mind clear as a crystal ball."

"It doesn't work like that. Not all the time."

"Fine. Then a nice, big glass one. Good and cracked a little, just like old Fortis himself."

"What does it mean, Fortis?" I look at him. I wish he would just be straight with us for once.

"What it means, I don't know." He doesn't slow down. "Maybe you can tell me when you get back. Off with you, now. Up the hill, my brave little Grassgirl." He motions to Lucas. "Let your friend 'round through the gate and get going."

"What do we do when we get up there?" I stare in the direction of the Icon, even though I can't see it. Not from here. From the looks of the incline, we will have a steep hike up to the top.

"I don't know." Lucas holds up his wrist, speaking into it. "Doc, do you have any idea of what we're looking for?"

Doc's voice is crackling; the connection is weak.

"Based on what we know, you should be able to locate a physical space approximating a control room, Lucas. A power source that connects throughout the building. Even if the technology is not based on Embassy specifications."

Fortis grabs Lucas's wrist and loosens the strap. "Old Hux is right, but he won't be able to help you much, not past here. Radio silence. Hazard of the Icon pulse."

"I've got it." Lucas yanks his wrist free and begins to unbuckle it himself. He presses a button on his wrist cuff and the air seems that much quieter.

Doc is gone.

Fortis slaps Lucas on the shoulder. "Remember. It's nothing from this world. Don't expect anything you see to look like anything you know."

"I said I've got it."

Lucas is as cross as I am; as I push open the gate from the inside, he nearly trips on an edge of old bone. "Watch out," I say, and he only glares. Our current situation is enough to put anyone in a foul mood.

But we don't stop. We can't. So we hike in silence until the empty houses finally give way to the steep canyon roads, and then roads become trails, and the trails become mountainside dirt. Everything twists in front of me until the city becomes the wild. Rotting remains of dense moss and fern overwhelm the dead trees on either side of the curving road. Now I understand how this Mossy Fern street got its name.

My head starts to pound.

Lucas points to the remnants of a wooden sign. Part of an arrow, and the letters ORY.

"There. The steepest incline, it must go to the Observatory."

"Lead the way."

He's right.

We're here, only I don't know what I'm looking at.

Through the empty parking lot, past the few outlines of rusted cars, there it is.

An observatory. People used to look into the heavens from here. Now the heavens have occupied it, and it observes us, visible for miles around. It reminds me of the Santa Catalina Presidio, almost, except the ocean doesn't stretch out in front of it, only a great lost city. I see the reason we are here, jutting up into the sky above the older building. The blackened metal of the Icon unfolds like an ominous shadow over everything else before us.

"Just keep walking," mutters Lucas. He sees it too.

I nod.

As we near the building, everything becomes darker, stranger, more damaged. The pounding in my head grows stronger. The building no longer looks like an observatory. It looks like an abandoned military plant.

We mount the cracked concrete stairs that lead to the central complex. The doors are chained shut. Lucas rattles them, but I don't waste my time.

I make my way around the side of the building, until I find myself on a concrete platform behind the Observatory, on the edge of the hill overlooking the sweep of the city.

The Hole.

I can see the wash of buildings, the white haze of horizon where they cling to each other in clusters that are nothing like anything found in nature. Shells of abandoned business centers rise up like ancient obelisks and arti-facts from a time that doesn't matter anymore. Closer to the hills beneath the Observatory, the pale sprawl gives way to curving hillsides of scrubby green trees and twist-ing dirt paths. I can see all the way from the mountains in the east to the water in the west.

Beyond that, I see the faint, jagged outline of Santa Catalina Island, only a brief disruption in the horizon.

I look at the Hole, all of it, and that's just what it is. A hole. I try to imagine it alive, free again from the constant fear of death.

I can't.

I can't escape the feeling that it's over, that this once-great city will never be anything again. Because as I stand here at the Observatory, the main thing I can observe is that the city is dying.

The Icon, the machine that pulses right behind me, is killing it—what was left of it to kill.

Like the dead houses on the way up the hill, only every-where, and worse.

"There you are."

Lucas has found me, but he's found something else, too. He stumbles backward, staring up at the sky.

I follow, turning reluctantly toward the Observatory.

Toward the Icon.

I half expect to see inhuman guards, shielded Sympa

298

soldiers, or maybe some alien tech that will keep us from entering. Then I remember that no humans could ever walk where I am standing, and that there is no way anyone operating the Icon would have planned for security here.

But when we get closer to the Icon, what I see is more frightening than any security system. The ground in front of us is completely covered with rubble. Partial walls rise into broken windows, as if an earthquake has hit the building. The front doors are wide open. One has fallen, the other hangs on its hinges.

"Easy enough." Lucas sighs, grim.

Neither one of us wants to go any farther.

But we do.

We walk straight toward the largest building of the central compound.

Lucas goes first, shaking his head as if he is trying to get something out of it. "Feel that?" A drop of blood slides down from the inside of his ear.

I nod. Because my entire body is trembling—even my heart is vibrating. It's all we can do to stay on our feet. No one can tolerate the energy this close to the Icon.

Not even us.

"We shouldn't be here, Lucas," I say, reaching toward his ear. He pulls his head away.

"Yeah. Neither should this."

He takes my hand and I let him.

"Let's look for the brain and get out of here, Dol."

We step inside.

The Icon has destroyed what used to be the Observatory.

What we see now looks like only part of the Icon—the part we can see from inside—but even this much is completely intimidating.

It's hard and sharp, metallic and silvery black.

The surface appears to pulsate, almost like a liquid, swirling and flowing in complex patterns.

I don't dare touch it.

The thing is like a jagged spike from a giant claw.

Long, protruding tubes like fingers run in and out of the building. The main part of the Icon body is long and broad and covered with nodes, a vertical strip of massive, circular steel rings. It's ironic; this part of the Icon, whatever it is, is the only thing that seems to be alive in the entire park.

The machine—I don't really know what else to call it—looks nothing like what I have seen from any distance, through any telescope. What can be seen from outside is just the shell. What we stand looking at remains hidden from the world, but more powerful than anything else in it.

It's not just the brains we've found. It has its own sort of heart, I think. We stand there watching it beat, feeling it pulse. Lucas raises his hand to his forehead. I feel it too, the strange energy coming from the Icon. I feel it probing at me, pounding at me, attacking me.

The power is incredible.

The power it has to stop everything that keeps me alive. It pounds out a rhythm like a heartbeat.

Something's there—deep in the center of this Icon. Something alive. Something powerful. Something that exists solely to kill.

I bring my hand to my chest to feel my heart banging inside.

Yes.

I close my eyes and remember the Padre and Ramona, and see the tiniest details.

Remember.

I know the Icon wants to control every pulse in my body, but I also feel something inside myself that pushes back against it.

My heart is not going to stop today.

I reach out in my mind and hold on to Lucas, next to me. Hand in hand, heart to heart.

He is frightened too, but we can't stop here, having come this far.

We pick our way through the debris and the wiring. The building is in ruins; the Icon tech has ravaged the old structure. Finally we agree we've seen enough, and it's time to go.

By the time we make our way outside, we see that the

walls of the Observatory aren't strong enough to tolerate too much fusion, and the concrete blocks have crumbled under the grip of the Icon.

Like a hand on a throat, I think.

"Look." Lucas points. "This thing has roots."

It's true. All around us, bits of black metal poke up from the cracked concrete. *There is so much more than we can see*, I think, as my head pounds.

Who knows where it ends?

Just then, my foot catches on something in the rubble, and I stumble. It's hard and metal, and when I bend to pick it up, it's cool in my hand. I'm already holding it when it occurs to me that it's a piece of the Icon. It vibrates, radiates its own kind of energy.

A breath. Or a pulse.

"Lucas?"

Lucas looks over at me. "Is that what I think it is?"

"This must have broken off when it landed."

I turn to throw it over the wall, out into the sea of dead city below. Then I stop. I can't bring myself to throw it away. Not after feeling it the way I do.

Which makes no sense, I know. The only thing the Icon has ever brought is death.

I should hate it.

Instead, I'm drawn to it.

"Dol? What are you doing with that thing? Get rid of it."

I can't. I don't want to.

I shrug. "Who knows? Maybe Doc can use it to figure something out. Maybe it will help." I force myself to drop the shard into my chestpack.

"Help what?" Lucas leans against the wall next to me. I look around.

"What Fortis is planning. To shut this place down, or blow it up? Whatever does the trick, I guess. You heard him."

When I turn his way, I see the wildness in Lucas's eyes. "Dol. Look around you. You really think you can just find the on or off switch for an Icon? You think you or Fortis or Ro or anyone can just blow it up?"

I stare at him, confused. "Isn't that the point? Why we're here?"

"Are you really that—"

"What, Lucas?"

"Stupid?"

I snort, but he keeps going. "You actually want to listen to Fortis now? Jump on the Rebellion's cause? Just forget about the fact of the Embassy, the Sympas, the weapons, the House of Lords—everything and everyone who controls the world we happen to be living in?"

Sympas. I've never heard him use the Grass word before.

"Lucas. If that's not what you want, then what are we doing here? In the Hole? At the Icon?"

"Isn't it obvious? I brought you here to show you how

303

crazy it was. To prove to you we couldn't win. To end it, Dol." He looks at me, sadly. "I just want it to end."

I know he does. But when I look at the Icon, in all its ugliness, I know he's also wrong.

"This isn't how it ends," I say. "Our story. Whatever it is."

"It could be. We could find a way."

I shake my head.

"We can't."

"What if Fortis is lying?"

"He isn't. You know he isn't. Besides, look around. This isn't a lie." I turn my back on the city, facing the Observatory now. Lucas doesn't. He closes his eyes to all of it.

"No. This is a nightmare."

"And it's not just Fortis. It's Doc, too. You have to trust Doc."

As I stare up at the Icon, I'm struck by how strange it is. That a machine has helped me find my way here, to where a machine has taken over our city.

Lucas's jaw is set. He shakes his head. "Fortis is not friends with Doc. Doc's a computer program. Nobody is friends with Doc."

"That's not true. You are."

Now we're both staring out at the city. Lucas is silent, so I say it again.

"You've known him since you were little—you said so yourself."

"That doesn't mean I'm going to blow up the Icon, just because some crazy Merk thinks it's a good idea."

"He's not a Merk. And that's not why you're going to do it."

"Yeah? Tell me. Why am I?"

"Because you can. We can."

"Stop."

"Only us. That has to mean something."

The whine of the Icon seems to grow louder and louder, the longer we stay there. Soon I will not be able to stand it.

"Does it?"

He's thinking, but I already know the answer. Or at least, the question.

What means something?

Of everything I have seen today, what matters?

I close my eyes and the fortune-teller enters my mind, unbidden. I can feel the jade figures in my bag. I try to remember what he said.

There's a girl, I think. *He said I have to find her. I'm not the important one. She is. But how can I do that? I can't even do this.*

Then I remember the gold cross, the one that belonged to my mother. The one the Ambassador pressed into my hand.

You lived so you can pay the debt.

I know why I'm here, even if Lucas doesn't.

I'd tell him, but the noise from the Icon is making it

impossible to think, and it's all I can do to grab his hand and pull him back toward the downhill trail.

This—all of it—is more than one person can bear, in one day.

More than I can bear.

There is so much to do, I think, *and no one else to do it.* It's not the way I wish it was, but the way it is.

We have to be strong.

My parents are dead. Our city is dying. This is about so much more than us.

RESEARCH MEMORANDUM: THE HUMANITY PROJECT

CLASSIFIED TOP SECRET / AMBASSADOR EYES ONLY

To: Ambassador Amare

Subject: Paulo Fortissimo, aka Fortis

Education: Doctorates from MIT and Columbia in astrophysics, neurology, genetics, and artificial intelligence.

Author of *Higher Power: Unleashing the Energy of Emotion.*

Special Scientific Advisor, US Department of Defense, through four presidential administrations, 2040–2056.

Special appointee to UN Commission on Near Earth Objects, instrumental in the detection and planning of response to NEO Perses.

Purported mastermind and author of research regarding Icon Children.

Location: Unknown.

Affiliation: Uncertain, but is known enemy of Occupation Government.

Highly dangerous.

Note: Standing Embassy order is to kill on sight.

By the time we reach the bottom of the hill, my heart is aching, my head is throbbing, my ears are bloody and ringing—and Fortis is gone.

"That Merk bastard." Lucas is furious and so am I. My book—my secrets—have disappeared with him, for now. At least he's left Lucas's cuff hanging on the fence.

Lucas points up at the sky, though, and then I hear it. Freeley is landing, well beyond the gates. The air churns violently in the deserted street, the noise growing so loud I clap my hands over my ears. The Chopper blows dead brush up around us, and I don't look to see what new bones have been uncovered.

"Doc must have given him the coordinates," Lucas

shouts over the noise of the engine, as we slip back beyond the fence.

Moments later, the Chopper doors slam shut behind me, and we pull up and away from Griff Park. I begin to shake—so strong is the surge of relief, and so exhausting was it to feel the Icon, all around me.

I see Lucas close his eyes in his seat, and know he feels it too. The release. The space.

Reluctantly, the Icon lets go of us—it doesn't want to, I can feel that much—and we climb up into the sky like one last lucky bird.

Freeley gets us home quickly, almost more quickly than I want him to.

Ro is watching when the helicopter lands. The closer we get to him, the better I can feel him. He is so much more than angry.

Lucas acts like he doesn't see him. Once again, Lucas and I have reached an impasse. We don't have the book, though we know Fortis does. We don't have a plan, though it seems both the Rebellion and the Embassy do. We can't fully comprehend the meaning of the things we've seen. Or those we haven't.

But.

Though the events of the day have been overwhelming and inconclusive, Lucas and I have shared them. They have sent us both into silence and hiding—from each other, from decisions, from what we must do and who we must trust—but that, too, is something we share.

He doesn't know what to think about me, any more than I know what to think about him. But for now, how we feel is totally beside the point. How Ro feels is what matters to me, and as the Chopper nears him—and the Embassy—I feel every bit of it.

He's hurt and he wishes I were hurt, too. I've never felt that from him, not Ro who would kill anyone who thought about hurting me. Things are changing between us. Maybe things have already changed. I close my eyes. I wish I could tell him. I wish I could make him understand the mess of feelings inside me. I wish I understood them, myself.

The Chopper lowers itself toward the barren concrete of the landing strip—Ro looms larger and larger—and I know there is no escaping what comes next.

I left him.

As always, in the right and wrong and good and bad world of Ro, there are no degrees to my decision. I prepare myself accordingly. I tell myself it will pass, like it always does. But it isn't true, not anymore. At least, I can't be sure.

When the helicopter finally touches down at the Embassy landing pad, he's gone.

The blades are still turning when I am up the steps and heading for the Embassy doors. Lucas has to run to keep up.

I'm not surprised when Lucas charms our way past the front entrance to the Embassy compound—but Ro's not inside the door, as I hoped he would be. The Sympa guards are there, however, so our day's adventure comes to a swift halt. Ro's not in any of the hallways I am marched through—also not in Examination Facility #9B, once my Sympa detail has locked me inside. I realize, all at once, that I may not be able to fix things with Ro, and I think how much has changed since we left the Mission.

I have to find him.

After my third try with the lock, I slump against my door. Then it occurs to me that there are easier ways to open doors now at my disposal. "Doc? Are you there?"

"Yes, Doloria."

"Can you open the door for me, Doc?"

"Of course I can."

I scramble to my feet, waiting in silence. Nothing happens. I sigh. "Doc. What I meant was, *will you* open my door?"

"I suggest amending your speech patterns to say what you mean—" The bolt reverses itself obligingly.

"Next time, Doc." I'm out the door before he can finish scolding me.

There are no guards posted outside my door—one of the benefits, I imagine, of being considered safely locked in a room. I've learned how to dodge patrols all the way to the library, but when I get there, Ro's not there. I don't find him in the glass prison classroom either, though Tima's there, and she manages to simultaneously not look up from her digi-text and yet still glare at me. I sneak up the back stairwell to the catwalk at the Presidio, but there is no sign of him. It's only when I reach the far end of the catwalk that I spy Ro sitting on the rocky shoreline.

I make my way down to him—once again, exactly as Tima has taught me—staying clear of the guards, keeping my head down, changing stairwells three times until I find the one that connects to the small strip of land behind the Presidio wing of the Embassy. The door slams shut behind me, but the wind is so loud Ro doesn't know I'm there.

The air whips all around us, as violently as if we were standing next to the helicopter.

It's not the wind; it's Ro. This is how it goes with him. It starts inside him until he can't contain it. Then it spreads, the red heat, first to the people nearest him, then farther. When the adrenaline pounds, he's so strong he could rip a steel girder in half.

That's also when he's chemically, electromagnetically insane.

I push the burning waves away, though they surge at me, pressing in on me.

I sit down next to him. He says nothing.

"I'm sorry." It's all I can say.

"Doc said the Sympas were shooting at you. I thought you were dead."

"But we weren't. Doc should have told you. When we were safe."

I see his hands. They're red and scarred. Burned, bruised marks in his own palms, from his own fists. I've hurt him.

No.

He's hurt himself.

That's what the Padre would say. Try to find the place where Ro ends and you begin. You are two people. You aren't the same person.

We aren't. I know we aren't, but it's hard for me to remember, because I feel everything he feels, more than I feel everyone else in the world. Maybe everyone else in the world, combined.

Two people. I say it to myself.

Not one.

Two.

But the Padre knows—knew—with Ro and me, it's more complicated than that.

314

Now all I can do is reassure him. "I was fine. You couldn't have done anything."

"That's the point. I couldn't do anything. I can't protect you from him." The idea is almost funny.

"Him? Lucas? You don't need to protect me from Lucas."

"You're right. I don't need to protect you from someone who takes you with him into the Hole and gets you shot at and whatever other trouble you were into today."

I steal a look out the corner of my eye, improvising my story as I go along.

"He seemed so upset. I only meant to go find him and talk to him. I thought I could convince him to come back into the library. Try again to figure out what was going on with the missing data. But Lucas practically ran straight into a helicopter, and before I knew it we were in the air..."

It's a lie, not one of my better ones, and we both know it.

"Tima's feelings are pretty hurt. She thinks you're going after Lucas. I don't know if you've noticed, but she..." He shrugs.

"Hard not to notice that." Her eyes never leave him. He's all she seems to think about, other than terrible disasters. Yeah, I noticed. But for Ro to see it too, that's really saying something.

He must be angrier than I thought.

"So." The word comes out evenly, with all the force of the other words, the words he won't say.

"So what?"

"Do you?"

"Do I what?"

"You and Lucas."

Ro's face is red and I stare at it as I have for years, even though he won't look at me. I try to decide if his face is getting redder. It's a sign, either way. How I know what I need to do or say.

But my pride has gotten the better of me, and I feel like I have to defend myself. "*Lucas Amare?* Love? Everyone on Earth loves him."

"So that's a yes." Ro scoops up a handful of rocks, throwing one out into the churning tides. The water is already so rough I can't see anything like a splash.

"Ro. It's not all like that. People follow him and shoot at him. Lucas is not exactly a person a girl can..." I sigh, because as I speak I realize it's the truth. "Not me, not Tima."

"Still not an answer."

I take a rock out of his hand and hurl it into the water myself. I'm furious. I can't speak, I can only shout. "We didn't do anything. There. Are you happy? Now it's my turn. Here's a question for you, Ro. Since when did you become such an ass?"

Now he looks at me. Finally. When he does, his face is so open I wish he hadn't. "Since I fell in love with a girl named Sorrow, I guess. Should have seen that one coming."

There.

He said it.

Love.

He loves me.

It's out now, in the wind and the water and on the shore in front of us. And now that he has said the words, I see it, coming from him in waves that are as real and as violent as the ones in front of us that crash against the rocks, over and over again.

It's red and pounding, distinctly Ro, but it's something new.

It's love.

He's telling the truth. He isn't confused. It isn't what he's always felt for me. Ro is changing.

"Doloria."

He holds out his hand for mine.

"I need you." His voice breaks as he says it. "Please—"

He leans toward me, bringing his face to mine. His hunger for me is overwhelming. Everything he wants wraps around me, a great cloud of Ro. A cloud of fury, like his name. A cloud of speed and sweat and grass and heat. And then—beneath it all—affection. Steady and real. The deepest, truest beating of his heart.

"Dol."

For a moment, I forget to breathe and I feel dizzy. Like my legs could buckle and drop me to the rocks. I could drown in the waves. I could lose everything.

But I let go.

I lift my mouth to his.

We kiss.

It begins as small as everything does, but it isn't enough. He isn't satisfied. The heat is raging inside him, and I feel like I will burn up and dissolve into ash. I'm turning cold, even though I'm burning.

His hands fall on my shoulders, slide down my arms. He tugs at my binding.

My fingers curl into a fist. I know he needs me. I know I calm him and soothe him and even, in a way, complete him. But my arm is frozen. My arm is ice.

Ro pulls his mouth away from mine. He doesn't take his eyes off me. I feel him fumbling at my binding. His fingers don't seem to work, and he pulls harder. He yanks the muslin loose, frustrated.

I look away from him just as the white fabric flutters to the rocks below us.

"Dol."

He pulls me closer to him. I try to let him take me back. I feel like a doll, like a thing.

I can't.

I can't bind with him, not like this. Not when it means

something more than our shared kitchen floor, our Mission childhood, our Grass brotherhood.

I don't know enough about how I feel. I don't know anything about myself. I only know I can't bind with Lucas and I can't bind with Ro. Even though there's part of me that wants to give myself to both of them.

What's wrong with me?

I shake my head.

"I can't."

It doesn't make anything easier. The red rage isn't gone. Neither is the love. Nothing's gone.

"Ro. I'm sorry. I shouldn't have let you kiss me."

"You feel it too. Don't pretend like you don't."

"I don't know how I feel."

"But I do. You're just afraid. You don't want to get hurt. You think if you love someone they'll leave. That I'll go and you'll be alone."

"Yes." It's true. I won't deny it.

"But I'm here. I stayed. I'm the one who stayed."

"Maybe I want everything to be the same."

"Look around, Dol. People are dying. The whole planet is dying. Nothing is the same."

"I know. That's why I'm so confused."

He looks away. Then he sighs, and picks up my binding from the rocks. Hands me the dirty fabric.

"Whatever."

I love Ro, I always have. We love each other, which is also something he knows.

But it doesn't seem like I should be reminding him of that right now. And that isn't what he means, anyway.

I begin to bind my arm. I want to tie off everything. How I feel, how he feels. I don't want any of it.

I knot the strip of muslin so hard I think the blood won't reach my hand. Maybe it's better that way.

"Let's get out of here," Ro says, chucking the last of the rocks. He watches it fly out at the waves. It's not the peaceful ocean of our Mission beach, up the Tracks by La Purísima. This water is pounding and restless and as chaotic as the Hole itself. As angry as Ro. As complicated as Lucas. As confused as me.

"Like I said, I'm sorry."

It's not what he wants to hear, and I'm sorry for that too. His face looks dark, and he sighs, shaking his head.

"It doesn't matter." Another lie. He begins the short walk up the shoreline, and I scramble after him.

"Did you figure anything out in the Hole, at least? Or was it all just fun and games, except for the getting shot at part?"

By the time we make it back to the medical wing, I've told him everything. About the Icon. About how it killed the boy, and not me. And not Lucas. How we hiked up to it, and what we saw.

About Doc and Hux and Fortis and the Rebellion.

"So there is something we can do." He stares up at the sky, the soaring top of the Presidio, thinking. "We've got to tell Tima. She'll know what we need. And maybe she has access to information we can use to hit it."

"Hit what?"

He looks at me like I'm stupid.

"For the first time in our lives, we can do something to actually help ourselves. To help everyone."

"We have to be careful, Ro. There are only four of us."

"Three. There's only three of us."

"What?"

"You're a fool if you think Lucas is going to help us blow his mommy's job right out of the sky."

"You don't know Lucas."

He looks at me, incredulous. "Lucas doesn't matter anymore. None of the Brass do. This is a Grass thing. I wish I was back at the Mission. I know a few people who could help."

"We don't even know if there still is a Mission." My heart twists as I think of Bigger and Biggest, left behind.

"It doesn't matter. This is our chance, Dol. We may never get another one. We have to do something. I'd get off this rock right now, except what I need might actually be here."

His eyes are flinty, hard as steel. Not a brown-gold fleck in sight. He's finally started to listen to the sound of his own angry voice. He's forgotten about his heart.

The Grassboy who loves the Grassgirl goes out with the tides. The Grass Revolutionary comes in with them.

Perhaps there is something more frightening than love, after all.

RESEARCH MEMORANDUM: THE HUMANITY PROJECT

CLASSIFIED TOP SECRET / AMBASSADOR EYES ONLY

To: Ambassador Amare

Subject: Lords/Icon Origins

Catalogue Assignment: Evidence recovered during
   raid of Rebellion hideout

Handwritten notes transcribed as follows:

DECRYPTED/DECODED SIGNAL FROM INCOMING ASTEROID
(UNKNOWN OBJECT 2042 /C4):

...

TARGET SCAN COMPLETE...

ADVANCED CIVILIZATION DETECTED

TECHNOLOGY STATUS...15.3X-B

INITIATE PURIFICATION PROTOCOL 1.334AXS39

TARGETS SELECTED...13

PURIFICATION COMPLETE IN 66 TPU

CONTACT ATTEMPTS INITIATED

...

CONTACT IS POSSIBLE...

WHAT IS "PURIFICATION"??

...WHAT DO THEY WANT?

TIMA

At dinner that night, the four of us can barely face each other.

Tima isn't speaking to Lucas or me. Ro isn't speaking to Lucas. Lucas isn't speaking to me. I'm not speaking to him. To make matters worse, Colonel Catallus is walking toward us. As if that wouldn't immediately kill all of our appetites.

Lovely.

"Do you want to tell them what we found today?" Ro looks at Tima as he shoves most of an apple into his mouth. "After they ran off and left us?"

"Ro," I say. "Quiet."

There is nothing Ro can say in front of Colonel Catallus.

We aren't free to talk here. He knows that.

Lucas glares at Ro.

"Not really." Tima puts down her fork. Her plate is untouched.

Colonel Catallus gives the four of us a withering look, positioning himself at our table, next to Lucas.

"I hear you left the compound today, Lucas." He picks up a sharp knife and stabs into a slice of meat drowning in pale gravy. "You too, Doloria. Though I have to say, I was surprised to see you take the same liberties as Mr. Amare. Not having the same—should we say, *protections*—in place that he does."

A threat. Of course.

When he eats, I hear his lips smacking and his teeth clicking. I want to tell him to eat with his hands. It would be more civilized.

"Speaking of which, have you discussed your little adventure this afternoon with the Ambassador, Lucas?"

"Should I?"

"Immediately. Did you not see any of my messages?"

Lucas holds up his leather-bound wrist, wearily. "As if I'd dare take off my handcuffs. You'd send the whole Sympa Guard after me."

Colonel Catallus doesn't smile. His mouth is pressed into a thin, watery line. "She's been trying to speak with you all evening."

325

"Funny. You found me easy enough."

"Lucas, please."

"I'm not pleased. But I am here if she wants me." He's as cranky as Ro today.

"She's terribly worried, not that I blame her. I can't imagine any mother being happy to hear her only son ran away to the Embassy City, only to be fired on by Grass Rebels."

I almost choke on my bread. Is it true? Is that who was shooting at us?

Colonel Catallus shakes his head in my direction. He's not interested in me, not now. Not in the same way he is in Lucas.

I look again to the medals and ribbons on his jacket. The shiny gold wings on his lapel catch the light.

Ro sets down his mug. "They weren't Grass." He looks at Colonel Catallus, who glares at him.

"I'm glad you have us to be worried about your safety, Furo. That's why I'm having you escorted to your rooms, as soon as you've eaten. Nobody leaves their quarters until we get to the bottom of today's little incident." He smiles at all of us, cold as winter. "Is that clear? Because I've also got a few rooms set aside for you in the Pen, if you'd feel more secure there."

Prison. Another threat.

With that, Colonel Catallus leaves us to sulk in peace.

Tima folds her napkin and lays it on the table in front of her. "Ro, do you want to go up to my room after dinner? I'm sure no one would mind, seeing as we're not the ones in trouble here."

Ro stops midway through shoving half a baked potato into his mouth. "Me? With you? What did I do now?"

"Nothing. I thought we could hang out, get to know each other better. Since we had so much fun alone together, today." Tima attempts to flutter her eyelids, but it only looks like she's gotten a cinder in her eye. "And I say that to imply touching, in case it wasn't perfectly clear."

She twists her legs, and I see that she's stitched a seam up the back of each calf. It looks like she is wearing stockings. The stitches are precise, each one like a small staple. Red and white and yellow and green. The new tattoo makes me wonder.

Tima's losing her mind.

Ro tries not to laugh at the awkwardness of the question.

"Okay." He'd never touch her, not like that—and not for those reasons. But Lucas doesn't know that, and I guess Ro doesn't mind letting him think it.

"Tima—" Lucas starts. She cuts him off.

"Great. Let's go. We can talk. And I say that to imply, you know. Not talking." She stands up to go.

"Sit down." Lucas tries again. She won't.

Ro looks from me to Tima. "Sure. We can *talk*. I'd like that." He grins and stands too, wadding up his napkin and letting it drop onto his plate.

I shake my head. Lucas looks disgusted. "Come on, T. I said I was sorry."

She ignores him. They disappear out of the room.

"Well?" I look at Lucas.

"Well what?" He shrugs.

"We have to go after them."

"Already thought of that. Doc?"

"Yes, Lucas?"

"Lock Tima's personal quarters, will you? I'm afraid I've left something toxic inside, and I need to warn her." Lucas sighs and I try not to smile.

"Commencing room-scan for toxins."

"No, no. It's nothing that will show up on a scan, Doc. It's—a different kind of poison. Something new. Insidious." His mouth twists and I begin to think he is enjoying himself.

"I understand. Does this poison have a name, Lucas? I should file it in the Catalogue and Compendium of Toxins, in the Embassy Wik."

"Yes. It's called...*Amici Nex*." Lucas looks at me, arching one eyebrow. "And it's a real pain in the ass."

Doc's voice returns. "I see. The Death of the Friend. It is a strange name, is it not? Not at all like the others. *Oleandrin. Nerine. Nitriles. Isocyanides. Methanidiol.*"

328

"I know. It's really not like anything else. It gets you when you least expect it, and it's positively lethal."

Silence. Then, the grating rattles as Doc's voice returns.

"The plexi-door is sealed. I have placed a Classified level ten clearance on the entry. Would you like me to alert Timora?"

"No, let me. Thanks, Doc. You're a real lifesaver."

"Given Timora's natural sensitivity to risk, I understand this will be quite upsetting. Please proceed with caution, Lucas."

"I always do." He stands up, motioning to me. "You coming?"

I look at the row of Sympa soldiers standing by the door. "Sure. Me and your mother's army."

———— • ————

Lucas and I—and at least five soldiers—detour toward Tima's room on the way to our own. We can hear the screaming from the stairwell, two floors away. When we reach the hallway, I see through a window in the door that Tima and Ro are standing outside Tima's room, while she stares up at the ceiling in exasperation.

Lucas doesn't move from the stairwell. Instead, he turns to face the guards. "Leave us." He speaks slowly and clearly, with a low, steady voice. "Five minutes. That's exactly how long we'll be out here. Then you can tell anyone who asks that we're in our rooms. All four of us."

I can't bear to watch Lucas as he focuses his eyes on the Sympas. His pupils begin to dilate, and I have to look away when I feel the familiar warm pull.

Now that I know what it costs him, it's hard to watch.

"You can swear you've locked us up and thrown away the key. Because you will have. You know it's true." I catch one last glimpse of his dazzling Lucas-smile. "Have I made myself clear? Any questions?"

Nobody has any. Nobody ever does.

We catch up to Tima and Ro as soon as the Sympas are gone. I'm not sure either one of them saw Lucas dispose of the guards, and I don't tell them. Having to do it bothers him enough. Having to talk about it, that's nearly as bad.

"*Amici Nex*? There is *no such thing*, Orwell." Tima slams against her own door.

"It is not a common toxin, Timora. It is new. You may not have heard of it yet."

"It's a joke. A bad joke about a fight between friends. Between Lucas and me, Orwell." Tima is shrieking. Doc says nothing. She shouts louder. "How can you be so stupid?"

"Strictly speaking, I would have to note that my intelligence is artificial but unlimited."

I hear barking from the other side of the door.

"Just let me into my room."

"I am afraid you do not have the security clearance to make such a demand, Timora."

"Orwell! I'm going to kill you!"

"That is not possible."

"It is. I will find a way to do it, if it means I have to erase every drive in the Embassy Wik. You know I will. So let me into my room, now!"

Ro is trying not to laugh, leaning against the side of the door. When Tima sees us, she turns and pounds on her door again.

"Doc. I can take care of things from here." Lucas smiles.

"Would you like a hazmat team to meet you at the room, Lucas?"

"That won't be necessary."

There is a long pause before the round grating in the wall rattles again. "Was this in fact a joke, then?"

"Something like that." Lucas winks at Tima. She punches the door, one last time.

"Was I sufficiently funny?"

I smile up at the grating. "Very. You were the funniest of all, Doc."

The door slides open, and Tima lunges toward it. I see a glimpse of her room—of action figures and old comic book covers and games. Miniature tanks and tiny toy soldiers.

Brutus, her dog, comes bounding out into the hall and into Tima's arms, licking her face.

"If you liked that joke, I have an even better one." And with that, the door slides shut and locks itself again. "Now try your own doors. All of you." Doc sounds pleased.

"We're screwed." Lucas shakes his head.

"Screwed but alone," Tima points out, though she never takes her eyes off her dog. "Probably for the last time in a while, after the stunt you and—you two—pulled today." She won't say my name.

I sigh.

"Did anything really happen today, when we were gone?" Lucas asks her directly now, because in all the chaos, she has forgotten to ignore us.

"No," says Ro.

"Yes, actually." Tima looks at Ro. "That's what I was going to tell you, when you came up to my room."

"Really, because I thought you said we'd be doing something else. Other than talking." Ro is teasing her, but she shuts him down with a look. That kind of look, she's good at.

"Since I got here, I've spent a lot of time in the library. I've read literally thousands of digi-texts on computers, and how they work. It's sort of amazing—did you know there is actually a language designed just to communicate with computers, to tell them what to do? Imagine if it were that easy to communicate with people."

"It is. It's called words." Ro rolls his eyes. She pinches him in the arm until he yelps.

"Tima?" Lucas is impatient, shoving his hands through his hair. His nervous habit.

"Sorry. My point is, I've figured out how the Embassy computers work, how they're connected, and where things are stored. Classified things."

"As in?" I nudge her.

She looks at Lucas, embarrassed. "I should have told you, but I didn't want the Ambassador to find out. It's how I get around the guard patrols. I found a way into the security logs."

Lucas raises an eyebrow. Tima keeps talking.

"It's this thing, where people used to break into private computers and look at encrypted information. They called it 'hacking.' Anyway, I used hacking to access things I'm not supposed to see. We're not supposed to see."

Ro snaps back to attention. "So what did you see?"

"Not as much as I'd like. I used Catallus's terminal to look around in his encrypted files, but I only had a few minutes and didn't get too far."

Lucas explodes. "You used Catallus's private digi? Are you insane? Do you know what he would have done to you if he'd found out?"

"Yes. And I don't want to think about it. But I found something. Well, to be more accurate, I read something. About us. And the Lords."

"What thing?" Lucas asks.

I look at her. "Tima?" The energy is rising around us.

My face is growing flushed—but so is hers.

"Not so fast." She takes a breath. "I also went back to the Hall of Records."

"How?" I think of the Sympas in the stairwell.

"Orwell and I did. When I asked, he said it was time, and he took me. Opened every door."

"Where was I during your little recon mission?" Ro looks insulted.

"You went to your room to mope." Now she finally glares at me. "Ro's horrible, you know. When you aren't around. I don't know how he exists in the world."

Ro turns red. "That's not tr—"

She cuts him off. "Anyway, I think I figured it out."

"What," Lucas asks.

"It. Everything." Tima looks smug.

I can't stand it. "Go on."

She tries to play it cool but I can tell she's excited. "I could tell you, but I might as well show you. You're not going to believe this." She looks at Lucas. "But everything is in my room. Can you tell Doc to let us back in?"

Lucas sighs, and thinks for a moment. "Doc?"

"Yes, Lucas?"

"I need to get into Tima's room now. There's a book of jokes I wanted you to have. I left it inside."

Nothing happens. Doc is wising up, I think.

"A hundred and one jokes," Lucas adds.

Still nothing. Lucas sighs.

"A thousand and one."

The door slides open, almost begrudgingly.

Tima runs back into her room, and all anyone can do now is follow.

Brutus the dog, last of all.

EMBASSY TELEGRAM

MESSAGE MARKED CRITICAL
CLASSIFIED TOP SECRET
AMBASSADOR EYES ONLY

From: General Ambassador to the Planet Miyazawa
To: Ambassador Amare, Los Angeles Icon

Leta,

I received your messages regarding the purported Icon Children. Understand you have identified four possible candidates.

It is imperative that you maintain close supervision without raising alarm.

Test. Verify. Then reverify.

Most important: tell nobody. This must remain between us. If the opposition finds out, we will have a full-scale uprising.

If the Lords find out who and what they are, and what they can do—God help us all.

—M

26

LUCAS

The door slides shut, and I look around Tima's room. I notice the familiar circular gratings, but they are pulled out, wires dangling.

Tima follows my look with a shrug. "I don't like people, or machines, listening in on me."

"Agreed." Ro nods, approving.

"Anyway, we can talk here."

"So talk," Lucas says, evenly. He doesn't want to hear another word, but he can't admit that. Not to us.

She shoots him a hurt look. "I am. I mean, I will. Listen to this—our birthdays are the same day because we were all cooked up in the same lab, on the same day." Tima grabs a Wik drive, quivering with a heady mix of fear and excitement.

Brutus licks her hand, and she scratches his ears.

"And based on this new bit of research I've so cleverly uncovered—not by moping, I might add, or by showing off for some girl"—she pauses to glare at all of us—"I've made a few educated guesses about why we're all here. Why we're all different. I think we share a lot more than a birthday."

We sit on the floor, and a silver digi is laid open between us. Four more sit in a stack, nearby.

"Wait, back up. Did you say cooked? You mean, from the flesh market?" Ro is the one who speaks.

"I can't believe we didn't think of it before. It explains everything, at least about our birthday. We're from the same cycle in the lab."

"Not me," says Ro. "I don't have your birthday."

"At least, not so you know. But there's a Costas on the receipt, I'll show you."

She jams a drive into a vid-screen. Immediately, text flashes, and she begins to scroll rapidly as she speaks. The words are flying by.

"I don't know why the full lab report is missing. The Wik doesn't give a reason."

"Of course it's missing," says Lucas, dully. He looks exhausted, like he already knows he doesn't want to hear anything Tima is about to say.

"But I did find a form ordering payment to our parents. Wandi and Ruther Costas." She looks at Ro. "Maria Margarita and Felipe de la Cruz." She looks at me. "Peter and Lia Li—those are my parents," she says, glancing up. "And one Leta Amare. I think we all know who that is."

Brutus barks.

"We're a science experiment? Some kind of—research?" Ro's head is in his hands, as if he were trying to keep it from exploding. "I'm just another piece of Sympatech?"

"No, not Sympatech." Tima says the words slowly. "Human tech." She looks around. Waiting.

Lucas gets there first.

"It can't be Sympa. We were all born a year *before* the Lords came," he says, quietly.

Slowly, the implications of the truth begin to unfold, for all of us. "Which means somebody knew what was going to happen, before it all happened." I almost can't believe the words coming out of my own mouth.

"Someone knew the bastards were coming." Ro whistles.

Tima continues. "There's more. When I searched Catallus's files, I found something. It looked like Catallus's private stash. There was a big section called 'Icon Children.' Since they were all labeled 'Ambassador Eyes Only,' I'm guessing he stole them. There were a lot of files, and I only had time to copy a few. About us. And the Lords." She holds up a portable drive and plugs it into the vid-screen.

I find myself forgetting to breathe.

"Some of the files are tagged as though they were scans of pages from what I think is the book Dol lost. If it is, she's right, it was some sort of a notebook."

Tima zooms through a few pages. I see what looks like scribblings written by some kind of mad scientist, with blotches and sketches and things I can't understand.

"This is really high-level research, way beyond anything I've studied. Math formulas, electrical schematics, genetic code, a lot of rambling on about DNA."

"Okay, now you're just talking gibberish." Ro shakes his head.

"Fine, let me keep it simple. For Furo." She sighs and clears the screen. "Somebody really did figure out the Lords were coming. They also learned about the Icons and what they could do." She pulls up a file. "Look at this. As far as I can tell, these are transcriptions of communications from the Lords. To somebody on Earth. *Before* they arrived."

Lucas looks closer. "What? How would that even be possible? The Day was a surprise attack. Nobody knew what was happening before it was too late."

Tima shakes her head. "I don't know, I didn't have time to read all the files. But this looks like somebody actually *communicated* with the Lords and decided to help them."

Ro leans forward, a grim look on his face. "Who? Catallus?"

"It doesn't say. Whoever wrote these notes also knew a lot about how the brain works. You know how the Icon can kill people and shut down everything around it? Look here." She scrolls to a new image. "It says that with a little help, people could do the same thing. Or, actually, the opposite thing. And I think that's what we are."

"So we're some kind of anti-Icon?" Ro looks up when I say the words.

Tima nods. "Whoever knew the Lords were coming, figured out how to design people who were not only immune to the Icons, but who could cancel them out."

"That's impossible." Lucas's face has turned ashen.

"Insane," says Ro, shaking his head.

"You mean, it's incredible." Tima sighs, and I feel a wave of admiration from her.

I try to wrap my mind around it all. "Think about it, how long would it take to design four *human* emotional time bombs? How many failed experiments?"

"If it's true, it must have taken years to just get to the point where we were created." Tima's eyes dart as she speaks. "Imagine the resources, the planning, the information required to know *how* to design us. Let alone *when*. To know what we were meant to fight."

"Do you think our parents knew?" I'm reeling.

Ro is on information overload. He's fuming. "My parents were killed on The Day. They weren't cooperating with any secret plan. They would have hated everything the Embassy stood for."

"How can you be so sure of that," snaps Lucas. "Seeing as they're dead and everything?"

"I'd rather they were dead than running the whole

Embassy for a bunch of No Face parasites. I don't know how I'd live with myself, Buttons. If I ended up like you—"

Lucas lunges for him, but Ro is ready. Within seconds, they are rolling on the floor, knocking over stacks of books, destroying Tima's carefully arranged nest.

Brutus barks madly, circling them.

Tima clings to her vid-screen. The metal box goes flying. Ro picks up a piece of the box and and pulls himself to his feet, rushing Lucas.

"Stop it! Just stop!" Tima screams, springing between them. They don't have time to stop charging, so she closes her eyes tight, bracing for impact.

They both barrel straight into Tima—until they are thrown onto their backs, hard.

I stand there watching in shock. The boys are equally confused.

Ro's nose is bloody and Lucas has a gash in his lip. "What was that?"

"That was you two being idiots."

Brutus growls, and Tima picks him up. Though he's full-grown now, he's not more than the size of a puppy.

"You threw me across the room without touching me." Ro looks at Lucas, who shrugs. "Both of us."

"And you deserved it. Clearly whoever grew you in the lab forgot to grow you a brain, either one of you." Tima looks like she wants to fight them both herself.

I scoot next to her, carefully, picking the box up from

342

the floor. I flash back to the image of Tima in the testing room. I don't know how she did it, but in any event, she doesn't seem to be processing what she did. "Tima, forget it. They're morons."

Lucas frowns. "You honestly think we were designed by somebody—and at the same time—to be some kind of sleeper cell of human weapons?"

"That's what it looks like." Tima nods.

Ro is enjoying this. "All I need to know is, who and what are we supposed to destroy—where, when, and how." He looks at Lucas with a cocky smile. "I have a good idea who and what I'd like to get rid of first."

I glare at him. "Quit messing around."

Ro winks at me. "Who's messing? I'm ready. I guess you could say I was born ready."

Ro's mood is improving by the minute, and I can't figure out why. Ro can't say anything more, though, because Lucas cuts him off. "This is ridiculous. There's no conspiracy. Why does everyone always think the entire planet is out to get us?"

"Lucas," says Tima, putting her hand on his arm.

"We were born on the same day. That's all. That's all we know. Period. What does that mean, except for the fact that our parents needed assistance to give birth? My mother was in public office before I was born. Of course she would have had access to all the best fertility Medics. That's not a crime."

"Nobody is saying it is. But you have to look at the facts, Lucas." Tima sounds sad, the way she says it.

"I know the facts, Tima. You just said them to me."

"Not just that. Not just that we were grown in a lab. But what it means, think about that."

I see her mind spinning. I can see the connections she is making, from idea to idea, thought to thought.

"Somebody needs us," I say, slowly.

Tima nods. She doesn't speak, but I know what she's thinking. *We have a purpose. We have a meaning. There is something we can do, if only because someone thinks we can do it.*

Ro looks somber. "It means we have to figure out our next move. Because we have one. Whoever made us, made us for a reason. We just have to figure out what that is." Ro looks at me, meaningfully. He wants me to tell Tima about what we learned at the Icon, which I will. But it all still makes no sense to me.

"Why the Ambassador?" I say. "Why would she want to make us, when all she and the Embassy have ever wanted to do was control us? We're a threat to them. We've always been a threat." I think of today when I speak. We are the only Icon Children, as far as we know. We are all that can stand against the Icons and the House of Lords.

"Maybe they were afraid we'd all end up slaves. Maybe they—someone—was hedging their bets. So they put together some kind of hidden fail-safe, in case The Day went wrong. In case the Carriers came and destroyed our whole world." Tima says the words slowly, but my mind is racing right along with her.

"Which they did," Ro says.

"But who?" I say, though as I say it I know she can't answer.

None of us can, not yet. But we will.

"You're all as crazy as she is," Lucas says.

I put my hand on his arm. "Lucas. She's right."

Lucas refuses to look at anyone.

Tima throws up her hands. "It doesn't matter what I say to you, does it? This isn't logical. You won't listen to me, you won't even listen to her."

It's a minute before I realize she's talking about me.

Lucas looks at me and shakes his head. "You're not thinking straight. You saw what I saw, but you don't understand. None of you do."

"Then tell me. Help me understand, Lucas."

"There's no point. You're not yourself, you're crazy. You're all crazy. I don't want any part of it."

Lucas is right. I don't feel like myself.

I feel a lot of things, but crazy isn't one of them.

———— • ————

That night, I can't sleep. I am afraid if I sleep, I will dream. I am afraid if I dream, I will see The Day. Only this time,

I know what the Icons look like, what they feel like—and I won't survive that dream.

At night, I can't defend myself. I fall asleep sitting up in my bed, pinching the insides of my thumbs, trying to keep myself awake.

Instead, I dream of Tima.

"Tima?" I see only the door to her chamber, locking and unlocking, as if Doc were still playing a joke on her. She stands with her back to me, slight as a reed, slight as ever. Her shoulders are sharp as blades, pale as moonlight.

A shadow spreads over them, and I watch it unfold in front of me.

Thread moves everywhere across her like veins, like water. Rivulets of brilliant color grow down from her shoulders in two epaulets. She stretches out her arms, tipping back her head.

She is screaming. Brutus is barking.

The stitching pierces her skin evenly, quickly. A hundred times. A thousand. More.

"Tima," I say again. "What's happening?"

She makes a strange sound, like choking. She turns to me. I see her neck marked with a vivid red thread, ear to ear beneath her throat. A new pattern.

"I don't like that one, Tima. It's scaring me." The stitches multiply, and the gash deepens. Her eyes are wide, her breathing shallow. I reach to touch her throat with my hands. That's when I see it isn't thread at all.

It's blood.

My hands are covered with blood.

I open my mouth to scream, but I can't, because my mouth is full and my voice is muffled with thread. Red thread, endlessly spooling out of me. I gag and choke on it, my stomach convulsing.

I'm still trying to find my voice when I realize someone is knocking.

———— • ————

"I made a mistake, Dol."

That's what Lucas says, the moment he comes into focus at my door. It's the middle of the night, and I can barely remember who he is or where we are or why we are standing there, anyway.

"What?"

"You need to listen to me. I told my mother about Fortis and the Observatory. And us. Everything."

The world snaps back into place—its terrible, habitual place.

"What do you mean, you told your mother?"

"After all that talk about joining up with Fortis and the Rebellion, and then Tima's crazy conspiracy theories, I didn't want you—us—to end up on a futile suicide mission."

"Are you joking?" I know he's not.

"I thought she would know what to do. But she lost

it. She started screaming, and called in her cabinet, and locked me out of the room. I don't know what happened after that, although I heard her say something about the Presidio Pen." He can't look at me, not in the eye.

The Pen. The Embassy lockup. He doesn't need to say it for me to understand.

"You've got to get out. I'll go find Tima, you get Ro. That's all I can tell you. There isn't much time."

"Why, Lucas? Why would you do something like that?"

"I told you. I had to. I wasn't going to sit by and let Fortis bring the wrath of the Lords down on the entire city. You think you've seen the worst of them, but you haven't. You don't know what they're like. You don't know anything."

"I was right there with you at Griff Park, Lucas. I know everything you do."

He's rambling. "No, you don't. You haven't seen the Pentagon. You haven't seen their mother ship—the size of it, the power, the complete control they have."

"Lucas." My mind is racing. His mother knows. *The Ambassador knows.*

"You think the Icon we saw yesterday is the worst of it? You think destroying that—thing—will make a difference?" He looks ill.

"Please, Lucas." I have to think, but there isn't enough time. I don't know what to do.

He won't listen. "Remember 6/6, Dol. The Day. They'll

strike back, and hard. I don't want that on my head." He softens. "And I don't want you in the Pen. So we have to get you out of here. Now."

I can't move. I can't breathe.

Lucas grabs my hands and pulls me out the door. "For once, will you just trust me?"

We are running before I think how ironic the words are.

RESEARCH MEMORANDUM: THE HUMANITY PROJECT

CLASSIFIED TOP SECRET / AMBASSADOR EYES ONLY

To: Ambassador Amare
Subject: Lords/Icon Origins
Catalogue Assignment: Evidence recovered during
  raid of Rebellion hideout

Handwritten notes transcribed as follows:

EARLY COMMUNICATIONS WITH OUR VISITORS IS PRODUCTIVE.
THEY MEAN BUSINESS.
RESISTANCE IS NOT AN EFFECTIVE OPTION. BETTER TO LET
THEM COME AND TRY TO MAKE THE MOST OF IT.
METHOD OF SUBMISSION IS ESPECIALLY TROUBLING.
COUNTERING WILL BE...DIFFICULT.
NOTING A LACK OF EMOTION IN COMMUNICATIONS.
AI?
POSSIBLE WEAKNESS.

FORTIS

Three of us sit in a gloomy gray cell in the Presidio Pen, just as Lucas said we would. Concrete walls, a solid metal door, a disgusting sink and toilet are our only companions.

We wait in the cold, damp silence.

It's me who finally breaks it. "I should have known. You can't run from Sympas."

"Why not? We have before." Ro shrugs.

I flash on the guards stepping out of the shadows at the bottom of the stairwell. On Lucas's face, as he tries to influence them. His eyes widening in surprise when he can't focus enough to do it.

I stare at the rough cuffs around my wrists. The skin beneath them is pink and raw. Here I am, shackled again, just like the first night I came to the Embassy.

Tima's words are quiet. "No. She's right. You run and they'll kill you."

After I'd seen them kill the Padre, after I'd seen the fortune-teller slump, after my attacker at Griff Park went limp—I didn't even try to get away. Sitting here now, I wonder if I should have.

"I'm sorry," I say, miserable.

"Yeah? You should be. I never trusted him." Ro glares at me through a cut eye and winces in pain when he leans forward. His shirt is ripped and bloody.

I look away. "I hate seeing you like this."

"This? This is nothing. The other guy—guys—they definitely got the worst of it." He tries to raise his arms over his head—Ro's victory gesture—but the cuffs won't let him, and he gives up.

Tima has her head down, making herself small. She is talking to herself. "I can't stay here. I have to get back to Bru."

She stares at the cuffs, pushing them back and forth.

When she speaks, she ignores me. "Dol knows why we're here, Ro. She was with Lucas last night, and he's not here. Even you can do that much math."

He looks at Tima. "Or maybe Superfreak here upset the librarian. Didn't put your little boxes back in the right place?"

I raise my voice. "It's not what you think. Lucas came to warn me—to warn all of us—but it was too late."

"If he needed to warn *us*, why was he in *your* room instead of Ro's or mine? *We* didn't do anything. *We* shouldn't be here." Tima's eyes are blazing.

"He—Lucas—" I still can't believe it as I say it. "He told the Ambassador everything. The visit to the Icon, what Tima learned from the records, Fortis's plans. Everything."

Tima's mouth drops open. "There m-must be a good reason," she stammers. "Lots of reasons. He didn't want us to go. He didn't want his life to change. He didn't want us to hurt his family."

"Listen to yourself, Tima. Wake up." Ro stands and starts to pace. "I knew we couldn't trust him. He set us all up. Us, the Rebellion, Fortis. We've been sold out." He pounds on the door.

I see the metal bulging and denting. I see his fists turn red with blood. I'm too exhausted to stop him.

As we sit in the dim light, I consider our options. "Look, I know we don't want to talk about this, but with Lucas—"

"Gone rogue?" Ro slams the door again.

"I think we have to." I look at the two of them. "Tima, is there even a small chance that we can destroy the Icon?"

Tima looks at the ground, composing her thoughts. "Yes, actually. Very small. A lot of variables. We'd need help. I don't like risk, but I would try."

"What about the risks? What if Lucas is right and the Lords retaliate? Think of how many people could die. It's more than just us in danger here."

"I've thought of that," Tima responds. "Then again, what if the Lords need us, or at least some of us? Think about the Projects." She pauses. "And tactically, our best chance to move is now, while we still have the element of surprise. What's left of it."

I look at Ro, sitting with his eyes closed, head against the door, nursing his banged-up hands—serves him right.

"And?" I look at him, pointedly.

"Come on, Dol, you don't have to ask me what I think. I've always wanted a chance to fight the No Face. If we get it, I say we take it and don't look back." He slams the door again with his fist, just to make his point.

I nod. "Agreed." We know what Lucas thinks. Now we know what the rest of us think.

Then the door knocks from the other side. Ro freezes, staring at it. I feel a familiar surge of warmth, and I wonder—

A voice echoes into the cell. "Right, then. I'm going to have to ask you to stop doing that. If you break the door over my head, Ro, I won't be able to open it."

"Fortis?" I stand up, pressing my ear against the door. I've never been so happy to hear the Merk bastard's voice.

Ro grins—even Tima looks relieved.

I hear him working with the door on the other side.

"Good thing I didn't come empty-handed. It's a bit sticky, this one. It almost gives a fellow the impression they've gone and locked you in. Not too hospitable, that."

354

I hear the sound of flint, or maybe a match striking—over and over—followed by the faint splutter of ignition. The scent of sulfur wafts up from beneath the door.

"Stand clear, then, love."

I step away, pushing the others back with my arms.

There is a pop, and then a flash of light. Smoke snakes up from beneath the shaking door. Slowly, it swings open—

And I see Fortis and Lucas standing in the opening.

"The cavalry, as they say, has arrived." Fortis looks out of place in the full Sympa gear he's wearing. Lucas, next to him, looks a bit better in his.

Nobody is speaking.

Fortis cocks his head and says to himself, "Thank you, Fortis. We owe you our lives."

He smiles. "Hello to you all, and again, you're welcome."

I fling my arms around him, though it crosses my mind that the last time I saw him, he abandoned us at Griff Park. Fortis has more than evened the score, I think. But nobody says anything to Lucas. Not even Tima.

"What's he doing here?" Ro growls.

"I'm here to save you." Lucas crosses his arms. "Of course, if you'd rather stay here, be my guest."

"Let me think about it. It's a tough call." Ro's eyes narrow.

Lucas looks at me. "You should think about it. What you're doing is suicidal."

Fortis raises an eyebrow. Ro, a fist.

"Lucas—" I begin, but he cuts me off.

"No. You're about to do the one thing that could wipe out the entire planet. There has to be a better way."

Fortis steps between Lucas and Ro this time.

"All right, children. That's enough. I'm here because your *friend* Lucas here told my friend Doc—who woke me up and tossed my toasty arse out of a warm bed to come paddle in the cold all the way out here and save you people." He gestures to the door. "Now, if you don't mind. Less talk. More walk. Follow me, or I'll leave you to rot."

I feel a surge of adrenaline and anxiety. The Sympas are getting closer. "He's right, we have to go now."

We walk down a corridor where he unlocks a door leading to another corridor and a dead end. I look at Fortis. "This was your plan?"

He responds casually, inspecting the wall. "Yes, actually. I think I've got it." He cocks his head at me. "Oh, and by the by, this one—little Grassgirl—is on the house." I barely have time to curl myself against the floor when the wall blows and I feel the concrete rubble raining all around me.

I cough. Dust fills my lungs and stings my eyes. I look up to see that Ro and Tima are out through the wall—or the hole that has replaced it. Lucas sits motionless, eyeing the gray dust that covers him.

I look at him, but he ignores me.

Fine.

I step toward the hole, but Fortis intercepts me, grabbing my arm before I can go through it.

"One thing—though I know we have to go. The Sympas won't be far behind."

"They're going to know you were here, Fortis. What if we've endangered the whole Rebellion?"

Fortis shrugs. "They'll just know a Merk came and blew you out of the Pen. So what? That's our bread and butter, love. Fortis the Merk would never pass up an opportunity as rich as this one." He eyes Lucas. "Brass Buttons over there makes it all worth my while, as far as anyone knows."

"Great." Lucas is despondent.

"Here's the thing. There's one part of this plan you're not going to like." Fortis looks me squarely in the eye. "You're not going to survive the escape. In fact, you're going to have to let Hux kill you."

"Excuse me?" He isn't joking. "That doesn't make sense. Hux isn't going to kill me. Neither is Doc or Orwell, for that matter. He isn't even real."

Fortis lowers his voice. For once, he sounds as serious as things are. "You can't think you're going to run wild and free in the peonies after this, can you? You're messin' with the big dogs now. You, Doloria, are going to have to die. You more than anyone." He wags his head toward Ro and Tima. "More than the rest. Believe me, I should know."

A thought comes to me. A glimmer, something familiar. I don't know why I didn't see it before.

"You mean, I have to die like you did?"

"What's that?" He knows what I'm asking, but he's going to make me put it together myself.

"You designed Doc, didn't you? You're his friend, the one who left. The one who's dead to him." I try to remember the exact words, but I can't. All I remember is that Doc had a friend, and lost him. Fortis. It has to be.

Fortis shrugs, but I don't stop. "You named him. The science fiction books—and the jokes—and all the Latin—that's you. Doc is yours."

"Ah, there's a story there, love. A good one. But first I have a little question for you."

"What?"

"Can you shoot a gun?"

Without another word, he shoves a Rebellion pistol into my hand and pushes me through the hole in the wall, hard.

There is a loud thump and the wall next to where I was standing turns to rubble.

The Sympas are here.

I take off running as Fortis fires. As I round the corner, I know there are more feet coming after me than just Fortis.

Out of the corner of my eye I see Lucas right behind him.

———— • ————

We don't resume the conversation until we are in sight of Fortis's boat—at least, the boat he hijacked from the Sympas. Searchlights crisscross in the air above us, slicing through the night with laser precision.

I try not to look at the dock, where two Sympas lie facedown along the foaming shore. "Casualties of war," says Fortis, grimly.

He climbs through the shallow, rocky water, not far from where I stood with Ro yesterday.

"Come on. Hurry it up, then, they're fast buggers, the whole lot of them. Fast and rather unfortunately armed." Fortis stands there in the center of the skiff, waving us in. His long coat flaps like ragged wings around him. Ro leaps into the boat, nearly capsizing it. I scramble along the rocks after him, carefully hoisting myself over the side. Tima and Lucas stand on the shore.

"You coming?" Tima looks at Lucas, then at us.

He doesn't say anything.

"Lucas?"

He shakes his head. "I'm not going with you."

Tima nods.

"I'm sorry," he says.

She looks at him for a long moment, her silver hair whipping in the wind. "I know. But I have to go."

She leans in to kiss his cheek, and he pulls her into an awkward hug. They cling together, just for a moment, but I have to look away. It's so personal, and so not something for me to see.

Or feel.

Maybe they're more like Ro and me than I thought.

I hold out my hand to Tima, and she takes it. We aren't friends, but we aren't enemies. Not anymore.

As I pull her into the boat, Tima calls over my head to Lucas. "Take care of Brutus for me—"

I hear the shout back—"Promise."

Brutus. That's when I realize, between Lucas and her dog, Tima's leaving the only family she's ever known.

I look back at Lucas. His green-gray eyes meet my blue-gray ones.

We don't say goodbye. We can't.

But inside, I can feel him, pulling back. This is the way our separate paths must take us.

My mother may live in the past, but she pulls me one way. His lives in the present, and she pulls him the other.

So I let go. It's all I can do.

Lucas looks small on the shoreline and only gets smaller, the farther we drift away.

———— • ————

"Were you serious—I mean, about me dying?" I scoot in the boat until I am next to Fortis, or nearly next to him. As close as the wet bench seats will allow.

Tima stares back at Santa Catalina. Ro stares the other direction, toward the Porthole.

Fortis keeps his eyes on the shoreline and one hand on the motor as he talks. "I did it, long ago. It's bloody difficult, what with all the ways the Embassy can track a person. Your digital signature, it's everywhere. But Hux can do it. He's done it before."

"Once?" I ask, looking at him.

He nods. "Like I said, you'll never be free. Not until you're dead."

"You make it sound so easy."

Fortis holds up his wrist. On it I see a leather cuff, exactly like the one Lucas wears.

"Did you—?" I point to the cuff.

He nods. "One a my earliest designs." He raises his voice, speaking into his wrist. "What do you say, Hux? Can you hook a mate up?"

"Yes, Fortis."

As I look over the edge of the boat into the black depths,

I think of how many times I have come so close to making the digital record real. A stray bullet could have found me, instead of the old fortune-teller. The Icon could have killed me, instead of the boy at the fence. I could have drowned in this dark water, sinking down until the cold and quiet consumed me.

I am lucky to be only this kind of dead, I think. *Who knows what lies ahead?* I pull myself out of the thought and back into the boat. My knuckles are white as I hold on to the seat.

"How long will it take, Hux?" Fortis looks grim.

"Doloria will die in four minutes. The record will reflect this."

A wave hits the side of the boat and I grip tighter. "Super."

"As the deceased, do you have a preference as to the terms of your tragic loss? A heroic narrative? A casualty of battle? Bringing what the ancient Greeks would call *kleos*, the eternal glory that awaits all warriors?"

I consider. "Just something simple." A simple death for a simple Grassgirl.

"There are so many choices," Hux offers, affably. "An electrocution. An explosion. A decapitation. A drowning, I believe, is the most appropriate."

I imagine each in turn, overwhelmed. I don't respond.

"I will include the digital record of your chestpack. We

will find it at the site of the accident. Digitally speaking."

I don't know what to say. "Thanks, I guess."

"All right. I understand. Sarcasm. The discourse of human cessation is typically thought to be uncomfortable to humans."

"Exactly." I turn to Fortis. "One more thing. Why me? Why did you say me, more than the rest?"

"You haven't figured it out?"

I shake my head.

"Just wait. You will, Doloria Maria de la Cruz." He grins, but his eyes aren't smiling. "It's something you carry within you. The most important thing. The one thing that I hope will save us all."

My mind flickers to the old fortune-teller, and the girl he spoke of. The one who matters—who is not me. I put her out of my thoughts, because in this boat, in this bay, there is no room for anything else.

"And that's why I have to die?"

He's not making sense, but he keeps going. "They know it too—or they will, soon. And when they do, they won't stop until they find you. Trust me, little Grassgirl."

Trust me, Dol.

I know Fortis is speaking but the voice in my head is Lucas's.

"Doloria," says Doc.

"Yes?"

"I have digitized and catalogued the contents of your chestpack, according to the data from your last night at the Embassy. They will be recorded in the Embassy Wik."

"Okay," I say.

"And Doloria?"

"Yeah?"

"I will be sorry to end your life."

I smile and look at Fortis, who seems more and more like the human twin of Doc. Or maybe his brother.

"I know, Doc. I'm sorry, too." I realize how distressing it is, just as my death becomes official.

Maybe Fortis is right. Maybe I do have something inside me, something to offer.

I hope so.

"I am searching my drives for something appropriate to say, to mark this event."

"I'm not sure there's anything in the classics that applies here, Doc."

"How about goodbye?"

I shake my head. "I don't like that word. Sometimes I feel like it's the only word I know."

My eyes are watering. *It must be the air*, I think. *I would never cry at my own funeral.* At the same time, I feel a new connection to my parents, to the millions who have died since the Lords came. I think of the meaninglessness of their deaths.

I promise to make this one count. "No goodbyes, Doc."

364

I hear the voice crackle. "In that case, how about hello?" I take the wristband from Fortis's hand and hold it up to my ear. It's all I can do to nod.

"*Salve*, Doloria Maria de la Cruz. I will see you again, soon."

"*Salve*, Doc."

"It is done. Your files have been deleted and replaced. As far as the world knows, Doloria Maria de la Cruz dies tonight. The Grass Rebellion was to blame."

I stare down at the dark, churning water and wonder if he will be right.

RESEARCH MEMORANDUM:
THE HUMANITY PROJECT

To: Ambassador Amare

Subject: Lords/Icon Origins

Catalogue Assignment: Evidence recovered during
raid of Rebellion hideout

Handwritten notes transcribed as follows:

WHAT HAVE THEY DONE—

HOW CAN THEY KILL ENTIRE CITIES—

WOMEN, CHILDREN, INNOCENTS—

MISJUDGED INCOMPREHENSIBLE CRUELTY

OF LORDS' METHODS—

NOBODY MUST KNOW—

WHAT HAVE I DONE—

—ACCELERATING RESEARCH—

MUST GATHER THE CHILDREN—

TEST—

TRIGGERS—

NO TIME, MUST JUMP-START—

THEY AREN'T READY BUT—
THIS MUST BE STOPPED—
I MUST STOP IT

6/6 6/6 6/6 6/6 6/6 6/6

ALL FALL DOWN

Fortis turns to me. "Now. Open your chestpack."

"Why?"

"I need to take a look at the shard."

"The what?"

"The broken bit of the Icon. The piece you brought back to Santa Catalina."

"How do you know about that?"

"Hux was the first one to notice. You think you can bring somethin' like that into the Embassy without settin' off a few bells and whistles? He scanned it for me, straightaway, and we've been usin' the data to plan our attack."

I open my pack.

There it is, luminescent in the moonlight. It's not very

long, but I can feel its peculiar weight the moment I reach for it.

"There you are," Fortis says, with a gleam in his eye. I hand it to him. Fortis rolls the shard through his fingers—then kisses it.

"This little beauty is absolutely critical. We're not sure what it is, exactly, but we've been tryin' all sorts of explosives against its data profile. I think we've finally gotten it right—light enough to carry, but causin' enough damage to do the trick."

Ro sits forward. "Military grade? There's an abandoned base near the Mission, I know there's a lot of good stuff there."

Fortis nods. "Believe me, I'm fully aware of your Grass contacts, Furo. Half those crazy buggers are with my people now." Ro grins. "We've got a plan in place, all right. When we get to the Cathedral, you'll be able to talk to our munitions team about how it all fits together. And how the Icon will come apart."

Tima is bouncing nervously. "I've thought a lot about how the Icons work, and I'm pretty sure they're all connected, somehow."

"That's what we think," Fortis offers.

She takes a deep breath. "I read about the initial invasion, how the Icons landed a few days before 6/6. The Day."

"To link up," Fortis muses.

She nods. "Like a web, covering the planet. Once they hooked up—it was all over."

I turn to Tima. "When I was there—really close—I had this creepy feeling it was alive. Like it was aware of me, or something." I know how it sounds, but feel like I have to say it. "And, well, living things can die, right?"

Fortis nods. "Clever girl."

Tima is so excited she jumps up and almost falls out of the boat. "I don't know why we didn't see it before. It's obvious. We need to disconnect them."

"It's possible you're right." Fortis strokes his chin.

Ro looks up. "So what you're saying is, if we take them out one by one, the network is weakened. And eventually the whole network comes down."

"As far as we know," says Tima.

"How many are there again, anyway?" Ro looks at Fortis.

Fortis frowns. "Thirteen." The word is like a death sentence. But I refuse to accept it. I've already died once tonight.

So instead, I smile. "Fine. Number one, here we come."

We don't say a word about the House of Lords. About silver ships disrupting our horizon, sliding over our city and across our sun.

About the very real possibility that we could fail—that we could find ourselves responsible for sentencing the Hole to become a Silent City of our own.

Human death by inhuman hands, and on a catastrophic scale.

We don't talk of retaliation.

I try not to even think the word.

Why should I? I tell myself. *What are words to a Silent City?*

But the things we don't say tonight are louder than the things we do.

The Cathedral is alive with activity. We can barely keep up with Fortis as he makes his way through what once was the chapel.

"We'd hoped to have a bit more time to prepare, of course, but Lucas gave us a new deadline when he had his little heart-to-heart with dear old Mum." Fortis sighs. "They won't be able to move on us without GAP clearance, but we need to go now."

"Right now?" Ro is hopeful.

"Before first light, my friend."

Tima catches up to Fortis. "I agree. And Dol's death won't stop them from increasing security around the Icon, soon enough."

Fortis nods. "Sad but true. People 'ave no manners." He claps Tima on the back. "No time to lose, then."

Fortis points to a group around a wide table. "Maps, schematics, communications. Tima, you're with them." She nods and heads off in that direction.

Fortis takes Ro by the arm and gestures to the other side of the room, where people are stocking backpacks. "Gear, camo, explosives. Arm up and get ready." Ro disappears.

"What about me?" I'm hesitant. The whole room is overwhelming, tonight.

"You? Clear your head. You're the one with the big finale."

"Me? What do I do?"

"You blow the place up, love."

With that, Fortis is gone.

I look around the crowded hall, trying to get my bearings. Everything is different from the last time I was here. The people are moving with purpose. Crates are stacked in one corner, full of salvaged equipment. In another is a makeshift kitchen, where what was formerly an altar is now lined with bread and plates, surrounding what looks like potato-cheese stew.

My favorite.

I breathe in the smell with a pang of regret, as it takes me back to the Mission. My birthday dinner seems like a lifetime ago.

Ten lifetimes.

An older man with graying hair shuffles by on his way to eat, and I notice him stealing a glance at me out of the corner of his eye, like he knows who I am.

Like I'm something special.

I smile at him and he smiles back, standing up that much straighter. The feeling I pick up from him—from the entire room—is so positive, I try not to fight it. It's almost like, for the first time, I'm helping people. Looking up, not down—forward, not back.

What's wrong with a little hope?

I don't answer, and instead grab a hunk of bread.

Three hours remain.

Three hours until we go to face the Icon. Someone has erected a countdown clock, fixing it in place with twine wrapped around the organ, over by the front altar.

Every time I go to look for Tima or Ro, they're somewhere new. Our lives have immeasurably broadened, just like that, in the span of a few hours.

Tima talks to five people at once, while reading maps and drawing grids and making neatly inked rows of calculations. Based on my description of the Icon—and the scans Doc made of the shard—Tima works with Fortis to make final adjustments for the optimal explosive and placement. The perpetual motion of her body, the flightless flight of her fingers, have suddenly found a purpose. She is radiant, beautiful in a way I haven't seen before. Her newfound confidence suits her. I wish Lucas could see her like this.

I wish Lucas were here to see all of this.

Ro's not one for the main table. He'd rather keep to the side, finding his way to the edges of the crowd. He finds other things there, too. Soldiers. Scavengers. Rebels— some of his old friends from the Grass. Ro is bright as a candle, full of energy. He circles around the place learning everything he can, getting ready to take the Icon himself— with or without the rest of us. He studies triggers, ranges of impact, detonators.

This is his time. I don't get in his way. These are his people. People to burn with.

Not me.

But I see how his energy is infectious. I imagine a fire spreading inside the Cathedral from person to person, and I know Ro is the origin.

Two hours to go. When I approach Tima at Fortis's wide table, she almost seems happy.

"There's so much to do," she says, looking up at me. "Strategically speaking."

"Is there?"

"Tactical. Munitions. Support. We've got to get you in and out before they notice. You and Ro. Before the Embassy can deploy." I can see her mind racing.

Me. Ro. They.

Of course. Of course it's us. Only an Icon Child can

get close enough. It's us against the Embassy and the House of Lords.

Us against Lucas and the Ambassador.

Just as it always has been.

"Right," I say, so she doesn't notice I'm trembling. "Where are we going in?"

"Pretty much retracing your route from last time. Through the gate, up the hill, straight to the Observatory, to the Icon. If we're lucky, the Ambassador won't have moved on it yet. Fortis and I have come up with a plan, and it's sort of brilliant. Though it would help if Lucas were here."

"We can do this. We'll be fine."

I catch a glimpse of Fortis through the crowded space of the Cathedral. He's deep in conversation with Ro.

"Tell me, what do you know about Ro and his contacts with the Grass Factions?" Tima leans in closer, so no one can hear what she is saying.

"Nothing. He doesn't like to talk about them with me."

"Can they be trusted? Now that they're here? They say they have explosives, but I'm not so certain."

"I don't know."

She looks at me steadily, taking my hand. It is tiny and cold and flutters beneath my fingers. "Yes, Doloria. You do know. Or at least, you can know. Check it out for me, will you?"

I don't want to; I don't like to do it to Ro. But Tima doesn't let go of my hand, and I know she is only trying to help, so I do it anyway.

I calm my mind and reluctantly allow myself to feel. I open my heart and am flooded, drowning in the sadness inside me, all around me. The tears come, and I close my eyes and reach for him. All the way across the hundreds of people in the dimly lit room, which smells like candle wax and smoke and dirt and chickens. Mission smells. Grass smells.

I let the smells fade first, then the people.

They disappear, one by one, until it is just Ro standing there. Ro and me.

I see the flashes in a fraction of a single moment.

The Padre's *pistola*. A cellar beneath an old cafe. Bundles of dynamite and bricks of something that looks like clay, where there should be wine. A ratty group of men and women, crouching around a table scattered with junk tech and industrial scraps and spools of wire.

Ro's mouth twists into a smile, and he nods at me from across the room. I open my eyes.

"Yes," I say. "You can trust them. I do."

Tima pulls me toward her in an awkward, jerky hug. It's a strange sensation, like being gripped by a stick. "Everything is going to be all right."

"I know," I say, though it's a lie.

"Better. At least, better." When she pulls away, I see

that her eyes are bright and wet. "He'll come back." Tima says it without looking at me.

I nod, but we both know that's a lie, too.

When only one hour remains on the clock, Fortis calls the three of us over to the munitions area.

"Try to measure twice and cut once and all that. You can't uncut, and you certainly can't un-explode, so let's do this right." He looks at Ro. "You have everything you need, then?"

Ro holds up two large backpacks stuffed full of plastic explosives, and a second, smaller bag. "Explosives and detonator."

Tima gives him a sketch of the Icon. "Here's where you need to set the charges." She hands me a map. "Here's the route—you know the way, so you lead."

Fortis nods. "Once you get there, Dol, you need to keep an eye on the entrance, make sure no surprise visitors stop by. We don't know what the Lords will do, or if they even monitor the Icons around the clock. We don't think so, since there already is a sort of foolproof defense in place—"

"You mean, the whole dropping dead thing?" Ro winces.

"That's it. But they've surprised us before."

I remember the lifeless plants, the bones, the desolation. "I don't know who they could send in to stop us.

Lucas and I could barely handle it ourselves. No Sympa could."

Then Tima and Ro and I raise our eyes to each other, at the same moment.

Lucas.

"You don't think he would, do you?"

"He's the only one who could," Tima says, grim.

"I hope he does." Ro shakes his head. "Lucas, Sympas, the Lords themselves. Bring it. We're doing this."

"Tima and I will be in communication as long as possible. As you know, once things break up, you're on your own." Fortis softens. "Don't worry, duckies. You're more than prepared. Everything in your lives has brought you to this point." He leans closer. "I'm not a sentimental sort, but I won't deny it'll be a bit sad if you blow yourselves up along with the Icon."

"Gee. Thanks, Fortis." I'd laugh, if it weren't true.

Fortis grins. "Yeah, all right. Just stick to the plan, and stay alert, and try to come back alive."

Ro looks at me. "It's a promise."

Five minutes later, we are saying our goodbyes.

The ceilings of Our Lady of the Angels are so high you would think they could hold anything. It's not true. They can barely contain the noise. What begins as shifting and muttering becomes stamping and shouting. Now Fortis is banging a fist against the old altar. It is no kind of service the Padre would recognize, and Fortis is nothing like a priest. I wonder what the Padre would say if he could see me here, tonight.

Fortis raises his voice to be heard over the others, in our new congregation. "Tonight's it, then, my friends. We've worn their collars and carried their yoke long enough. Thanks to a strange twist of providence," he says, looking at us, "we've got one shot to take the Icon down, an' show the No Face we haven't given up yet."

He raises his glass first to Tima, who stands next to him—then Ro and me, who stand side by side. "To the human race, then."

Ro finds my eyes in the dim light and hooks on to me.

"There," he says.

There, I think.

We can do this. We're together—just like always, like the Mission.

Home.

But now it is finally time to go. Ro and I are surrounded by those whose most desperate wishes for the future go with us. "You can do this," Fortis says, clasping one hand to my shoulder. "You too," he says to Ro.

"I'll be right there with you," Tima says, shoving my headset into place behind my ear. "Until the very last second before the pulse cuts us out." She smiles at me, a quick and rare thing. "Don't be scared."

"I won't," I say. "I'm not."

I look at her eyes and see that she is crying.

"You were meant for this, you know." She wipes her face with her hand.

"So were you," I say, nodding toward her own headset. I put my hand on her shoulder and squeeze it. "See you soon."

She turns to Ro and holds out her hand to him—but instead, he flings his arms around her in a massive bear of a hug, until her feet lift right off the ground.

I smile, but I can't stomach any more goodbyes. So without waiting for Ro to catch up, I step out into the night.

I touch the walls beneath Our Lady, carved in the stone. In the night, her halo becomes lost in shadow. I think of Lucas vanishing on the distant shore, of Tima and her bloodred thread. My mother's necklace. Ramona. The Padre. Everything disappears, sooner or later.

Anything can go, anytime.

That's the thing about triggers and feelings, I guess. Colonel Catallus was wrong. The trick isn't having them. It's keeping them. Owning them.

They don't make you weak or sad, angry or afraid, even heartbroken.

They make you.

I am powerful because of who and what I am. Not because of who I am not.

I'm not going to apologize for what I feel.

Not anymore.

How we feel—at least, for Ro and Tima and me—is our only chance to win back our freedom.

And after tonight, the only thing gone will be the Icon.

That's what I tell myself, anyway, as Ro emerges from the Cathedral behind me, and we disappear into the darkness of the Hole.

———— ◆ ————

I am really here, and I am really carrying a backpack stuffed full of bricks of plastic explosives, salvaged from abandoned military bases. CL-20, according to Ro, Fortis's explosive of choice. It looks like putty or clay, something that would belong to a child, not a troop of guerilla warriors.

The pack feels heavy, but I don't mind the weight.

Ro, who hasn't taken a breath or a break since we started walking, is so far ahead of me he disappears around the bend.

"Hurry up. We don't have much time." I hear his voice floating behind him. "What's wrong with you? You're never this slow. I'll race you to the top." He takes off running, even with his heavy pack. He's excited, and his loping gait reminds me of our childhood together, of racing and playing in the Mission hills.

Making forts, not bombs.

He's right, I'm never this slow.

But I don't hurry. Something feels wrong.

I stop.

Because the moment I step into the moonlight at the corner of the trail, I see a dark figure sitting on top of a boulder in front of me. Before my eyes can adjust, I know who it is.

I'd know him anywhere.

I'm frightened and overwhelmed and it's all I can do not to start sobbing.

"Lucas?"

As I approach, he slides off the boulder, looking more like a young boy than I have ever noticed. He's wearing Sympa camos and carrying a pack. "Dol. I've been waiting for you."

Instinctively, I back up. I hear Ro and Fortis and Tima in my head.

Lucas can come inside the radius of the Icon.

Lucas is the only one they could send to stop us.

Lucas can't be trusted.

He steps up toward me in the darkness, and tries to slide his arms around me in an awkward hug.

I push him away, because I don't know if he's here to help me or kill me.

What a trio we are.

Me, recently dead. This boy, who just wants to be loved. The other boy, who races me up the hill. *Who decided we were the ones who had to shoulder this burden? What business is it of ours, what happens to this place? For that matter, to the Hole itself, our people, our planet?*

I don't know what to say, so I turn and walk until Lucas falls into step next to me.

"Why are you here, Lucas?"

"I came to try to talk you out of this. One last time."

"Message received. Now beat it." I keep walking.

"Look," he says, catching up, "I got you out of the Pen, right? I came all the way out here to see you. But my mom knows everything."

"Thanks for that." I don't look at him.

"They'll be here soon, in force. The Embassy, or worse."

The Lords.

He doesn't have to say it. We all know.

"So go home."

"No." Lucas grabs my arm, and I yank it away as hard as I can.

"Lucas. Of course your mom doesn't want this to happen. She doesn't want the Lords upset—maybe they'll decide she's expendable."

"That's not what this is about."

"I get it. She's comfortable. She's got you to think about. Why wouldn't she do everything she can to keep things the way they are?"

"You don't know my mom," Lucas says quietly, but I can see my words are sinking in.

"I know she held us hostage. I know she's trying to

383

keep us from doing what—if Tima is right—we were literally born to do. I know she works for the Lords, Lucas. The Ambassador, and the whole Embassy. GAP Miyazawa, all of them. I know they aren't keeping us safe."

"Yeah, then what are they doing?" Bright spots of red appear on his face.

"They're keeping us enslaved—because they're afraid to let go of the small amount of power and privilege they've got. And you—"

I realize I'm shouting.

Lucas looks at me, daring me to say it.

So I do.

"You're not as different as you think."

It's too late for this or any other kind of conversation. We've chosen our sides, and they're not the same. I'm tired of pretending the truth is not true.

Lucas doesn't give up, though. He doubles his stride, until he's practically backing up in front of me, along the trail.

"Please, Dol. Listen to yourself. You say we were born to do this, but you don't know why. We don't know who engineered this. This isn't destiny, it's a joke. A cruel joke. We have a choice. You were born to be Doloria de la Cruz, and nothing else. Walk up that hill, and you're making the choice to end it all. And I can't bear to see that happen."

"Maria." I stop walking.

"What?"

"Doloria Maria de la Cruz. I'm named after my mother, and I'm doing this for her."

I see his face in the moonlight and realize he is crying.

"For my father and my brothers. For the Padre, and Ro. Tima and Fortis. Bigger and Biggest and Ramona. For all the Remnants who got shipped off to the Projects."

I look at him.

"And for you, Lucas."

I see his face falter. With those words, I realize I'm done talking. From the quiet that surrounds me, I see he's done following.

The Observatory comes into view in front of me. The white stone domes, the obelisk, the wide steps—all of it dominated by the ugly scar of the Icon. Beyond the crumbling debris lies the cool sweep of the city, mostly dark where it should be light. Only the far, far distance, where the thin, rugged line that is Santa Catalina Island, glistens with moonlight.

Ro must already be inside.

The closer I get, the louder the hum of the Icon echoes in my mind. It seems stronger than before, buzzing like an angry wasp, like it knows why we're here.

It becomes more difficult to walk, and my pack feels heavier, but I don't stop.

I refuse to stop.

"Dol, wait—"

I turn to see Lucas running after me. I wave him away; I don't have the energy for him anymore. "It's too late. You can't keep this from happening."

He stops next to me, breathless. "Dol. I don't want you to get hurt. I couldn't—I don't want to live with that."

"Lucas. Please."

"It's too dangerous."

"One of us has to do it. I'm not afraid. I'd rather it be me." I turn and walk away, because as I say the words, I know they're true. I don't want anything to happen to Ro or Tima. Or Lucas.

Even now.

"Okay, fine. You're right," I hear behind me, his voice cracking. I stop and look at him.

He raises his voice. "I've been a coward. Too afraid of losing what I have—and disappointing the Ambassador."

"Your mother."

He nods. "Everything I did was because I was afraid of what would happen if things changed."

"That doesn't make it right."

He nods again, rubbing his eyes with his sleeve, and takes a deep breath. "There's more. About my *mother*," he says. "When you left, I went to her private office. I went straight to her safe, the one hidden behind our family portrait."

"And?"

"Private digi-text. The files my mom had re-Classified, rerouted to her office. Doc cracked the safe. It had something to do with calculating the average time each of the numeric tabs had been pushed. There's some kind of digital imprint that remains. Apparently each time a touch pad is activated, there's this—"

"Get on with it, Lucas. I have to keep moving." I don't have time to hear it.

"I found another box of drives. It might as well have been labeled 'everything I never want Lucas to read.' There were records, more than you want to know. Things I wish I didn't know, still."

"Like?"

"Tima was right."

"About our parents?"

"About everything."

"What's that supposed to mean?"

"It means there's more to us than we thought. More than what Tima knows. And more than Fortis is telling you." His face darkens.

"What are you saying?"

"We're not just meant to be a weapon. Like Tima says, whoever made us also made a bargain with the House of Lords. And like she didn't say, I think the Ambassador knows who it is."

I freeze. The hair on the back of my neck begins to prickle, a thousand tiny needles in my skin.

How is it possible? How is there a kind of humanity this low? So low it doesn't even deserve to be called human?

"What kind of bargain?"

"The kind that brought the Lords to our planet in the first place."

Is it true?

Could it possibly be?

I want to cry but I push it back. We can't stop now. I'm sure of that, more determined than ever.

I look at Lucas. "You're telling me we might have something to do with the very reason the No Face came?" He nods. "Then we'll also be the reason the No Face leave."

He says nothing.

We watch the moonlight reflect on the white stone of the building before me. My head is pounding, but my heart aches at the sight.

"It's beautiful, isn't it? Too bad we're going to have to blow it up." I tighten my pack.

"We?"

"Ro and me."

"How?"

I motion to my pack. "I have enough CL-20 in here to rip this side of the mountain in half."

He shakes his head. "You can't."

"Don't start. I told you. I can, Lucas. I have to."

"Not without me." He reaches for my pack and slings it over his own shoulder.

I smile, in spite of everything.

"You'd do that? Stay and help?"

He shrugs. "Not much for me back at the Embassy. Seeing as, according to them, I helped three fugitives escape the Pen."

We take off toward the white domes.

"Don't worry," I say. "You get caught and I'll come back for your trial and testify. The truth is, you were really no help at all."

His laugh dies out as the pulsing of the machine noise takes over my brain. I try not to wince as we cross into the thick, buzzing atmosphere of the ruined building. Every cell in my body starts to writhe.

I want to scream.

Hell, I think. *That's what this is.*

I would almost rather be dead.

"Buttons? What's he doing here?" Ro holds a thick tube of plastic explosives in each hand. He looks so surprised to see Lucas, I'm afraid he's going to drop one. Or hurl it at Lucas.

"It's fine, really. He's here to help." I look over at Lucas. "Right?"

Lucas motions to Ro's ears, where the blood is spattering

down to his shoulders. "Let's just get this done before our heads explode."

Ro considers him for a long moment, then hands him Tima's map.

One by one we place the thick cylinders of explosives.

One bound to each of the snaking, cylindrical black tendrils that work their way down into the rock and soil of the cliff beneath the building.

We attach most of them to the body of the Icon itself, jammed into the pressure points that Tima has so carefully mapped out. Like some kind of art project, everything is placed just so.

We shove all the remaining cylinders at the base of it, just to be sure.

One detonator, strapped to that.

Ro lays it gingerly in place, a carefully constructed contraption, spring-loaded and running on a mechanical timer—no electricity. With a sense of pride, Ro explains the process as he adjusts the trigger. "Fortis is a genius. Because Icons interfere with chemical reactions, he designed the detonation to work incredibly fast, before the Icon's field can interfere. Once the detonator is tripped, the chain reaction will take over, and everything will go off before the Icon can shut it down. It won't know what hit it."

All we have to do is set the timer and get out.

The three of us stand there, for just a moment. It feels

like madness—standing this close to an Icon, with the power to destroy it. I hold only a stopwatch in my hand. A coiled spring, like the detonator. Very simple. The technology is more than a hundred years old and still reliable.

"Ready?" says Ro.

"Ready," I repeat.

Lucas nods and says nothing.

"Detonation will be in one hundred twenty seconds, on my mark." Ro's voice—steady and sure—ripples over everything we do and say.

"Mark." Ro flips a switch and stands up, satisfied.

I click the stopwatch. The numbers spin past me, sprinting down the screen.

One press of a button, and everything has changed.

—————— • ——————

We run. I don't look back as I tumble through the hall and down the concrete steps, or as I race past the brass plates of the planets in our solar system embedded in the walkway, or as I cross the grass near the obelisk that marks the way to the deserted parking lot.

I keep running until I am halfway down the shortcut, the back side of the hill, toward the place where Tima promised she would meet us, to take us to a Rebellion safe house.

No Freeley. No Embassy Chopper. Not tonight.

Lucas is right behind me, and we both turn to look back. "One minute," I say, almost to myself. "This whole place is about to be a cloud of ash."

I turn to Lucas and wipe the blood dripping from his nose with my hand. Then I push a strand of hair out of his eyes.

Ro comes tearing after us, breathless.

"What are you doing? Come on!" He grabs me by the hand and pulls as hard as he can. I go flying. He doesn't even notice Lucas. He doesn't care if Lucas comes or not.

Ro keeps running, pulling me after him. He's not stopping for anyone, not now.

We sprint down the hill, outside the fence, and away from the Icon. We run well clear of the blast zone, and duck behind a big rock.

I look at the stopwatch.

10

5

1

All we get is silence.

There is no smoke and ash, where there should be smoke and ash.

"Something's wrong. The first blasts should have come by now. I staggered the timing. One supporting leg at a time." Ro can barely say the words.

We're all panting.

"Maybe you hit the wrong time. Maybe the detonator misfired. Maybe there's a loose connection." I try not to imagine the worst, that the Lords discovered what we were doing and found a way to stop it. "It could still go off any second. And the Embassy will be here soon. We have to go. We can always try again."

"No," Lucas says. "We've gone too far, risked too much, to leave without making sure this is going to work."

Ro tries his earpiece. "I got nothing."

I tap mine, but I can't get reception.

Lucas raises his wrist, shouting into his cuff. "Doc, Fortis, what's going on?"

We hear static, then Fortis's voice erupts into the air. "Well, my darlings, I think the better question is what's not going on, and why."

More static.

Fortis speaks up again. "Hux, you ran the numbers over and over, what's wrong?"

I hear a loud buzzing sound—then Doc's voice. "It's quite possible the assumptions underlying my calculations were off. I've tested the Icon sample—and done extensive measurement of the Icon's effect—but there is always a small margin of error."

There is only silence on the line.

Silence and static.

I grab Lucas's wrist. "Doc? Fortis?" I finally hear Fortis.

"Yes, Dol. I'm not going to lie. This is a bit of bad news."

"What are you saying?" I can barely think. "There must be something we can do."

I hear Fortis hesitate, through the static. "It's up to you. I can't make you do it. The only way it will blow is—"

"One of us will have to blow it." Ro says the words.

"That's it. Manual."

My heart sinks. Lucas drops his head into his hands. Ro stands.

"I'll do it. It's my responsibility."

No. Not Ro. Not my oldest friend. I can't bear to imagine life without him, even if the Icon is destroyed.

"Fortis, it's not worth it. We need to figure out something else." I tap my earpiece, over and over. "Tima, you there? Doc?"

No one answers.

Ro takes my hand. "Dol, don't. You know there's not another way. It has to be one of us. It's not going to be you, and I'm not going to let Buttons here get all the glory."

"Come on, Ro." Lucas is ashen.

Ro won't even look at him. "Shove off. This is my fire. I need to light it."

I yank away my hand. "Ro, listen to me."

Then I stop, because I hear something.

"Is that—"

Ro listens. "Barking?"

"Here?" I think of the dead Sympa, and the blood coming out of our own ears. Nothing could survive where we have been. We barely did.

But it's true. The sound is coming from one of our packs. Ro bends down and opens the nearest one—and Brutus sticks his head out and licks Ro on the mouth. "What is Lucas doing with the dog?"

"How is that dog even alive?" *It's a miracle*, I think. Curled in the pack on Lucas's back, that small, mangy dog survived the Icon.

"Brutus!" Tima appears on the hill behind us. She's dragging a handful of face masks, and what looks like a pack of medical supplies. I recognize the cross on the gear.

Tima pulls Brutus all the way out of the bag, and he licks her face with a howl. "Good boy. How did Lucas get you here?"

She turns to me. "What's going on? Why is there no explosion? Where's Lucas?"

Ro and I look at each other in shock.

Because Lucas is gone.

Tima picks up in a heartbeat what is happening. "No. Absolutely not. He can't do it. I won't let him."

Before I can say anything, she shoves Brutus into my arms and takes off running, faster than I knew she could. She disappears up the hillside into the dark, scrambling toward the Observatory.

Brutus howls.

"Wait!" Ro shouts and climbs after her.

"Ro, stop." I pull his arm toward me. I can't let him go. "Please, Ro, it's too late. We'll never stop her, and Lucas is too far ahead."

He stands, fists clenched, jaw tight. "This isn't happening."

I pull him down, no longer able to stand. The dog clings to my chest, whimpering.

"It is. And I am not going to let you throw your life away. Not yet, anyway."

He slumps next to me, defeated. I put my arms around him and utterly and completely lose it.

I can't take it anymore. I no longer have the will to protect myself from the pain of my sadness, and it all comes crashing in.

My parents, the hundreds of millions of people who have died, the Padre, Ramona, and now Lucas and Tima. I feel the power of the sadness grow, bigger than myself; I can't contain it.

I weep.

I don't stop when I hear the first explosion. Or the next. Or the next.

I don't stop when the debris rains down around us, and I first smell the smoke.

I don't stop when Ro, covered with ash, stands up to see if the Icon is still standing.

Or after that—

The silence.

EMBASSY TELEGRAM

GENERAL MESSAGE
CLASSIFIED TOP SECRET

From: GAP Miyazawa
To: All Icon Ambassadors

All,

I received the following message from the Lords regarding Project productivity. They are not happy. Orders are to increase Project staffing 20% to bring up production. I don't care where you get the people.

If you value your position and your life, make it happen. Amare and Rousseau, I'm talking to you.

—M

BEGIN MESSAGE

CURRENT ICON PROJECT PRODUCTION IS UNSATISFACTORY.
GLOBAL OUTPUT AT 84.7%.
MINIMUM IS 90%.

LOS ANGELES: 78%
NORTHEAST: 95%

LONDON: 84%
PARIS: 75%
MOSCOW: 81%
SHANGHAI: 89%
TOKYO: 91%

END MESSAGE

THE VIRUS

I'm not sure how long I sit, stunned and in shock.

Brutus whimpers until he pulls me out of my daze, and only then do I look around.

A thick, gray-white ash is accumulating everywhere, blanketing the trees, the rocks, the ground. Black smoke clouds the air, and I can't see more than a few feet ahead.

Ro stands silent, staring up the hill.

I think of the massive gash we have blown into the side of this mountain. I think of the people who have died here, because of the Lords, and of how many more may die now, because of what we have done.

If Lucas is right.

Was right.

What have you done, Doloria Maria? There will be reprisals. Consequences. The House of Lords will not let this go unpunished. If they find you. If they strike.

If.

It comes back again to those two small letters. If I've done what I think I've done. If the Lords do what Lucas thought they would do.

That's when I turn around and begin climbing my way up the hill, back the way I came.

I can't see anything until I get to the top of the hill. And then I see everything.

Or, rather, almost nothing.

No buildings. No Icon. No friends.

Lucas is not anywhere. I don't see any sign of him or Tima.

"Lucas! Tima!" I yell, though I know it's useless. Tears are drying on my cheeks, smeared dirt covering my face, and it takes me a moment to notice I don't feel the pain or pressure of the Icon's energy.

I close my eyes.

Through my grief, I feel an incredible wave of relief. Our plan worked.

The Icon has been shattered, severed from the earth, and the Lords have lost their power over us.

At least here, at least for now.

But now we know we can do it. Will do it.

One Icon at a time.

Lucas and Tima, their sacrifice means something.

It has to.

I put Brutus down and he runs ahead into the smoke. Where the Icon stood, just minutes ago, there is only a black crater. It looks like a giant has grabbed the Icon and ripped it from the ground—and then used it to smash everything in sight. Fires burn where there is any part of the building still standing. The dead trees surrounding it have toppled. Everything—the sky, the rubble, what's left of the brown, scrubby brush, me—everything smells like smoke.

Ash floats through the air like snow. It falls along the scattered piles of concrete and pieces of the Icon, slowly covering the ground. It almost makes everything look peaceful.

Almost.

I walk closer to the center of the blast, where the Icon stood. Where the detonator was.

Where Lucas was.

All that remains of him and Tima is in the ashes floating around me.

Gone.

Like the Padre, like Ramona Jamona.

Like everything I love.

I feel my eyes start to burn.

"We can't leave them." I say it out loud, because I can feel Ro standing behind me. He must have followed me back up the hill.

I expect Ro to be cheering. Fire and force took down the Icon—just like he's always wanted.

Instead, when I turn to him, he's crying.

I walk past him to the deck, to where the crumbling stone balcony gives way to the burning, smoking hills and the silent city below. My foot strikes something, and I stop. A shard, the last remaining bit of the old Icon. Just like the one I'd found before.

I pick it up, feeling the weight in my hands.

I feel it burn and hum, beating with its own quiet life, still.

I feel the loss of Lucas. I feel Tima's sacrifice. I feel all the pain I've locked up inside myself. My parents, my Padre, Ramona. A billion people no longer in the world. Parents, children, grandparents—our invisible history now.

A billion forgotten faces. A billion lost stories. A billion reasons to hate and kill.

The spark inside me is growing. The shard of the Icon is turning hot in my hands.

I feel sorrow, but I feel rage too. I feel fear, but I feel love, and it is stronger, perhaps strongest of all. I feel everything I have come to feel in everyone I have come to love.

I stretch my arms out to the sky and the city and the distant water. I don't push them away. I want to feel, I want to let myself feel everything there is to feel. Everyone.

I push the last shard of the Icon up above me.

My whole life, I've been afraid it would overwhelm me. That the feelings are too big for me, the people too many, the pain too great. I spent every minute of every hour of every day protecting myself from having to feel all the life there is around me.

Because feelings are memories, and I don't want to remember.

Because feelings are dangerous, and I don't want to die.

Tonight is different. Now is different. What we have lost, we have lost together. I want to feel the loss. I want to feel the Hole. I want to feel the great goodness of life, of the things that remain when the Icon is gone.

I want to feel it all.

"Dol? Are you okay? What's going on? We can't stay here."

I don't speak. I can't.

I feel like my hands are on fire. Between my arms, where I hold the shard, a great ball of energy forms. It leaves my body, spreading wide across the hill, across the city, across the horizon. Pulsing as brightly as the spark of life itself.

I am an Icon.

Not the House of Lords' Icon, but your Icon.

Feel what I feel, I think.

Feel what you are.

This is your sorrow as much as mine. Your love, your rage, your fear. These are our gifts, and our gift to you.

I hear the beating of the energy as it radiates outward, flapping in crescendos and waves like the wings of a bird. Like the collective heartbeat of the city.

I am spreading like a virus. Not me—the feeling. The idea. I smile to myself, thinking someone should tell Colonel Catallus. I am more than dangerous. I am contagious. He had no idea how contagious I actually am.

I understand now. I know what to do with my gift. It seemed like too much for one person, because it was.

This feeling doesn't belong only to me.

I was meant to share it.

I take my gift and project it out. I am not the Weeper, not now. We all are. We are all Weepers and Ragers, Freaks and Lovers.

Come.

Come and be free.

I belong to you. This, too, is you.

One by one, I feel them. Curious. Slow.

They are ragged and gasping. They are weeping and afraid. They are worried and cautious. They have been

405

beaten like dogs and are afraid of being beaten again. They are sick. They are poor. They've lost their mother, their son, their brother. They huddle together on a bare mattress in a dark room behind a barred window. It hurts to breathe. It hurts to hope.

But they can feel it.

This is who we are. This is what we have become. This great pain is life. This joy and this fear and this rage.

This hope.

It belongs to us.

Chumash Rancheros Spaniards Californians Americans Grass The Lords The Hole. Us.

The pattern belongs to us.

We are here again, as were our mothers, as were their mothers before them. We have lived and died and lived again.

We were here first, and we will be here last.

Feel what you have lost, I think.

Feel what you have lost and don't lose it again.

Listen to your own voices.

You are not the No Face.

You are no Silent City.

Let your hearts beat.

Be brave. Be alive. Be free.

My hands drop and I collapse against the remnants of the rocky wall in front of me. The wave passes.

It has left me.

I can feel the tears running down my face. Even Ro is still crying, next to me. I know this as clearly as if I was looking at him.

"My God, Dol. What have you done?"

I can't find the words. I reach for him and he pulls me to him with strong Ro arms. I am exhausted.

I weep in his lap, not as Doloria Maria de la Cruz, the Icon Child, but as Doloria Maria de la Cruz, the girl.

I am both.

I hear Brutus barking and whining, behind me. "Bru, are you stuck?" I walk toward the sound, climbing through rubble and smoke.

Ro follows.

I see Brutus digging in the dirt and debris. He looks up at me and keeps digging.

"Let's get you out of here." I reach down to pick him up. "Come on, Brutus." When I bend down, my heart stops short, and I can't breathe.

I see a hand, coming from a gap in the rubble. A wrist, with three dots.

They're here.

I have spent my tears, and all I can feel is a sharp pain in my chest. "Ro," I say quietly.

"I know. I see them, Dol. I'm sorry."

Ro carefully lifts a splintered support beam that seems to be covering Lucas.

I recognize the tile flooring around us and know this was close to where the detonator must have been.

The gap beneath the beam is dark.

In the shadows, we see Tima curled around Lucas. They aren't ash—but they aren't moving, either. They look almost like they could be sleeping. Lifeless, but frozen.

Tears run down my cheeks as Brutus jumps out of my arms and races over to Tima, licking her face.

She lies there, motionless, but the dog doesn't seem to notice. He won't give up on her.

Then she starts, and pushes him away.

Before she can say a word, Ro and I are upon them. I am holding Tima's hand when she opens her eyes.

Moments later, we are holding Lucas's hands when he opens his.

I don't let go of either one, but I read the shapes in their minds, like pages from a book.

Lucas, resetting the detonator.

Tima, throwing her arms around him.

A bright flash, then nothing.

I smile, but the tears won't stop.

They don't stop for any of us.

The lights come slowly, one at a time. Ro sees them before I do.

"Do you see that? What is it?" He points out past the tops of the burning trees and the smoking hill.

Tima looks where he points. "Torches, I think. Or flares."

Lucas squints, next to me. "Who has a flare?"

I stare in wonder. "What's happening?"

We watch the lights as they appear below us. First one, then another, until whole streams surge through the streets and veins of the Hole like a flood, like blood. They push their way up the twisty paths of Griff Park. They blanket Las Ramblas and the alleys and the streets.

Nothing stops them.

Nothing, and no one.

They have power. They are power. They feel it now.

They come by the tens, by the hundreds. Old men with dark eyes and leathery hands and black nails, spittle in their lips. Old women with brown skin and no chins, barely walking. Graying hair pulled back in a low, oily twist. Walking from their hips, stiffly, as if each thick-ankled step pains them. Which it probably does. The world is made up of these men and women, I think, whole armies of them. Women who have borne children and buried them. Men who have endured the march of time and still they march.

And then the young men and the young women, with covered heads and straw hats and muscled legs and glasses and no glasses. Some walk, some run. They are fat and they are bony. Even smaller children race between them. All they have in common is the forward movement and the look in their eyes.

It is enough.

We watch as the light moves through the city, nothing paranormal, nothing supernatural. Only something natural, something distinctly human.

Only—

The clouds flash with electricity. We look up at the sky. Tima's face twists in concern. "Was that—lightning? But there isn't a storm."

The ground begins to rattle beneath our feet.

"Dol? You getting anything—" Ro shouts to me. I fall to one knee, pressing against the earth.

I feel nothing, nothing human.

Only energy in its purest form. Heat and power and connection. I pull my hand away, quickly, shaking off the burn. "I don't know. Something's wrong."

Lucas stares up at the sky in horror.

"It's them. They're here."

Then the clouds part, and one by one, the silver ships arrive. They hang low over the city, sliding across the horizon, blocking out the low-hanging moon.

This is what we feared most. I just didn't expect it so quickly. The Lords have massed their ships like they did on The Day. They have come to put down this Rebellion. To make an example of us.

They have come to use their greatest weapon, our greatest fear.

"Can they do it without the Icon?" I whisper.

Nobody dares answer.

Have we done enough?

Silence falls over the Hole. In the streets, the people stand motionless.

"Ro! Lucas!" I stretch out my hands, but Tima is already coiled against Lucas's body. Ro dives toward me, as if he could shield me from the Lords themselves.

"Don't look—" shouts Lucas. As if that could stop The Day from happening all over again.

My heart is pounding.

I don't take my eyes off the ships.

My heart is pounding.

I watch as the Carrier ships align in a perfect circle over the Hole.

My heart is pounding.

I watch as a stream of light unites the ships, like the spokes of a wheel.

My heart is pounding.

I watch as the sky flashes blinding white, so bright that my eyes blur.

My heart stops pounding.

My heart stops.

411

My heart

My

A sound like thunder echoes across the sky. I feel a jolt of energy coursing through me, almost lifting me off my feet. It's as though all the energy from the Lords' ships is flowing through the entire population of the Hole, to me. We are all connected. And I accept it. I take it in and release it back into the heavens.

The clouds break open, and the air fills with rain.

I exhale, and slowly, slowly—my heart begins to beat again.

Silence.

Then I watch in awe as the ships slowly, grudgingly, rise to the clouds and disappear.

A cheer builds from the city below, the streets singing and shouting, laughing and catcalling.

They've failed. The Lords. They've retreated.

Ro grabs me into a hug the size of the city, and we roll in the rubble like puppies.

Because the Hole remains.

Tima jumps onto Lucas's back, screaming at the top of her lungs. I can hear her voice carry over the hilltop and across the city. Brutus barks, chasing wildly after her.

Because today is not The Day.

Lucas trips over Ro, and Tima lands on me, and all four of us become one pile of tangled limbs, laughing.

Because we are not a Silent City—not today, not ever again.

We lie back on the dirt, staring up at the sky, panting. I find myself caught between Lucas and Ro, one hand tangled in Lucas's gold hair, one wedged beneath Ro's back.

Today, right now, they feel exactly the same to me.

Alive.

We stay like this for a moment. Still. Then Tima sits up and raises her arms to welcome the rain. "Even the sky is happy for us." Ro smiles at me with a look of wonder.

"What did you do, Dol?" Tima turns to me, a shock of silver hair and wild eyes, curious.

I try to put the answer into words. "I don't know. I think, somehow, I passed our immunity on to them."

Lucas sits up. "The entire city?"

I nod. "With this." I hold up the Icon shard, now blackened in my hand.

"And this," says Ro, touching my heart with a knowing smile. It's impossible not to smile back.

"It's our city now," says Tima. Lucas nods, but as he turns his head toward the coast and Santa Catalina, I see his eyes and feel what he feels.

There are many ways to lose a family, I remember.

Ro stands up, holding out his hand to me. "That's one down. Only twelve more to go."

I take his hand and offer mine to Lucas, who grabs Tima. We pull each other up.

As I make my way down the hill, I hold on to my friends, hand in hand, and know Tima is right.

There is no way to stop the demonstrations now. They will say what they will. They will speak the truth and nothing else.

The Projects will be empty, I think.

The Embassy will be powerless, I hope.

At least in the Hole.

For now, for a moment, this moment—the Hole has found its voice.

———— • ————

We know the plan. We do as we said we would. By early light, we have found our way back to the Cathedral, past the fires and the torches and the singing and the celebrations. When I look up toward the Observatory, I see it is still lit with a bonfire as big as the Icon itself.

Inside the gates of Our Lady of the Angels, Tima is so happy to see Fortis she flings her arms around him and kisses him on both cheeks—even though he's already juggling a flask in each hand.

Ro disappears into a tightening circle of his Rebellion friends. They grab him, hoisting him off the ground, and he dives back into the throng of them, as if they were all made of the same wild energy.

I don't need to listen to know he is busily embroidering our story, watching it grow like wildfire with every retelling.

Let him.

I stumble toward the others, but I find my legs won't support me any longer. I am so exhausted I can't speak, I can't move.

Lucas sees my legs buckle before I can hit the stone floor. Wordlessly, he scoops me up and carries me away through the crowd. He knows. His chest is warm and steady, even though he's scorched and bruised from the blast. I listen to the beat of his heart, all the way until he leaves me, curled against the low cot.

"There," Lucas says, pulling a thin army blanket up to my chin. He looks at me, affectionately.

There, I think.

Home.

I can't say anything now—not to Lucas, or to anyone—and he doesn't make me try. So instead, I lie there in the darkness, numb and still, until Fortis awakens me.

Time to leave the Hole behind.

By noon light, we have found our way back to the Tracks. There are no carloads of ragged Remnants, headed to the Projects. The Sympas are on high alert, though, and the Tracks are still dangerous. We slip back to the last Embassy prison car, where a certain Merk and a coat of explosives and pack of four thousand digs sees to it that four exhausted prisoners are transported back to a long-forgotten Mission in the Grasslands.

La Purísima.

What remains of it. The fields are torched. The flocks are scattered and gone. The trees are charred black sticks.

Yet Bigger and Biggest are having bowls of bread and milk in the kitchen when we arrive. The glass has been broken from the windows, but Bigger has covered them with burlap, all the same. Bigger knocks his bowl off the table, he is so surprised. I can't tell which one of us is happier to see the other.

Biggest, as she always does, takes one look at me and makes me a bed in front of the oven.

The goats lap up the spilled milk, and I try to choke out the words to introduce Bigger and Biggest to my friends.

That night, I sleep next to Ro and Tima and Lucas and Fortis on the warm tiles of the kitchen floor. I wake up to find that Fortis has drawn his insane coat, full of strange wonders and secret curiosities, all the way over me. I'm so drained, all I can do is lie there and breathe. Only one thought struggles to the surface of my mind.

They aren't perfect. They aren't much. They didn't grow me in their bellies or a lab or adopt me through the

Embassy. I don't know the total truth of them, or the truth behind the truths.

But it doesn't matter. For better, for worse, here we are. What we have is one another.

This is my family now.

EMBASSY CITY TRIBUNAL
VIRTUAL AUTOPSY: DECEASED PERSONAL POSSESSIONS TRANSCRIPT (DPPT)

CLASSIFIED TOP SECRET

Performed by Dr. O. Brad Huxley-Clarke, VPHD
Note: Conducted at the private request of
Amb. Amare
Santa Catalina Examination Facility #9B
See adjoining Tribunal Autopsy, attached.

DPPT (CONTINUED FROM PREVIOUS PAGE)
Catalogue at Time of Death includes:

45. Grass Rebellion propaganda flyer, text-scan follows:

YOU CAN'T KNEEL TO A LORD
WHO WILL NOT SHOW HIS FACE.

YOU CAN'T PRAY TO A GOD
WHO HATES THE HUMAN RACE.

BIRDS

Birds used to sound like rubber squeak toys, the kind you'd give a dog. They sounded like the rapid flutter of wings or a folded paper fan. A bicycle tire that made the same noise in the same place as it turned, over and over. A monkey having a tantrum, some of them. An old mattress right when you sit on it. Sometimes, early in the morning, they sounded like all those things at once.

This is what the Padre told me.

I think about it, as I scrub the dirt from my arms and legs, in the dripping faucet in the barn. I grab another handful of straw, and smile as I remember the hot showers and pristine plumbing of the Embassy. My stomach roils, though, at the thought of the Ambassador, and I close my eyes, willing the memories away.

Lucas has been gone for a full day now, nearly twenty-four hours. He's gone to see about his mother, if there's anything or anyone left to see. When I'm honest with myself—really honest—I don't know if he's ever coming back.

I force myself to think about the birds again.

Birds.

I wonder if my father heard many birds. I spent an hour, this morning, rummaging through the Padre's desk, learning what I could about my family, from the old photographs the Padre kept for me. Old photographs and older papers. My father worked for the Forest Service of the Californias. Apparently he would sit for long hours in the middle of the Grasslands, holding binoculars to his eyes, hoping to keep the trees and the animals safe from forest fires. My mother sketched him that way, sitting in a tree.

My own father was waiting for disaster but looking in the wrong place. He wasn't looking at the skies. He was looking at the trees.

I turn off the dripping faucet.

I wonder, as I pull on my clothes and wring the water out of my hair, what pulled my father to the wilds?

Perhaps it was the same thing that drew him to my mother. I imagine many sunsets and sunrises between them, between all of us, in the life I lost, unlived.

She would have taught me how to draw. He would have taught me how to use the binoculars. I would have listened to the sounds of many thousands of birds.

I wonder what it is I'll miss, when all this is gone. Like the birds. If things don't work out for us, or the city, or the Rebellion.

Ro, and Lucas. When they aren't attacking each other.

Tima's hands.

Fortis and his magical jacket.

Doc and his jokes.

I think of everything we have lost, and everything the Lords have left us.

Somehow there is still so much more to lose.

I am listening for the birds in the silence, when I hear the sound of footsteps behind me. I feel the familiar warmth, spreading from the outside in, and then from my inside out.

I can't believe it, but there's no other feeling exactly like his. It has to be true.

I say it before I see him.

"Lucas?" I fling myself toward him, hurtling myself into him. "I was starting to think you were dead." The words don't carry enough weight. They can't. They're only words. They don't hurt the way the not-knowing did.

He smiles. "I'm not. I'm here."

The flush creeps from my heart to my cheeks. "What

happened?" I look up at him, reaching my arms more tightly around his neck.

"I found my way to Santa Catalina, but I couldn't cross. They say the Embassy is empty. I didn't stay long, and it took me a while to get out. They've closed the Tracks for good now, Dol. The day after the blast."

"And your mother?" I hold my breath.

"She's gone. GAP Miyazawa recalled her to the Pentagon. I don't know what's going to happen now." His words are grim, but not unexpected.

Casualties of war, Fortis would say. I know it means something different to Lucas, whatever she was or wasn't to him.

"I'm sorry."

I put my hand on his cheek. His mouth twists into a smile. The barest part of one.

"I like you," he says. "How long am I going to have to keep acting like I don't?"

"You're not doing a very good job." I smile back at him.

"I'm not?" He looks surprised, and I laugh.

I pull my head back to where we can lock our eyes together. "I like you too, Lucas." I smile.

We kiss.

We really kiss.

Kissing Lucas is like kissing a kiss itself. There's no way to explain it any better than that. And I don't even want to try.

All I want to do is kiss him.

This is more than a kiss, I think. *It is real and it is happening to me.*

It has fallen on me, as sudden as ships out of the blue sky. Like monsters. Like angels.

I feel his hand as it loosens my binding, unwrapping the long, thin strip of muslin from my wrist.

I let him do it. I want him to do it. I take my other hand and fumble at it, helping him pull it free.

Then his hand covers my smaller one, and he stops me before my binding drops to the floor.

"Doloria."

I look up at him and take him in, the dark blond hair that falls long into his face. The various cuts and bruises he earned in the blast. The worry in his eyes and the care in his smile. He's as beautiful to me as the Observatory, as the Cathedral, as the Hole itself. And he's here in my Mission barn, which means he's not in Santa Catalina.

"Everyone thinks you're dead, you know."

I smile up at him, sadly.

"Maybe they're right. Maybe I am. Maybe I've become someone else." *Like a butterfly and a cocoon. Like the water cycle. Like the Chumash*, I think.

Lucas nods. There is always a part of him that seems to understand the words I cannot say.

Then my smile fades, because in the distance, out of the corner of my eye, I see Ro watching us. He's alone in the meadow, and we're alone in the barn.

Still, I see the emotion in his face, naked and unabashed.

He wants to kill Lucas.

And as much as my heart aches, I know some things will never change.

EMBASSY CITY TRIBUNAL
VIRTUAL AUTOPSY: UPDATE

CLASSIFIED TOP SECRET

Assembled by Dr. O. Brad Huxley-Clarke, VPHD
Note: Conducted at the private request of
Amb. Amare
Santa Catalina Examination Facility #9B

Deceased has been positively identified as Doloria Maria de la Cruz, an adolescent girl from the outlying Grasslands community of La Purísima.

Identity has been confirmed by Dr. Huxley-Clarke and verified by the Embassy Labs.

Further information has been sealed as Classified.

This case has been closed.

Remaining inquiries can be directed to Dr. Huxley-Clarke, VPHD.

Thank you.

EPILOGUE

THE GRASSLANDS

Feelings are memories. Memories are also feelings. I know now that what we feel is all we have. It's the only thing we have that the House of Lords never will.

I want to remember everything, as we follow the old Route 66 east through the dark heat of the Mojave Desert in the evening. The desert hides the last remaining Rebellion Choppers; Fortis says we'll ride all the way to Nellis, to meet the one waiting for us. Our donkeys are slow and tired, but we don't stop moving, and I don't stop remembering, and feeling.

Clouds settle and sit on the tops of the mountains like hats, like curls. They hang low over the sandy scrub, shadows unfolding on the rolling hills beneath them. There is gray and green and silver in the brush, earth appearing only beneath and between the growth. In front of me, a red-brown dirt road leads to red-brown dirt hills in the distance.

As we ride it grows darker. Everything divides and aligns into neat lines, same as the headless mountains. Snow falls on the dirt hillsides in white stripes. Across the valley, on the other side of highway lines and power lines, white snow and red dirt line the sides of the plateau mountain. Bits of white fluff appear on cactus tops, on brush.

We reach the sign for Death Valley. The hand-cut sign is old, a lone piece of debris from a less complicated age, before The Day.

Then I think of the book in my satchel, the one that Sympas have killed for and Grass have died for. The one Fortis gave back to me, only days ago. The one I'll carry with me, wherever this road takes me.

The others are waiting for us on horses of their own, the Desert Grass. As we take the turnoff to their camp, Furnace Creek, I think again of the sign, how old it looks. Like an important memory I don't have, from a family trip I never took. A place I might have visited along with my brothers, had things been different.

It doesn't matter anymore, whether it happened to me or not. It happened to some of us, so it happened to me. I know that now. I accept it.

It's who I am.

I remember it, the same way I remember *Chumash Rancheros Spaniards Californians Americans Grass The Lords The Hole.*

Maybe Tima is right to have that tattoo. Maybe there is such a thing as a world soul, after all.

I remember it all.

I remember my parents, my brothers, the ache of the not-knowing. The Padre and the Mission and Ramona Jamona. Bigger and Biggest at La Purísima. Doc. Fortis. Silver-haired Tima at the lunchroom table. Ro falling asleep next to me, warm as sunshine. Lucas with a smile on his lips and clouds in his eyes.

More than anything, I remember this feeling.

I want to remember this feeling.

I remember hope.

EMBASSY TELEGRAM

From: GAP Miyazawa
To: All Icon Ambassadors
Notice of Promotion

Colonel Virgil William Catallus has been assigned the position of Acting Ambassador, Los Angeles Projects.

Military presence will be increased until the Rebellion can be put down, and the Projects are complete.

We will not be stopped short of our Unification goal.

Ambassador Leta Amare has been found guilty of Treason and sentenced to Death, by order of the House of Lords, Origin Office, Commanding Lord Null. Acting Ambassador Catallus will execute the sentence at his discretion.

May Silence Bring Her Peace.

ACKNOWLEDGMENTS

SPECIAL THANKS TO MY OWN PERSONAL ICONS

Icons was represented by the always wise Sarah Burnes at The Gernert Company, who was in turn helped by the ever clever Logan Garrison. Internationally represented by the inexhaustible Rebecca Gardner and Will Roberts. Represented for film by the steady-handed Sally Willcox, CAA.

Edited by the incomparable Julie Scheina, as assisted by the tireless Pam Garfinkel. Editorially directed by the generous Alvina Ling. Art directed by the talented Dave Caplan. (*That cover! That cover!*) Cover font designed by the innovative Sean Freeman. Guided through copyediting and proofreading by the (oh so!) patient Barbara Bakowski. Publicized by the fearless Hallie Patterson, overseen by the savvy Melanie Chang. Marketed by the always original Jennifer LaBracio. Supported for libraries and schools by the one-of-a-kind (two-of-a-kind?) Victoria Stapleton and Zoe Luderitz. Published by Megan Tingley and VP Andrew Smith, each iconic in their own ways.

Adopted and adapted for film by my genius friends at Alcon Entertainment, Broderick Johnson and Andrew Kosove; and at 3 Arts, Erwin Stoff; and at Belle Pictures, Molly Smith, who were happily willing to continue the partnership we began with the *Beautiful Creatures* movie.

Read and reconsidered in all its draft-y infancy by–chronologically, FYI–Kami Garcia, Melissa Marr, Raphael Simon, Ally Condie, Carrie Ryan, and Diane Peterfreund. Thank you all!

Promoted online by Victoria Hill, Giant Squid Media ("Get Kracken!"). Photographed for the Web by Ashly Stohl.

Cajoled into being by Dave Stohl, Burton Stohl, and Marilyn Stohl, Virginia Stock, Jean Kaplan, the Cabo Collective and all the rock star readers, librarians, teachers, students, journalists, and bloggers who have supported me ever since the *Beautiful Creatures* novels.

Ensured production continuity via the Linda Vista Local 134: Melissa de la Cruz, Pseudonymous Bosch, and Deb Harkness, with help from P, N, and I. Via the NY chapter: Hilary Reyl, Gayle Forman, Lev Grossman, and the (even honorary) Punks. Via the SC/GA chapter: Jonathan Sanchez, Vania Stoyanova, and everyone at YALLFest.

Special thanks to Dr. Sara Lindheim for her Latin translation expertise.

And, of course, special thanks to my brilliant family, Lewis, Emma, May, and Kate Peterson, and my Motel Stohl honorary family—you know who you are—who always have been and always will be the whole point.

TURN THE PAGE FOR
A SNEAK PEEK OF *IDOLS*,
MARGARET STOHL'S RIVETING
SEQUEL TO *ICONS*!

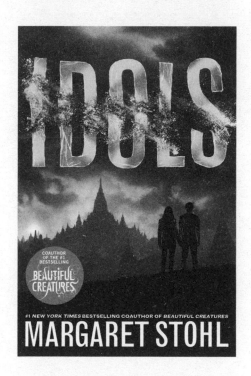

AVAILABLE JULY 2014
HOWEVER BOOKS ARE SOLD

PROLOGUE

PICK A GOD AND PRAY

I want to close my eyes but I don't.

I refuse. I won't let darkness be the last thing I see.

So I watch while my world spins out of control. Literally. While our tail twists and our alarms scream and our lights flash and the impossibly loud roar of our failing rotors fills my heart with terror.

Not now, I think. *Please.*

Not like this.

We have twelve more Icons to destroy. I never bound with Lucas—and Ro's never forgiven me for kissing him.

I'm not finished.

But with every turn, the rocky desert floor beneath us lurches closer. And out the window, all I see is a dark kaleidoscope of stars, ground, moon—in a whirling, chaotic blur.

A cloud of smoke chokes my lungs. I grasp Tima

with one hand, clutching my gear to my chest with the other. The outline of the Icon shard in my pack is unmistakable as its sharp edges push against my ribs. I always know it's there—along with the power it once seemed to give me, back in the Hole. Even now, I couldn't forget it if I tried.

It doesn't matter, I tell myself. *Not anymore.*

Nothing does.

The Chopper drops again, and in the front seats, Ro and Fortis almost hit the glass window. Wedged as I am behind them—between Lucas and Tima—my head slams into the back of Ro's seat.

"Bloody hell!" growls Fortis.

I feel Lucas's fingers on my shoulder and his fear in my chest. Brutus barks wildly, as if he could attack our fate and chase the end away—when in reality he's scrabbling just to stay put in Tima's lap.

Stupid dog. Stupid fate.

Stupid, stupid Chopper.

"Hold on, mates, this may be a bit of a rough landing!" Fortis shouts over his shoulder, with the sudden flash of a grim smile.

"I thought you said you could fly this thing!" Ro screams at Fortis, and I feel the clash of panic and anger coming off him in powerful waves.

"You want to take a crack at it?" Fortis barks, too busy fighting the controls to look up.

"Dol." Lucas finds my hand and tightens his grip on me, lacing his fingers through mine. He radiates little of his natural warmth tonight, but I know it's there.

The tiniest of sparks, even now.

We're together, I think. *Lucas and me. Ro. All of us. It's something.*

Grassgirl, Hothead, Buttons, Freak.

The night we fell out of the sky, at least we were together. At least we had that.

The moonlit landscape of wind-sculpted rock and canyons whips around us, and I wonder if this is the end. I wonder who will find us.

If anyone.

Our seats are shaking violently now. Even the windows are rattling. Tima tightens her grip on me, closing her eyes. Her fear hits me with such force that her touch almost burns.

As she touches me, a new idea claws itself into my mind.

"Tima, we need you—" I search for the memory of her at the Icon, how she used her fear to shield Lucas and Brutus from the explosion.

I reach out to her.

Try. Just try.

Tima's eyes flash open. She stares at her blood tattoo, the colorful streaks and patterns on her arm. She grips Brutus tight.

Tighter.

I hope she can do it. We're going down fast.

"It's no use. You can't fly a bird with broken wings," Fortis shouts. "Hold on, children—pick a god an'—"

Pray.

Pray, I think as we slam into the canyon wall.

I'm praying, I think as I listen to the violent clash of metal and rock.

Chumash Rancheros Spaniards Californians Americans Grass The Lords The Hole. Chumash Rancheros Spaniards Californians Americans Grass The Lords The Hole. Chumash Rancheros Spaniards Californians Americans Grass The Lords The Hole—

I recite it in my mind, the only prayer the Padre really taught me.

I pray as I feel the streaming heat of spreading flames.

I pray as I close my eyes to a flash so bright it burns through my eyelids, thin as onion skin, as paper.

I pray as I fall into the silence.

Pick a god—

I don't know a god. Just a girl.

So I squeeze her hand as the Chopper hits the ground in a ball of fire.

GENERAL EMBASSY DISPATCH:
EASTASIA SUBSTATION

MARKED URGENT
MARKED EYES ONLY

Internal Investigative Subcommittee IIS211B
RE: The Incident at SEA Colonies

Sirs:

I have, after great expense and effort, located and infiltrated the secure archives of Paulo Fortissimo. I believe their relevance to the disastrous recent situation in the Colonies will be instructive, or, at least, illuminating. It is to this effect that I offer my services, in the name of our dear mutual friend, the good Dr. Yang.

Now commencing decryption of files. Will immediately send all relevant materials as they are unpacked and decoded, in chronological order.

Following, you will find transcripts, beginning with initial contact with Lords (done via AI/virtual), research notes, personal journal entries, etc.

We can discuss compensation in due time. Recommend destroying all files immediately after review, Physical Humans being as swayed by emotion as they are. The final decision is, of course, at your discretion.

Yours,
Jasmine3k
Virt. Hybrid Human 39261.SEA
Laboratory Assistant to Dr. E. Yang

1

WRECKED

I am lying facedown in the dirt. I taste it. Dirt and blood and teeth as loose as old corn. Every bone in my body aches, but I am alive. Death would hurt less.

I feel hands rolling me over, pressing against my arms, my legs. "No, don't move her. She's in shock." *Fortis*.

A blur of dirty blond hair comes into view in the darkness, and I feel the familiar warmth surge into my cheeks as a hand touches my face. "Dol? Can you hear me?"

Lucas. I move my lips, trying to make a word. At the moment, I think, it's harder than I remember. "Tima—" I finally croak.

He smiles down at me. "Tima's fine. She's still out, but she'll be fine."

I roll my head to the side and I see her lying in the dirt

next to me. Tima, her scrawny dog, cactuses, and stars. Not much else.

Brutus whimpers, licking Tima's tattooed arm, which looks like it's bleeding.

"Fine? You don't know that," says a voice in the night. *Ro.* I see that he's just on the other side of Lucas, tossing dead tumbleweeds onto a makeshift fire. Ro doesn't feel just warm—not to me. He's smoldering. I could feel him anywhere.

Lucas rubs my hands between his. "I do know that, actually." He looks over his shoulder. "Because if Tima wasn't okay, we'd all be dead right now. Who do you think broke our fall?"

Tima. It must have worked. She must have done it.

I remember now the bright blue light expanding outward from Tima just as we hit. The muted, violent shock as we landed, the heat of the exploding Chopper—then nothing.

I sit up, weakly. I don't know how we got here, but we're clear of the wreckage, which is still burning black smoke in the distance. I can smell it from here.

I cough it out of my mouth.

Lucas pulls me up until I am leaning against the side of a rock. Ro is there a second later, forcing a canteen to my lips. The cold water chokes my throat as it goes down.

I can't take my eyes off the burning Chopper. The

burning metal carcass that was our only chance to escape the Sympas and get to safety is going up in flames, like everything else. Then—

POPPOPPOPPOP

A string of rapid noises catches me off guard. It sounds like gunfire, but it can't be. Not out here. "What was that?"

Fortis sighs from the darkness nearby. "Fireworks, love. That's our live ammo, burning up with the bird." He disappears toward the fire.

POPPOPPOPPOP

There it all goes, I think. Our dreams of living another day, popping like bubbles. Like a pan of hot corn set in Bigger's fire.

POPPOPPOP

Gone, gone, gone, I think. Our chances of success in our impossible mission to rid the world of twelve more Icons.

POPPOP

Our shot at making it to the next Icon—let alone coming up with a plan of destroying it.

POP

I try not to think anymore. It's all too bleak. I only watch. The flames would be higher than a tree—if there were any trees around here. But all I see in the firelight, aside from the five of us, is a flickering blanket of desert floor that rises and falls into a sheet of continuous cliffs and rocks and mountains. An uneven expanse of unkempt scrub and shale.

Nothing like life—as if we've landed in the Earth's own graveyard.

I shiver as Fortis returns from the glowing wreckage, dragging two charred backpacks with him. His ripped jacket flaps and drags behind him, like some kind of maimed animal.

"Where are we?" I ask.

Ro flops down next to me. "Don't know. Don't care. Doc?"

Lucas sighs. "Offline. Still. Ever since we took off."

"What do we have?" Ro calls out, and Fortis shakes his head, dumping the packs next to us.

"Not much that didn't burn in the fire. A piss pot an' a pea pod. No real rations. Less water. I'd say we have enough to last two days, three tops." Fortis taps on his cuff, but all I hear is a flash of static.

Lucas tosses a branch into the fire. "All right, then. A couple days. There has to be something around here. Someone, anyway."

"Who knows if we even have that long?" I look up at him. "We barely escaped the ambush at Nellis—and now this? The Sympas will have us back in the Pen before we have the luxury of starving to death."

"Maybe there's a Grass camp nearby?" Ro says it, but we're all thinking the same thing.

There isn't.

There's nothing out here. We knew that when we left Nellis Base—when the Sympas attacked and we didn't care where we ended up. But we should have, because now here we are.

Stuck.

Ro tries again. "We can't just sit here waiting to die. Not after what we did to the Icon in the Hole. We gave those people a chance—we gave ourselves a chance. If we don't take it, who will? What then?"

We all know the answer to that. *The Lords will destroy our people while the Sympas laugh.*

Ro turns to Fortis. "There has to be a way out of here. A Merk outpost? Geo station? Anything?" Ro is relentless. Inspiring, almost.

And absolutely crazy.

"There's your fightin' spirit," Fortis says, clapping him on the back. "An' here's my fightin' spirits." He pulls out his flask, slumping down to the desert floor next to me. *And that's his real answer,* I think.

"Ro's right. We can't give up." I look at him. "Not now. Not after everything."

Not after the Embassy. The Hole. The Icon. The Desert. Nellis.

Fortis pats my leg, and I wince. "Give up, Grassgirl? We're only just gettin' started. Don't send me off to an early grave yet, love. I'm too young and too pretty to die."

The fire throws shadows on his face, hiding his eyes, grossly exaggerating his stubbled, bone-tight features. At this particular moment, he looks like some kind of evil puppet from a child's nightmare.

Barely human.

"You know, you're not all that pretty," I say, my throat still full of dust.

He laughs, more like a bark, pocketing his flask. "That's what my mum said." As he draws his arm around me I can only shiver.

Then Tima groans awake, clutching her arm, and I forget about everything but staying and being alive.

Return to the haunting world of the *New York Times* bestselling Beautiful Creatures series with *Dangerous Creatures*, the first book in Kami Garcia and Margaret Stohl's brand-new series featuring fan favorites Link and Ridley!

Available May 2014
however books are sold

⊰ BEFORE ⊱
Ridley

There are only two kinds of Mortals in the backwater town of Gatlin, South Carolina—the stupid and the stuck. At least, that's what they say.

As if there are other kinds of Mortals anywhere else.

Please.

Luckily, there's only one kind of Siren, no matter where you go in this world or the Otherworld.

Stuck, no.

Stuck *up?* Maybe.

Stupid?

It's all a matter of perspective. Here's mine: I've been called a lot of things, but what I really am is a survivor—and while there are more than a few stupid Sirens, there are zero stupid survivors.

Consider my record. I outlasted some of the Darkest Casters and creatures alive. I withstood whole *months* of Stonewall Jackson High School. Beyond that, I survived a thousand terrible love songs written by one Wesley Lincoln, a clueless Mortal boy who became an equally clueless quarter Incubus. And who, by the way, is not the most gifted musician.

For a while, I survived wanting to write him a love song of my own.

That was harder.

This Siren gig is meant to be a one-way street. Ask Odysseus and two thousand years' worth of dead sailors if you don't believe me.

We didn't choose for it to be that way. It's the hand we were dealt, and you won't hear me whining about it. I'm not my cousin Lena.

Let's get something straight: I'm *supposed* to be the bad guy. I will always disappoint you. Your parents will hate me. You should not root for me. I am not your role model.

I don't know why everyone seems to forget that. I never do.

No matter what Lena says, she was meant to be Light. I was meant to be Dark. Respect the teams, people. At least learn the rules.

My parents disowned me after the Dark Claimed me as a Siren on my Sixteenth Moon. Since then, nothing rattles me—nothing and no one.

I always knew my incarceration in the sanitarium that my Uncle Macon called Ravenwood Manor was a temporary pit stop on the way to bigger and better, my two favorite words. Actually, that's a lie.

My two favorite words are my name, Ridley Duchannes. Why wouldn't they be?

Sure, Lena gets the credit for being the most powerful Caster of all time. Whatever. It doesn't make *me* any less excellent. Neither does her too-good-to-be-true Mortal boyfriend, Ethan "the Wayward" Wate, who defeats Darkness in the name of true love every day of the week.

So what?

I was never going for perfect. I think that should be clear by now.

I've done my part, played my hand, even thrown in my cards when I had to. I've bet what I didn't have and bluffed until I had it. Link once said, *Ridley Duchannes is always playing a game.* I never told him, but he was right.

What's so bad about that? I always knew I'd rather play than watch from the sidelines.

Except once.

There was one game I regretted. At least, one that I regretted losing. And one Dark Caster I regretted losing to.

Lennox Gates.

Two markers. That's all I owed him, and it was enough to change everything. But I'm getting ahead of myself.

It all started long before that. There were blood debts to be paid—though this time it wasn't up to my cousin and her boyfriend to pay them.

Ethan and Lena? Liv and John? Macon and Marian? This wasn't about them anymore.

This was about Link and me.

I should've known we wouldn't get off easy. No Caster goes down without a fight, even when you think the fight is over. No Caster lets you ride off into the sunset on some lame white unicorn or in your boyfriend's beat-up excuse for a car.

What's a Caster fairy-tale ending?

I don't know, because Casters don't get to have fairy tales—especially not Dark Casters. Forget the sunset. The whole castle burns to the ground, taking Prince Charming down with it. Then the Seven Dwarfs go all ninja and drop-kick your butt straight out of the kingdom.

That's what a Dark Caster fairy tale looks like.

What can I say? Payback's a bitch.

But here's the thing:

So am I.